THE SILENT

CHILDREN

THE SILENT CHILDREN

AMNA K. BOHEIM

Matador
9 Priory Business Park,
Wistow Road, Kibworth Beauchamp,
Leicestershire. LE8 0RX
Tel: 0116 279 2299
Email: books@troubador.co.uk
Web: www.troubador.co.uk/matador
Twitter: @matadorbooks

ISBN 978 1784625 160

British Library Cataloguing in Publication Data.
A catalogue record for this book is available from the British Library.

Typeset in 11pt Aldine401 BT by Troubador Publishing Ltd, Leicester, UK

Matador is an imprint of Troubador Publishing Ltd

To those who have kept their silence.
To those who have had the courage to speak out.

CHAPTER ONE

There it was, waiting for me. A letter. From her. My estranged mother.

Cold, stark. Distant.

As I walked into my apartment on Sunday, happy and relaxed after a sailing holiday in the Ionian Sea, a letter from my mother was the last thing I needed. Her stationery, her handwriting with its left to right sloping swirls, her preference for blue ink – none of it had lost its familiarity.

For two days the envelope remained unopened on the table in my hallway. On the third day I forced myself to read it.

Annabel Albrecht
Himmelhofgasse 15, Ober St. Veit, Wien
18th August 2004

Dearest Max,

I am writing to inform you that I am dying. The doctors, however, cannot tell me how long I have left – whether it's a week or a month or a year.

Reflection is something that comes naturally as one's life comes to an end. I have thought a great deal about your long-gone father and brother – and, of course, I have been thinking of you. The reality is that I love you and always have done – you are, after all, my son.

1

I recognise that in your eyes, I may not have been the best of mothers, and I know our last argument was particularly heated. But there are two things I want to ask of you – dying wishes, if you want to be sentimental about it. The first is for you to visit me so that I have the chance to explain everything. At the very least, please call me. The second is that I need your help. Enclosed is an old photograph taken just before the war. I remember the boy in the picture. I must find out if he is still alive. He has some information – a missing link – that I think will help reinforce my story.

I'm not asking for sympathy or forgiveness. But I would like to hear your voice – better still, to see you one last time – so at least I can explain.

Yours,
Mama

If I had felt any guilt or self-reproach when I began reading her letter, it was entirely consumed by anger by the time I got to the end.

Almost a year before, we'd had a serious argument and we'd been estranged ever since. It was unlike our other quarrels, filled with general pettiness. On this occasion, her words, then mine, were laced with something more like hatred. Such was the nature of our row that if she were a man, I would have hit her. I couldn't remember how it started, but I do remember her saying that she wished I had never been born. I had stormed out of her house and refused to speak to her until I got an apology. But none came, so our silence became the norm. Now, here she was with a letter, absent of apology, asking me to contact her – worse, to help her.

A letter seemed too old-fashioned an approach to smooth

over our rift, but then again, that was her style. Maternal instinct just wasn't part of her make-up. From a young age, I had turned instead to her closest friend, Vivienne Fuchs; she was like family to both of us and more of a mother-figure to me. And my mother seemed to encourage it, never showing any jealousy or a wish to close the distance between us.

The admission of love in her letter did surprise me. Even so, this supposed love that she was now pronouncing felt shallow, almost an afterthought. I had wondered if her own childhood had made her like this, if that was the reason for her destructive way when it came to our relationship. But my mother's character was quite unique; it didn't need excuses. Nor did I need her rambled explanations or lectures. Besides, if her desire to reach out to me was so important, then surely she should be the one to phone me.

But I couldn't help wondering: if this message of hers was so important to explain, why had she left it so late? So I put off the phone call. Usually work would have been a distraction, but with it being August, little was happening, and my mother's words, and the strangeness of the photograph she had enclosed, teased away at my mind.

Although faded in places, and dog-eared and creased, the black-and-white image was clear enough. At first glance, it was nothing more than an innocent picture of two children: a boy and a girl standing side by side in a garden. The girl was a little taller than her companion and had her head turned to one side, her eyes wide open as she laughed. There was a clarity about her, save for the whitish blur of her hands, suggesting she was engaged in an animated conversation with someone off camera. This girl was, of course, my mother, but a version I never knew, in the way she smiled with her eyes, her innocence, her ease with the world.

The boy's posture contrasted sharply with my mother's. His arms, stiff and rigid, were clamped to his sides. He stared into the camera with no hint of a smile on his lips. Yet there was something else that troubled me. I studied the photograph more closely and found myself focusing on the boy's expression: he looked whitewashed with fear.

On the other side of the picture was a name and date – *Oskar Edelstein '38* – written in pencil at the top. Underneath it, scrawled in black ink, were the words, *You knew*. The script was quite different from my mother's neat hand. Even though the writing was childlike, there was something disturbing in the way those two words were written, with their forced indentation and jagged strokes, leaving an impression that I couldn't shake off.

By the end of the week I had resolved to call my mother.

I picked up the phone, hesitating for a few seconds before dialling her number. I reread her letter while the low beeps of the Austrian ringtone sounded down the line. Just as I was about to hang up, my mother's housekeeper, Ludmilla, answered:

'Albrecht Residence.'

'It's Max. Is my mother there?'

Ludmilla replied with a stifled cry.

'Hello, Ludmilla?'

'Oh Max. I ...' She cleared her throat.

'What is it? Ludmilla? What's happened?'

'Your mother passed away last night. Frau Fuchs is here ...'

There was a scuffle with the telephone receiver and a muffled conversation. Then Vivienne came on the line.

'Max? I was just about to call you. I'm so very sorry.'

OBER ST. VEIT, VIENNA, 1937

Annabel stands on her tiptoes by the window, her head barely rising above the windowsill. It's chilly and although the little seven-year-old is wearing bed socks and a thick nightdress, she shivers. It's no use: she's far too short to see anything more than the spiky silhouettes of the treetops. Quietly, she grabs the stool in the corner, her cherubic hands gripping the edge as she struggles to carry it without making a sound. Heaven help her if Maria hears her. She sets it under the window and clambers up on her knees.

That's better.

She presses her nose to the glass, the warm air from her nostrils and open mouth casting miniature clouds on the windowpane. She's lucky it's a clear night. The half-formed moon washes a glow across the sky, but she still has to strain her eyes to look into the garden below.

Annabel's certain she heard something. She'd struggled to go back to sleep, awoken by Mama's return home from dinner with the Zuckerkandls at the Palais Leben-Auspitz. Mama's kiss, her accompanying heady mix of spiced perfume, cigarettes and the sweet hint of wine, stirred Annabel from a dream of dancing elephants and Oskar and Eva dressed as pirates. And just as sleep drew her away, she thought she heard an animal scream out in the night. Well, she couldn't ignore it, could she?

But it's no use; there's nothing to see.

Wait a minute! She sees a flash of light bobbing in the dark, then glimpses a white shirt limping along and the shiny crown of a bald spot.

'I know you,' says Annabel, moving a lock of her blonde hair out of her eyes. Maybe Fritz, their butler, is on some errand for Papa. It must be

important, as it's awfully late. *Her gaze follows him as he strides across the lawn. He stops, then looks over his shoulder. Annabel ducks down for a moment; then slowly, she raises her head and takes a peek again.*

'Papa!' She could squeal in delight, for she hasn't seen him in days. Annabel would run out to him if she knew no one would wake up, but she daren't because it'll make Maria cross. She'll just have to wait until morning, when he'll come into her room to say hello.

Now Papa's rubbing his head with a towel, and she thinks he looks funny in his shirtsleeves and with his braces hanging down. He must have had a long journey home. He was in Germany – Munich or somewhere – Annabel couldn't really remember, although she'd asked him, and had asked Mama a dozen times while he was away, which drove Mama quite mad.

Papa turns to Fritz and puts an arm around his shoulder and Annabel sees the lava tip of their cigarettes hovering in the night.

Last Christmas, Papa had given Fritz a sum of money so he could buy a house for his family, declaring, 'Fritz, you're like family to us and a brother to me.' Annabel and Mama had stood there in the kitchen as Papa made his speech, going on for far too long as usual, his hands clutching the butler's hand as if he were unwilling to let go. Annabel's tummy had rumbled and she'd shifted from foot to foot, wondering how on earth Papa could have a brother when they'd all died in the Great War. Mama soon clarified things though.

'What rubbish,' she had said quietly in Annabel's ear. 'Your Papa always comes out with these things whenever he drinks too much port.'

Well, that made far more sense and Annabel had just giggled.

She likes Fritz, but amongst the ones downstairs it's Eva she absolutely adores.

Annabel's drawn back to Papa and Fritz out in the garden, smoking. Papa still has his arm around Fritz's shoulders. Heaviness lines Annabel's eyelids. She yawns then slides off the stool to climb back into bed. Drawing the bed sheets up to her chin, she fights the Sandman to stay awake, for the excitement of Papa's return is just too much.

CHAPTER TWO

'May her soul and the souls of all the faithful departed, through the mercy of God, rest in peace. Amen.'

The priest's words felt like frigid water dousing me. I looked down at the walnut coffin. Too polished, I thought. The priest made the sign of the cross. Others followed suit. I didn't.

It was strange to think of my mother lying cold in what was really a glorified wooden box. Lifeless. Silent. Her words, her mannerisms reserved for memory alone. I glanced up and caught Vivienne's eye. She mustered a half-smile which I reciprocated.

I was an outsider observing an alien ritual. I surveyed the other mourners flocked around my mother's resting place in Hietzinger Friedhof, their dress and solemnity complementing the bleak September day that threatened rain. There were one or two familiar faces, now etched with age. A couple betrayed their desire to leave with a shuffle of their feet. Others dabbed at their eyes. An old flame of my mother's cast a white lily into the grave. I watched as it landed on top of the coffin. Then he threw a handful of earth inside and glanced at me to ask if I wished to do the same. I shook my head, catching the shadow of disapproval crossing his face. I disliked these burial rites, as well as my family's neoclassical memorial with its golden relief of the Son of God. They removed any sense of meaning. It was as if they were telling me what I *should* feel for my dead mother.

The formalities fulfilled, people turned to leave. Soon it was just Vivienne and me left to pay our final respects. At that moment I was aware of very little other than the morning breeze on my face and Vivienne's rose-scented perfume.

I regarded my mother's name – *Annabel Maria Konstantina Albrecht* – engraved on the stone underneath those of my ancestors.

'What is it?' asked Vivienne.

I looked up at her. She was quite different from my mother. Age had softened her features but her eyes remained the same: bright emeralds – that was how I had referred to them as a child. My gaze wandered back to the headstone.

'She just wouldn't …' I took off my glasses, wiping them as I considered my mother's reasons for leaving the way she did. 'She didn't even leave a note.'

'I know, Max.' Vivienne said. 'She knew death was close by. Perhaps she wanted to meet it on her own terms.'

I kicked at the gravel. 'Is it wrong to feel so numb?'

Vivienne touched me on the arm, as if to say, *Enough*.

I glanced back towards the grave once more. There were no grandparents, aunts or uncles from either side to speak of. I was all that remained of *Familie Albrecht-Gissing*.

We turned to wander down the narrow pathway towards the cemetery's exit, glancing at the headstones, memorials and vaults weathered by time: *Olbrich, Novotny, Moravec, Schmidt, Wagner*. Names relegated to history. There was one in particular that caught my eye: a sombre memorial to *Feist*, the final resting place of three family members, including *Chanoo Wolfgang*. He too had passed away in the same car accident that had killed my brother and father. Chanoo: the first name stood out amongst the Germanic and Eastern European names.

'He was your first friend. Do you remember?' said Vivienne.

'Vaguely,' I said. 'I must have been four or five. I was in the garden, playing, laughing, when Mama came running out to me with something like fear, or perhaps anger, on her face. I can't remember. Anyway, she grabbed hold of me by the shoulders, almost shook me.' I turned to Vivienne. '*Who were you talking to?* That's what she'd said. And I remember her eyes. There was something wild about them. But I didn't understand. So she asked me again, this time really shaking me. I was confused, so I said the first name that came into my head: Chanoo.'

'And then you cried,' said Vivienne.

'Were you there?'

She nodded. 'It was three, maybe four months after they died. I ran out to you and Annabel. She was holding you tight, whispering to you.'

'*Meine Maus.* Do you remember? That was Mama's pet name for me. *I'm sorry, meine Maus, so sorry*, she had said.' I squinted away the light reflecting in my glasses. 'She'd stroked my hair, then let go of me. She'd tried to smile, but I could see she was crying.' I offered my arm to Vivienne and she looped her hand through it, blotting her tears as we headed to the cemetery exit.

'When your father and brother passed away, it was a terrible time. But your mother's bravery, the way she recovered ... Well, it was admirable.'

'Was it?'

She nodded. 'She worked so hard to protect you from all of that darkness. You see, she wanted so much for you to do well. And you did.' She looked up at me, wearing a momentary smile.

I knew Vivienne was right. For all her distance, my mother had nurtured my ambition; she wanted me to go to the US. She even showed a glimmer of joy at the news of my place at Princeton – that much I recalled.

Vivienne hugged me. 'When I look at you I see you have the best of both your parents.' She was referring to my eyes, which mirrored the arctic blue of my mother's. With her near symmetrical features, her fair hair and skin, those eyes of my mother's had lent her a glacial air. On me, perhaps it was the darker features inherited from my father that blunted their edge. But there were mannerisms of mine that reminded me of my mother, my frown amongst them. Over the years I had tried hard to change them, to diminish the connection with her, but I could never quite get rid of them.

At the gates, friends of my mother's offered their condolences. In hushed voices they shared reminiscences, piquing my curiosity with their mosaic of memories, commenting on her sense of humour, her mischief, her taste in art and her coveted collection. My curiosity soon gave way to quiet impatience and I itched to leave. In that regard, my mother had saved me. She hadn't wanted an after-service gathering. She'd always thought them a waste of time. *Quite depressing, really*, she had said in the past. *The whispered conversations, as if people have a fear of waking the dead.*

As we watched the last car leave, Vivienne turned to me. 'Do you want to drive by the house? We can go together, if you like.'

I shook my head. I hadn't been there since the last argument with my mother. 'I'm not ready,' I said. 'Besides, I doubt it'll stay in my hands.'

'She'd never do that,' she said, her tone brisk yet warm. 'When are you due to see Frederik?' Frederik Müller was my mother's lawyer. Although she had considered him a friend, he hadn't attended the funeral.

'In a couple of weeks. I need to be back in London.'

'Wedded to your work? Always the same excuse.'

'I'm sorry,' I said, realising several months had passed since I had last seen Vivienne.

'Oh don't worry about me,' she said smiling, although I could see the disappointment shadowed in her eyes. 'The way you push yourself, you'll never meet someone.'

'I date.'

'Once in a blue moon, Max.'

'I think that's a bit of an exaggeration, don't you?' I shrugged off the faint echo of pain. 'It's not as if I have the time, with everything going on.' The truth of it was, I never gave enough time to the few girlfriends I'd had, and Lana, a girl I met during my summer sailing trip, had since returned to the US.

Vivienne arched an eyebrow at me as she removed her hat, revealing thick white hair drawn into its usual loose bun.

'You're the benchmark anyway,' I said, half serious. In my case, with most of the girls I met, when you rubbed away their sheen, there was nothing much left. 'Can we just leave the subject?'

Vivienne gave up her fussing. 'I know you can't wait to leave, but you can at least join me for tea before you go.'

I opened and shut my mouth before smiling at her. 'Am I that obvious?'

'You sometimes forget I know you inside out. Anyway, you can tell me about the photograph your mother sent you. I need something to take my mind off things.'

Rather than return to Vivienne's house, we settled on an anonymous cafe at the lower end of Hietzinger Hauptstrasse. I told her about the letter, my incredulity over its content, the way my mother had approached me, telling me how she'd always loved me.

'But of course she did,' Vivienne said, as I protested once more at her view of my mother. She put her cup of tea to one side and placed her hand on mine. 'It's just the way she was, the way she became. She had to harden up. But deep down she was

11

always the same Annabel.' Her voice faltered at the mention of my mother's name, so I quickly moved on to describe the accompanying photograph with the words *You knew* written on the back. I was certain she would know of Oskar Edelstein and what my mother had wanted to tell me.

'I know she wished to reach out to you. I imagine she wanted to say the same thing I've told you now,' Vivienne said.

I pressed her on the photograph – the *missing link*, as my mother had phrased it.

After thinking some more, she said, 'I do recall her mentioning this Edelstein fellow. Come to think of it, she was quite agitated. That's the word. All she said was that he had some information. I'm not quite sure what. And as for the writing on the back …' She brought her cup to her lips, hesitated, then put it back down on its saucer. She was about to say something but shook her head, a subtle shake as if to rid herself of something brewing in her mind. 'Perhaps she wrote those words as a child.' She fell silent and glanced towards the window, observing the remnants of blue sky nudging the clouds away. 'Oskar Edelstein … I've no idea who he could be. Can't have been a relative. A childhood friend perhaps, though no one I knew. But it seemed important enough for her to enlist your help.' She turned back to me. 'Please find him, won't you?'

I shrugged my shoulders. 'All right. For you.' I wondered why she considered it important to find the man, particularly given the likelihood that he would no longer be alive. I could only think that she wanted closure after my mother's death. She never liked loose ends, and Oskar Edelstein was just that.

After dropping Vivienne off at her house on Veitlissengasse in Ober St. Veit, I drove out towards the airport. I gazed at the passing architecture, taking in the switch from pre-twentieth century to post-war, low-rise office and residential blocks lining the outer districts of Vienna. If I were a tourist, I think I would like the city – its history, its grandeur. With the luxury of time, perhaps, I would come to be more accepting of it as the place of my birth, my hometown. But I had no such affinity with it now and any creeping sentiment was brushed aside when I joined the throng of traffic on the motorway. The blur of chemical refineries and industrial plants turned my mind to other things – to work mostly: the next set of meetings, our transaction pipeline, revenues and the all-important bottom line.

Air traffic congestion, the endless circling, the waiting for a gate at Heathrow and a snaking line at passport control were the usual greetings from the UK. By the time I got into central London it was late at night, and although it was raining, I needed to stretch my legs, so I asked my cab driver to drop me off on the Marylebone High Street. From there I walked the short distance to my home on Wimpole Street. I had lived in Marylebone for a few years, attracted to the area for its absence of statement cars and boutiques. I enjoyed its relative anonymity, the way it set itself apart from the wealthier London enclaves. I considered it to be London's best-kept secret. I liked the buildings too: the milieu of red-brick Queen Anne and Georgian town houses, many of them now converted into apartments. My place was in one of those, with a Coade-stone head above the white portico. With his long tresses and stern face, he reminded me of the Greek god Zeus. From time to time I would give him a nod, and I did just that on my return. Seeing him filled me with something like relief, and on entering my apartment I felt the same. On the surface, it appeared contemporary: white walls, stripped wooden floors, chic. Almost. Over the last year or so, the wear and tear betrayed my landlord's cheap renovation. That said, I still liked the place. I always tried to keep it simple and uncluttered, far away from the ornate world of Vienna and my mother's house.

I checked my messages before slumping in front of the television to catch CNBC and its bleached-toothed pundits drone on about the market's trajectory, but I couldn't really concentrate on what was being said. My thoughts strayed to the conundrum of Oskar Edelstein. It felt like a tenuous link with my mother, one that I didn't need. I would rather have forgotten about him. But I couldn't, not after Vivienne's request. Feeling frustrated, I switched off the television and went to bed.

For a while, the city's symphony of traffic and sirens kept me awake. When I eventually drifted off, I found myself wrestling with a dream sequence running on autoplay. Interspersed with flashes of gravestones, wreaths and ravens, I heard a muttered reference to *darkness* as I stood alone at the edge of my mother's grave. All the other graves and memorials had disappeared, leaving behind a wasteland swept by a breeze that rattled the branches of charred trees. Dusk had fallen, a golden streak spliced through the sky. I looked down at my mother's coffin. I took one step, and then another, my heart skipping a beat as I let myself fall inside, bracing myself for the collision that never came. I plunged deeper and deeper until I landed on my bed in my mother's home. Now I was a child again, woken in the middle of the night by a small stranger crouching in the corner of my room. I screamed out for my mother, but she didn't come, so I screamed and screamed again.

I woke up at the same point in the dream each time. After it had played through several times, I got out of bed and went for a run around Regent's Park. It was four in the morning but I didn't care; I cared even less for the scenes that featured in my dream. Still, as I ran through the paling darkness, I couldn't put thoughts of my mother out of my mind, nor her reference to Oskar Edelstein and the photograph with the words *You knew* on the back of it.

Papa and Annabel sit on her bed. It's their morning ritual, with Papa visiting her room the mornings he's home. Usually, they chatter about her day, his day, how her day's far more interesting than his day. When she knows he's home, she jumps out of bed before Maria clatters in. She washes her face, pulls on her clothes and does her best to make something of her mass of platinum curls, which never seem to grow out as Mama keeps promising. This day is no different, other than the fact that it's Christmas Eve. She's wearing a new dress – red satin and lined so it doesn't irritate her skin – and she has a new pair of black shoes with a red bow at the toe, made by Rudolf Scheer & Söhne on Bräunerstrasse, which, to Maria's and Mama's surprise, she had declared she simply loves.

Presents will come later this evening, but there's a package which Papa clutches behind his back.

'What's that?' Annabel says, twisting around, but it's too late – Papa moves the parcel away before she grabs at it.

'What's what?' he says, laughing, happiness shining on his face. He casts his hand up in the air, the package on show. Annabel springs up on to her bed to try to reach it.

'Not so fast, meine Prinzessin.'

Giggling, she grabs Papa's arm and then he grabs her and tickles her, burying his head in her hair. And then he kisses her cheek and she squirms from the sandpaper touch of his cropped beard, as light in colour as her hair. He lets go of her and laughs as she runs her little hands over his suit jacket and turns her attention to his head.

'Papa,' she says, 'your beard is thicker than the hair on your head.' Her seriousness borders on severity – one of the many things she's learned from her English governess,

'Really? I wouldn't have known if you hadn't told me.' He looks at his daughter with the same solemnness she is showing him, then whispers, 'What should I do?'

Annabel gets up from her bed and begins to pace her room. Rubbing her chin, she glances up at him. Bright-eyed, she says, 'Let's make a Christmas wish.'

'You know, you're absolutely right, meine Prinzessin. Where would I be without you?'

'Well, you'd be incredibly sad for a start,' Annabel says, her tone making her sound older than her years.

'That wouldn't do, would it?'

Annabel shakes her head.

'Come here,' Papa says. She perches on his knee and nestles her head against his chest, listening to the cadence of his heart. He holds out the golden-wrapped gift, tied with a red ribbon that matches the colour of her dress. 'You really want to know what it is?'

Annabel weighs it in her hands, turns it over, runs her fingers around its edges, trying to guess what it could be. She gazes up at him and he nods to tell her to open it. So she does, picking at the ribbon which comes loose easily. Unfolding the paper she takes out a deer-hide-bound notebook with thick, cream-coloured sheets inside, waiting to be filled.

'I know you like to daydream and to draw. Rather than taking my paper ...' Papa looks at her like Fritz does at times when he pretends to turn a blind eye to her mischief. 'I thought you could make better use of this. Do you like it?'

'I do, Papa. It's the best gift in the world.' Hugging him, she thinks of all the things she'll use it for: drawings, practising her handwriting, creating stories. She's so glad it isn't a doll or some other tiresome toy she's outgrown.

CHAPTER THREE

A week after the funeral, emptiness burrowed its way through me. While work offered some respite, my focus lapsed. Some people noticed, including my boss, but they chose to leave me alone. So I continued regardless, trying to apply myself to my job. Yet this only served to intensify my exhaustion. The descent into depression took me by surprise. Up until that point, I had never experienced anything as extreme. To discover that I could feel this way and be enveloped by something so crushing, pushed me down further.

My affliction couldn't have come at a worse time. Work had picked up significantly, and I was dealing with a high profile transaction for my firm. With one more meeting to go to finalise the whole thing I thought I could manage it. I placated my boss and colleagues, assuring them that I was more than capable. All I needed was a good sleep the night before the meeting – something easier said than done. When I finally fell into the depths of unconsciousness, my alarm chimed minutes later, dragging me to the start line of another day. I blinked in the light yet remained flat on my back. It felt as though my body was trapped under a rock.

Time ticked by; the rumble of rush hour faded away. It was the intermittent blare of a car alarm that made me clamber out of bed. In the bathroom I splashed water on my face, brushed my teeth, shaved. Things that usually came naturally now required effort. The shower did little to revive me so I twisted the tap to cold, willing the jet of water to shake me awake. Like a shockwave, it worked, though I knew the effect wouldn't last. The meeting was in our offices on Fleet Street. I managed to make it with two minutes to spare, ignoring my colleagues' grim faces as I took my seat. I didn't think to utter an apology. No doubt they took my blankness for nonchalance, which I'm sure irked them more. I should have bowed out then. But of course I didn't. I thought I could pull through.

My concentration lapsed after five minutes. I could feel myself ebb back and forth to the room and discussion. My team had little idea of the exertion it took to hold on to strands of conversation. Details, terminology, numbers floated about me. Once or twice I felt a dig under the table indicating that it was my turn to answer a question or to make a point. In response, I sat up, at once alert and attentive. Even that lasted only a moment.

The fact was, I couldn't help feeling that I didn't belong there. My gaze drifted around the room – the chestnut table, bordered by the Eames leather chairs, the suits, the ties, the watches. They all seemed to jar. A stream of sunshine bounced off the stainless-steel coffee machine standing on top of a side table at the back of the room. Someone asked a question. I caught the gist of it – something about valuation – but I was too distracted to answer. Then a voice in my head said, *You don't need to be here.* I got up, quietly excused myself and left the room.

My boss confronted me after the meeting, of course. He stormed into my office and slammed the door shut behind him. His wild gesticulations were enough to create an afternoon show for the junior analysts and associates sitting in their cubicles out on the floor. The more he shouted, the more his New Jersey background whipped through his words. Throughout it all I remained silent, watching him pace my office. There was very little I could say to defend myself, and I think eventually it was my passiveness that brought him to a halt.

He shrugged. 'You've had it tough recently. Take some time off. Take as much as you want. Come back when you're ready.' He then shot me a look. 'But if you pull a stunt like that again, you're out.'

He had given me a second chance. My boss was old school, not in the English sense of the word but in the way he looked out for me. I was in my early thirties and coming into my own at the firm. But despite my achievements and age, in his eyes I would always be the awkward Princeton graduate with the faint hint of a German accent I tried to disguise with an East Coast lilt. I'm not sure I would call this second chance he gave me an act of grace. What I do know is that if I were someone else, I would have suffered a different fate.

So I decided to go to Vienna. My mother's lawyer, Frederik Müller, had contacted me several times to arrange a date for me to see him. I had put off returning his calls due to work and, I admit, fear of the inevitable. My mother's desire to disinherit me had been no secret, and confirmation of it served little purpose. Nonetheless, I had promised Vivienne that I would return to Vienna. We had spoken on the telephone a couple of times since the funeral. Although she would never have said so, I could hear the loneliness in her voice. Each time we spoke she would ask, *Have you found Oskar Edelstein?* And each time my answer was the same: *No time, but I will.* Now I had little excuse. Before I left London, I hired an agency to trace him.

I arrived into Vienna International Airport on the morning of my meeting with Frederik Müller. I entertained notions of stopping by my mother's house beforehand, but decided against it. I saw little point. It wasn't that I didn't want to be there: I did. It was a contradiction that I tussled with, because the thought of losing the house chipped away at me. It was a piece of history that I wanted to hold on to – the way it represented the Belle Époque, a defining time when art, architecture and medicine broke boundaries. Its high-ceilinged rooms entertained all of that, with my grandparents playing host to the great and good of Viennese society. The house transcended the years. Situated on the hilltop of Ober St. Veit, it appeared oblivious to the changes happening around it, as modern residences and social housing had sprung up during the post-war years. I laughed out loud to think of my mother's dislike of those changes – the move into a different time, of new people arriving. *So cheap*, she had said on some occasions; *A disgrace*, on others.

I took a taxi to the First District and asked to be dropped off at the Hotel Sacher. For all its splendour I should have disliked it, but it seemed suitably placed in its location next to the Opera. I even went inside the red-canopied cafe to buy its famed cake to take back with me to London as a sort of peace offering to my colleagues at work. I then walked the short distance to Frederik's office on Neuer Markt, weaving around the huddles of tourists milling in Albertinaplatz and the Opera. Although it was late September, the sun had decided on one more encore before the onset of autumn, encouraging me to shed my pullover. Tying it around my waist, I took in the immediate sights as if I were a tourist, absorbing the hum of traffic, the footfall and chatter about me. It all carried the promise of summer again.

I turned up at Frederik's building ten minutes late for our meeting. I regarded the beauty of the building, the swirls of the cast-iron gate barricading the entrance. Apparently Frederik owned the entire nineteenth-century block, a piece of prime Viennese real estate. I looked upon it with a little envy. He had built up his practice from almost nothing and was now renowned as one of the leading lawyers in Vienna. Added to that, he had made a few investments along the way, which had proved quite fruitful. He would normally be the type of person I'd look up to, but by virtue of his relationship with my mother and my move abroad, I'd kept my distance.

I pressed the brass button on the wall. At the sound of an electronic buzzer, the gate and door behind it opened and I entered the foyer.

Frederik's secretary met me on the third floor. She looked like the trophy assistant: tall, blonde, a made-up face, and curves accentuated by her tight grey dress. If she'd offered a smile I would have found her attractive, but her lips remained pinched together as she nodded her head in the direction of the reception area. Barely blinking, she stared at me through her rimless glasses, reminding me of a Stepford wife. I smiled to myself, catching the glimmer of surprise in her eyes.

While I waited, I scanned the room: the twist of white calla lilies in the vase in the middle of the glass coffee table, the collection of newspapers and magazines positioned around it, the artwork, the furniture. All I observed seemed to be party to a certain public display of the wealth the lawyer had amassed over the years. It was as if every item of furniture and each object had been handpicked to convey sophistication and prestige. Yet to me, it all felt like an imposition, as though he were trying too hard.

Fifteen minutes later, Frederik Müller strode towards me with his wave of silver hair, his three-piece suit and the flourish of a handkerchief in his breast pocket.

'Max, how are you?' His nasal pronunciation revealed his Viennese roots. He took hold of my hand with both of his. His fingernails were manicured, their whites perfectly rounded off. There was little warmth in his handshake, although his crescent smile suggested otherwise. He surveyed my face. 'Working long hours as usual?'

I mustered up a brief smile.

'Let's proceed, shall we?' he said, leading the way to his office. 'This shouldn't take long at all.'

Even though his practice had taken off, he had remained loyal to my mother when he could have passed her on to a junior employee. I suspected this was on account of the kickstart she had given him at the beginning – that, and the fact that she had supported him through a difficult patch when he extricated himself from his business partner.

Just as we were about to take our places at the large table in his room, his mobile rang and he excused himself to take the call outside. While I waited for him, I glanced around his office, noting the law books, the first editions, the framed photographs with people of significance. Placed among them was a group shot from some kind of formal dinner. Sitting in the centre were my mother and Frederik. It must have been taken many years ago. Her hair was longer, and in her ringless hand she held a glass of white wine. I didn't want to have her gazing at me and I looked away, only to catch sight of her will on the table. Before I could take a closer look, Frederik returned to the room, grabbed his glasses from his desk and came over to join me.

'So ...' He put on his glasses. 'Did you ever see your mother's will?'

I shrugged. 'I think you know the answer to that one.' I fixed my eyes on Frederik. I assumed he was in on the whole affair.

He pursed his lips and proceeded to leaf through the document. 'There were some amendments, but nothing material.' He nudged his glasses up the bridge of his nose, then spoke without emotion as if he were reciting a list: 'The house and its contents are all yours. All her investments, cash deposits, et cetera, are to go to The Albrecht Trust. On that note, I'll continue to be a trustee. They're doing excellent work, you know.'

My grandparents had established an institution that had evolved from a basic orphanage to a leading light of charitable care, providing refuge for women and children, as well as counselling and financial support. There was no question that I'd continue to donate, but at that moment in Frederik's office, I had little interest in it, grappling instead with the news of my mother's bequest. My eyes flicked back to the picture of her on the lawyer's bookshelf. I could feel Frederik following my gaze, studying my reaction, waiting for a word or two in response.

'You expected more?'

His comment drew my attention away from her. I turned to him. 'I didn't expect a thing.'

He leaned back in his chair, throwing me a wary smile before stretching over to the edge of the table for the large folder brimming with official papers and envelopes.

'This is yours,' he said as he slid it over to me. 'Title deeds, house plans. It's all in there.'

I got up from my seat, tucking the folder into my bag, desperate to leave, to get some air. But one question stopped me from hurrying out. 'There was someone my mother mentioned before she passed away,' I said. 'An Oskar Edelstein. Does the name mean anything to you?'

Frederik removed his glasses, dangling them between his fingers. Glancing over to the photograph of my mother he said,

'She told me she'd come across a photograph – I never saw it – but she said something about tracking him down. I offered to help her, but she brushed off my offer. Finding the man seemed important to her though. Something about the need to make amends.' He glanced at me as he shuffled the rest of his papers. Part of me wanted to press him further, but thoughts of my mother's legacy loomed larger.

Uttering a brief *thank-you-and-goodbye*, I left the confines of Frederik's offices and turned right, down Neuer Markt. I had no idea where I should go and I wandered aimlessly, ending up at a cafe in front of the Donnerbrunnen. Sitting down in such a place seemed like a good idea; I thought it might offer some respite.

As soon as I stepped inside I relaxed a little. The air there was cooler and filled with the murmured conversations of only a handful of people. I chose a table tucked away in the corner with a view of the fountain and ordered a mozzarella sandwich and a coffee.

When my food arrived, I couldn't eat. The bread tasted as dry as firewood and I pushed away my plate. My mother's departure from her threats to disinherit me threw out question after question. My mind raced on to Oskar Edelstein. I wondered what Frederik meant about my mother wanting to make amends. I stirred my drink, the teaspoon chinking against the porcelain while I looked out towards the fountain, staring beyond the tourists grouped around it. They seemed to fade into the background as I replayed the scene in Frederik's office, frame by frame. I stopped mid-motion, the teaspoon suspended between my thumb and forefinger.

I left some money on the table, grabbed my bag and made my way out, breaking into a jog towards the U-Bahn station at Karlsplatz. On the way, I called Vivienne. She didn't answer, so I left a message telling her about my inheritance, that I was heading over to my mother's house and that I'd phone her in the morning. I knew she wouldn't mind.

'*Eva, you must sit still,*' *says Annabel.* '*Otherwise it's very difficult to draw you.*' *Although she's only eight years old, she thinks it's apt to adopt the tone Mama uses with Maria and the other staff at home when she issues instructions.*

'*Of course, Fräulein Annabel,*' *says Eva in return. She stifles a laugh, which Annabel catches, narrowing her eyes like she's seen Mama do when she's annoyed. And then she giggles because when Eva laughs, it's infectious and they can't stop.*

But Annabel must, as she's set on drawing her black-haired friend who she secretly wishes was her older sister. She is sketching in the book her father gave her. Her tongue pokes out of the corner of her mouth as she pencils in Eva's eyes, so large and almond-shaped.

'*I wish mine looked like that,*' *Annabel says out loud.*

'*Like what?*' *says Eva.*

The door opens. It's Maria, and although Annabel knows she shouldn't, she ignores her nanny and continues to sketch away.

'*Very good, Fräulein Annabel,*' *Maria says, hovering by her shoulder.*

Annabel's waiting for the next bit. Here it comes – the huff and puff of Maria's breath, the shift of her soft mass from one foot to another. Annabel looks up and sees Maria giving poor Eva one of her dagger stares while she says, '*I think you're needed downstairs.*' *In the past, Annabel's tried to argue with Maria to let Eva stay and play with her, but her protests never seem to dent Maria's will. Maria's like God, Annabel thinks to herself. Of course, she'd never say anything like that out loud. Not even to Mama.*

Eva nods and slips out of the room, sticking her tongue out at Annabel as she closes the door and Annabel stifles her giggles because it really wouldn't do if Maria caught her smirking.

'Is Oskar coming today, Maria?' asks Annabel.

'I believe so,' she says, picking up Esther, Annabel's doll, from the floor.

'Hooray! If the weather's nice, can we go outside? Please? Pretty please? We need to finish off our pirate game.'

'We'll see.'

'Yes then!' And Annabel races out of the nursery, clatters down the two flights of stairs and charges into Mama's drawing room.

'Oskar's coming, Mama, and we've got a ...'

Mama and the friend she's with – Herr Meyer – jump away from each other and Mama's fingers go to her throat, which turns almost crimson, the same shade as the dress she's wearing. The dress is one of Annabel's favourites: the colour, the way it shows off Mama's waist, the pretty flair of the skirt ...

Annabel's daydreaming is cut short by Maria slipping behind her into the drawing room, her bosom heaving with the effort of chasing after her young charge, and Annabel knows she's for it. She feels Maria's hands clamp around her shoulders, twisting her round to face the door.

'I'm so sorry, Frau Albrecht,' Maria says. 'It won't happen again.'

'I'm just leaving anyway,' says Herr Meyer as he walks towards them. He stoops down to Annabel and lifts up her chin. 'You're a bold one, aren't you?'

Unlike Papa, he always dresses as if he's on holiday. There's something horse-like about him, and his eyes are curious: one is green while the other is hazel brown. Both are fixed on Annabel. She doesn't know what to say, and looks to Maria, then to Mama.

'She's a free spirit. Like me,' Mama says.

Why must adults talk in riddles?

CHAPTER FOUR

I jumped on a train at Karlsplatz. As it rattled through the city's underbelly, the house continued to dominate my thoughts. With every flicker of light in the carriage, the house and its features blinked before me: driveway, windows, entrance, stairway, paintings, ornaments, photographs. The stops skipped by – Kettenbrükengasse, Pilgramgasse, Margaretengürtel, Schönbrunn, Hietzing, Unter St. Veit – then Ober St. Veit. From there it was a twenty-minute walk to the house, mostly uphill. But I didn't mind. Its distance from the tourist trails lent the streets a calmness. There were fewer people, less traffic, smaller boutiques and cafes. Even the whir of the passing electric trams was muted, lessening any anxiety I felt.

I approached Himmelhofgasse. My mother's house lay at the end of that road. I regarded the incline, the surroundings, the woodland crowning the hilltop. A breeze rippled about me with the air of an idle spirit as I walked on, taking in the pastel-coloured houses and the mix of conifers and deciduous trees lining the street. They stood like soldiers, ready for inspection, running all the way up the road as far as the house. I came to a stop, standing face to face with the wrought-iron gate. I placed my hand on the latch, then slid it open with all the apprehension of a son returning home after a long absence, and stepped into the horseshoe-shaped driveway.

My mother's ancestral home had a refined otherworldly feel about it with its white stone walls, now dressed with the orange-tinted green of a mature honeysuckle that climbed towards the roof. The windows sparkled with the kiss of the late afternoon sun, as if to say, *Welcome back.* I took this as my prompt and walked up the three steps to the door. I drew the house key from my pocket and held it in the palm of my hand, studying its turreted teeth. Placing the metal in the lock, I twisted it until it clicked, signalling my invitation to enter.

From the threshold I contemplated the house's interior: its white marble floor with its thread of grey veins, the curve of the staircase leading to the two galleries above, the Venini chandelier that hung from the domed atrium. The light from the doorway fell on two wooden carvings of a saint and an angel fixed to the wall on either side of a bench. It was another antique; my mother had had it reupholstered in crimson velvet that always made me think of blood. I glanced at the mahogany chest next to it. Lying on top were my mother's reading glasses and a stack of unopened mail.

As I shut the door to the outside world, the stillness struck me – not so much the quiet of inside, but a brooding silence that pressed down upon me. I placed my bag on the bench, then looked around once more. Despite the lingering scent of my mother's jasmine perfume, the permanence of her absence infiltrated the house, its corners, its eaves, floating in and around me, until I felt its chilled embrace. I slumped to the floor, my hands cradling my head. Tears seeped through my fingers. I felt like a young boy again, but this time alone. I couldn't move. I didn't feel like moving. I stayed like that, hunched against the wall mourning a mother who barely loved me.

When I eventually pulled myself up, a dull pain made its presence known in my lower back and shoulders. I had a throbbing headache and my mouth felt like straw. The dim light suggested it was early evening. I looked at my watch: it was shortly after six thirty. Pushing back my hair, I walked into the kitchen, half expecting to see Ludmilla, my mother's housekeeper, preparing supper. I gulped down a glass of water, then refilled it, sipping from it while I looked out the window to the garden beyond. The lawn had been mown, the roses, begonias, marigolds and other flowers were still in bloom and the garden furniture out on the terrace basked in the late sun.

I went through to the drawing room and drew back the curtains to let in what was left of the daylight. Musty air wafted about me, so I unlocked and opened the French windows, feeling the cooler air slip inside. I surveyed the room: its cream upholstery, the primrose walls with their treasured collection of art, including, on the wall opposite the windows, the most precious piece of all, worth far more than the house itself: Egon Schiele's *Mother with Two Children*. The painting always left me cold. Seeing it again after some time, I felt no different. Set against a mass of muddy charcoal, it depicted a woman with her offspring sitting on her lap, one blonde, the other brunette. While the artist had given the children a colourful vigour, his rendering of the mother – her pallor, the deadness of her eyes, her gaunt body – told a different tale. And she stared, not at the children but at some imagined point. What I would do with it – and the other things, for that matter – I couldn't even begin to consider. At that moment all I wanted was to feel the sun's early evening warmth on my skin.

I walked out on to the lawn and sat down on the grass. It was soft to the touch, as if no one had ever set foot on it before. Above me, the clouds skimmed across the sky, accompanied by the sound of the breeze tickling the leaves on the trees and the low chirrup of the birds. My gaze drifted to the house. It was funny how the ebbing light played the fool, creating silhouettes and movement in some of the windows. I closed my eyes, imagining my mother looking down at me from one of them. In a different world, she would be smiling rather than frowning … Picturing my mother's frown pierced the tranquillity of being outside, and feeling my tiredness return, I went back indoors, fetched my bag and headed upstairs, conscious of a heaviness pressing down on my body.

It was strange how my mother had kept my old bedroom. Over the years it had morphed into something like a memorial dedicated to my childhood and teenage years. The colours remained unchanged, with the walls painted a shade of light blue – her choice – and a cream carpet that she'd had cleaned every six months. An ancient hi-fi stood in one corner, along with a CD stand, packed with albums reflecting my hard-to-pin-down taste in music: Def Leppard, Guns N' Roses, Metallica, Nirvana, Pearl Jam, with a few Madonna and Michael Jackson albums thrown in for good measure. My desk was bare but for an old Pentax camera that had accompanied me on my year-long travels before I started at Princeton. Above it were three bookshelves filled with crime and spy thrillers; some were dog-eared and most were imprinted with coffee stains. The windowsill was home to my collection of model classic cars. I picked up a 550 Spyder and spun the tiny wheels with my thumb. As a child, I'd taken a lot of pride in my collection. Although I grew out of them I couldn't let them go, and so they remained on permanent display in my bedroom.

I put the model car back down, distracted by the glimpse of my bed standing opposite the window. My mother always kept my bed made, and even with her gone, it had retained its just-made feel. I opened the window and drew the curtains together, before casting off my clothes. I sank on to the bed and fell asleep as soon as my head hit the pillow.

Some hours later I woke up. I lay in darkness, unsure of what had stirred me. Sleep still clung to me, but I was conscious of my whereabouts. Moonlight spilled through a gap in the curtains, painting a translucent white streak across the floor. I was aware of my own breathing, the constant rise and fall of my chest.

It felt as though ... It was the feeling that I was not alone in my bedroom, that someone lingered by the side of my bed. I closed my eyes and listened. Silence permeated the room, but the sensation remained. Somehow, it felt worse with my eyes shut.

I froze.

Even swallowing proved difficult. Only the thump of my heart filled the stillness of the room, a sound that I wished would subside. I didn't know what was worse: keeping my eyes closed and letting my imagination agitate my fear, or opening them, only to see ... My heart drummed louder. My breathing came in short bursts. Fear or cowardice – whichever, my only thought was that an intruder had broken in. If I kept still for long enough, then whoever it was would leave. That was my hope, at least.

A draught grazed my face. I waited. Then I opened my eyes, careful not to move anything else. I saw – or I thought I saw – a shadow skim across the pool of moonlight, fleeting, retreating towards the bedroom door. Fear knotted itself around my body, squeezing the breath from me. I waited for the sound of an opening door. It didn't come. I waited some more. Locked in my bed, I gulped in air, trying to slow the beat of my heart. I searched the darkness, but without my glasses I couldn't see anything other than the straight-lined silhouettes of the furniture. As I lay there, the sounds of the house and outside seemed louder: the gentle wind disturbing the leaves on the trees; the creak and stretch of the house; the faint crackle of electricity through the wires. There was nothing to suggest that someone else was in the house. I tried to tell myself it was no more than my imagination, and that was the mantra I forced myself to repeat until my limbs loosened up. Then I reached for my glasses on the bedside table. With them on, I relaxed a bit. Whatever I sensed earlier had gone.

Tension seeped out of my shoulders and I switched on the lamp next to me, its light bringing back the familiarity of my old bedroom and belongings. Still, the experience left me unwilling to go back to sleep. In need of a distraction, I went to my bag in search of some reading for work, then returned to bed.

At first I found it difficult to concentrate, but as the nocturnal normality of the house grew on me, I was soon able to immerse myself in the research report on the company we planned to take public. Before I realised it, almost two hours had skipped by. It wasn't quite sunrise, but already I could hear the soft prelude to the dawn chorus. I'd had enough of reading. My headache had returned and the growl of my stomach reminded me that I hadn't eaten for some time.

I wandered downstairs. As I turned into the kitchen I noticed I'd left the light on. A casual drip told me that I hadn't properly turned the tap off either. Feeling parched, I filled a glass with water. Above the rush of the water's flow, I thought I heard something else. I lessened the stream and concentrated on the noise, but I still couldn't make out what it was. I turned off the tap. There it was again: a soft but incessant knocking. It didn't come from outside. Nor did it come from the kitchen. I glanced behind me, then turned around to face the empty gloom of the hall beyond the kitchen. A cold breeze wrapped itself around my bare legs. I shivered. As I moved to the doorway, the sound grew louder, conspicuous in the silence. Wood against wood: musical, a lullaby. It seemed to come from the direction of the drawing room. I walked down the hallway and paused under the atrium. I listened once more.

Knock-knock, knock-knock.

Its rhythm grew more urgent, hammering out some sort of code that I couldn't ignore. It seemed to surround me, and whether it was the noise or my tiredness, for a few moments I felt disorientated, as though I were standing on sinking mud, not solid marble. I wheeled around and felt the draught again, coming from the drawing room.

I went into the room, where my eyes immediately fell on the French windows. The doors were wide open and banging against the walls as though they had been flung open by a storm raging outside. Yet I felt nothing other than the same gentle breeze that had been blowing earlier in the evening. Still, the French windows swung violently back and forth as if they had a mind of their own. I went to shut them, fighting with the curtains which fluttered up like petticoats dancing to the doors' acoustic tune. Once closed, I pressed my forehead to the glass. The sky was edged with the faint pink of dawn, but the looming clouds made daybreak appear further away, and it was difficult to see anything through my ashen-faced reflection. I strained my eyes but there was no sign of an intruder. I stepped away from the windows, frowning at my own image staring back at me. I rubbed my eyes. My reflection mirrored my action. So did the stranger standing behind me.

I shouted out, jumping away from the window, my arms flailing to regain my balance. I shot a glance over my shoulder, scanning the room. Panic twisted my insides; my heart thumped against my chest. There was no one in the room except me and the figures gracing the Schiele on the back wall.

I couldn't think. My body shook, whether on account of the cold, the shock, or both I didn't know. I sat down on the sofa in front of the French windows, trying to regain some composure. My fingers trembled. I clasped them together, fingers clenching fingers, pinching at my skin. What was it? Real, imagined? The moment was swift, yet sent such a jolt of fear through me. I couldn't even begin to describe what I had seen, other than the blur of a face that wasn't my own. My brain processed the events of the nocturnal hours just gone by. That I heard something – yes; that I *felt* something in my bedroom – I couldn't be sure; that I saw someone – I couldn't have.

But. But …

I fought against my denial by ticking off my symptoms. Exhaustion had taken hold of me. I hadn't slept properly in days. I remembered a similar experience during my slog as a junior analyst when I had worked round the clock. There were times then when my weariness had played tricks with my mind. I just needed a break – that was all.

But.

It took a while for me to force myself off the sofa. When I did, it must have been close to six or seven in the morning. The start of a car engine on the road outside brought back a semblance of the everyday, of the real world, and helped restore my sanity. I left the drawing room and headed back upstairs to my bedroom and I climbed into bed. Pulling the duvet over me, I reluctantly drifted into another fitful sleep.

OBER ST. VEIT, VIENNA, 1938

Maria has a fever and is lying in bed with a flannel on her forehead. So Mama has put Eva in charge of Annabel, and that has made Annabel's day. Oskar has since come over with his mother, Claudia Edelstein. They've played endless rounds of hide-and-seek, but Mama's instructed Eva to take them upstairs because she simply must have some peace and quiet to talk to Claudia.

Sleet blurs the windowpane of the nursery and the dishwater gloom outside has turned everything grey inside. Annabel and Oskar are bored of playing with the toys on hand, including Annabel's puppet theatre; besides, Oskar wants to play with soldiers and Annabel has had to tell him innumerable times that she doesn't have any, and that's that. Eva intervenes and asks them to teach her a word or two of English.

'I like the sound of it: how do you do?'

They all giggle because Eva has an uncanny ability to mimic everyone and anyone, including Annabel's English governess.

'We'll play word games,' declares Annabel.

'I don't like word games,' says Oskar.

'Oh, don't be so down in the dumps, Oskar. I'll make it fun.' So Annabel sits down at the table and writes out the letters of two familiar words, each one drawn carefully before she turns them into an English phrase. Oskar and Eva look on and Annabel glances up at them, catching the awe in their eyes, and she can't help but glow with pride.

Oskar reads them out loud, struggling to enunciate each word.

'It's a silent K, silly,' says Annabel. 'Kneels. Not K-neels.'

Eva can read and does so silently over their shoulders. 'What does that mean, Fräulein Annabel?'

'It doesn't have to mean anything, Eva. They're just words, you see?'

'Sometimes I think you're just too clever for your own good,' says Oskar, folding his arms.

'Sometimes I think you can be just too grumpy,' says Annabel and she gets up to play with her doll, Esther.

CHAPTER FIVE

When I eventually woke up, it was late morning. In need of some fresh air, I opened my bedroom window and breathed in the sweet smell of damp grass, feeling my unease peel away. Rain sprinkled in from outside so I closed the window, knocking one of the model cars off the windowsill in the process. As I put it back in its place, I hesitated. All the cars were positioned with their fronts pointing to the window. They didn't look right at all and I turned them around, with their bonnets facing the room.

As I was on my way out to find a bite to eat, Vivienne called me on my mobile. She was rushing to the Albertina where she volunteered as a guide.

'You knew she'd leave me the place, didn't you?' I said.

'As I always told you.'

I heard the jingle of keys in the background.

'But are you quite all right? You don't sound yourself,' she said.

'I'm tired … and hungry too.' I came to a stop at Wolfrathplatz. 'Where should I go to eat?'

'I'm sorry Max,' Vivienne said, 'you could have come over. I should have asked someone else to take my place today. And then this blessed bridge match this evening – we always lose.' She muttered instructions to her cab driver. 'Come tomorrow, won't you?'

'I promise. But where can I get food?'

'Biedermayer – you remember it, don't you?'

'It's still around?'

'Of course – you never noticed?'

I hadn't. I only recalled the few times Vivienne had taken me there when I was younger. On walking through the door, I saw that very little had changed: the familiar smell of fresh brioche mingling with the aroma of coffee; even the clientele looked the same. I sat down and ordered a breadbasket, with a side order of prosciutto and cheese. When the food arrived, I tucked in as if I hadn't eaten for days. My late breakfast made me feel a thousand times better. I smiled to myself: the more I thought about it, the more the previous night resembled a fading dream.

After breakfast, I walked down to Schlosspark. The rain had stopped and I meandered around the park's many paths, avoiding the area by the colossal Neptune fountain where most tourists congregated. I tried not to think of anything in particular, just wanting to keep my head clear as I walked up to the colonnaded belvedere. I regarded the honeyed walls of the Schloss Schönbrunn down below, toying with the idea of staying for a coffee, but I didn't. There seemed to be a definitive shift in seasons – a cool wind gusted through the park while grey cloud hung low overhead – and here and there, ravens, perched on the ground in groups of twos and threes, lessened the welcome of the place.

Once back at the house I wandered through the rooms, opening up the curtains, letting in more light and air. I wanted the house to breathe again, to renew itself. Yet I still couldn't bring myself to go into the study. That's where they had found my mother and I couldn't help imagining her slumped over her desk, her eyes wide open. So I turned my back on the study and went to the library instead.

Three of the room's walls were home to hundreds of books from my grandparents' time, to which my mother had since added. Many were collector's items that she had catalogued and restored and kept to one side of the room. I decided to pick a book at random, so I walked around the library, running my fingers across the spines, taking in the smell of old paper from long ago.

My hand came to a halt at a copy of *Young Gerber* by the Austrian writer Friedrich Torberg. On opening it up, I saw that it was a first edition. I remembered reading it as a set text at school and despite my addiction to thrillers, I had enjoyed this book with its tale of teenage angst and suicide, driven by an archaic school system. Coming across it again, I had the urge to reread it, so I pulled it out of its resting place and went through to the drawing room. There, I kicked off my shoes and lay on one of the sofas, arranging my mother's precious cushions behind my head. I hadn't read a novel in German for a while, but once I got used to its style, I was soon immersed in it. I wasn't going to finish it in a day, but it didn't feel right to take it back to London with me, so I put it back in the library, promising myself I'd pick up where I left off on my next visit.

Although it was still early in the evening, tiredness nagged at me, so I decided to go to bed. Before heading upstairs, I checked and double-checked all the windows and doors, ridiculing myself as I went along. I half thought that I'd succumbed to madness, but laughing at myself helped, and as I settled into bed I felt my mind and body float into deep sleep.

I awoke with a start to the sound of shattering glass. I checked my watch. It was close to three in the morning. I slipped out of bed, reached over for my glasses, then crept towards my bedroom door and out on to the landing. Noticing nothing other than the rain pattering down on the atrium, I glanced over the banister to the hall below. There didn't seem to be anyone there, yet I was certain I'd heard something.

Caution made me hesitate before I walked downstairs, and when I did, I couldn't help pausing at every other step. At the foot of the staircase I stopped. The sound of scrapes and scratches against a windowpane rose above the rain. And from somewhere on the ground floor, a door creaked on its hinges. I surveyed the hallway. All the doors were shut, apart from the one to the study.

My curiosity pushed against my reluctance to enter that room. For a few moments I stood where I was, a tug of war playing in my brain. I shook my head in a bid to empty it of the grotesque pictures of my mother and approached the study. As I did so, the rain turned into a downpour, ferocious and brief, before it gave way to a lull that filled the space around me. Face to face with the door, I gave it a nudge, then pushed it a bit more, then gave it another shove, until it swung wide open.

The curtains were open, as was the window. I went to close it, checking for signs of anyone outside, but there was no one. Not wanting to linger, I tugged the curtains across the glass, thinking that intruders must have tried to enter the night before too. Perhaps they were checking the place out and I'd disturbed them. Perhaps I really had seen someone after all ... I tried to blank out the image. If my mother had had an alarm installed, this could have been avoided. I never understood why she hadn't got around to fitting one, but that was the way she was. I decided to call the police to report the attempted break-in, yet when I picked up the telephone on the desk, the line was dead. At least I have my mobile, I thought, swallowing my flit of panic. But it soon resurfaced. Something didn't feel right.

The desk, the bookshelf behind it – all seemed to be in order, with its array of files, books, photographs and family heirlooms of one sort or another. But it was the gap on one of the shelves that caught my attention. As I stepped behind the desk, the sole of my foot caught on something sharp. I winced and brushed the sole of my foot. Noticing a smear of blood on my finger, I glanced down at the wooden floor. A silver photograph frame lay face down, surrounded by a halo of splintered glass. I picked the frame up and turned it over. The sepia print showed my grandparents sitting amidst a group of young children who I assumed once lived in the orphanage. All grins. The picture of happiness.

My mind went to the task of clearing up the broken glass. I searched the kitchen and utility room for a dustpan and brush, but could find neither. The only place left to look was the cellar, a space so drab and uninviting that I could count on my fingers the number of times I had been down there. As I switched on the light in the cramped stairwell, the cellar appeared more neglected, damper, chillier than I remembered. Certainly, the naked light bulb's dirty yellow glow did little to cheer up the space, and the strange stale smell hanging in the air didn't help either, triggering a faint jolt of alarm inside me.

All the doors running along the right-hand side of the cellar corridor were closed, save the one leading to the furthermost room. I hurried over to it and found what I was looking for. Halfway back up the stairs, I heard what sounded like paint pots clattering to the floor. I stopped. More than anything, I wanted to tidy up and return to the comfort of my bed, but I couldn't shrug off the noise I'd just heard and so I went back down.

I flicked the light back on in the stairwell. This time, its beam appeared duller, emitting only a pitiful gleam at the entrance of the corridor. I peered towards the room I had left. Just get on with it, I thought. I went in and opened the cupboard where I had found the dustpan and brush. Nothing had fallen over – metal cans or otherwise. I couldn't understand it. I had heard something. I was certain. I looked beyond the room to where the corridor narrowed towards the wall at the far end. It was now blanketed in darkness. Although a part of me longed to leave, I kept going, tripping over forgotten household equipment and cardboard boxes. The corridor stretched another few metres or so, but in the feeble light, the distance seemed much greater, and the further I went, the more I felt the ice cold of the stone pervade the soles of my bare feet. It seemed, too, as though the stale air had morphed into something else, taking on a fetid odour. The narrowing space, the low light, the drop in temperature, the smell – combined, they sent a wave of despair down my spine that I tried hard to ignore. I moved on nonetheless, tugged along one step at a time.

Then something stopped me in my tracks. There seemed to be a pile of bedding or clothing on the ground in front of the wall. I drew closer.

It wasn't bedding or clothing.

I took another step. It looked like a person curled up on the floor.

It can't be.

I edged forwards. I pressed my hand over my mouth and nose, suppressing the stench and swallowing the sick that was pushing up my throat. I took another step and crouched down.

Oh God.

I fell back against the wall, smarting from the shock. I stole another glimpse. It appeared to be a child's body. Small, frail. Decomposing.

I retreated, my back slamming against the wall, fear sucking the breath out of me. The light behind me blinked on and off, creating random snapshots of the corridor and the body in front of me. It lasted only a few seconds, then darkness rushed in. I stood up, shivering as I backed further away, sliding along the wall. After a couple of paces the light flickered on, the bulb throwing a needle of light across the floor. I looked to where the body lay.

It was gone.

I couldn't have been more than three metres away, but there was nothing there: no pile of clothing, no body. Just a vacant space in front of the wall. I was certain of what I saw. I couldn't believe that I had imagined it.

I inched towards the end of the corridor again, wanting, yet not wanting, to see the body again.

The light petered out, plunging me back into darkness. Fear crept up on me once more, paralysing my limbs. The dark inked over any remaining certainty I had. I wanted the light to return. I tried to sweep away my misgivings and began to count the seconds out loud to give me something else to concentrate on. One, two, three … Twelve seconds later, the light flickered on and off. I looked back to the stairwell, wishing for the assurance of a steady beam. But the light continued to sputter as though a moth was dancing around it, conjuring illusions out of the shadows, weakening my resolve.

I still couldn't move.

Then I became aware of someone else in the corridor.

Through the flitter of shadows I struggled to see anything at first, and then … in the corner, I caught sight of … the light dimmed … and returned. It seemed … It seemed that a child was standing there. I quietly drew closer. It had its back to me. My fear ebbed away as I assumed it was a runaway, hiding in my mother's cellar. I edged forward, careful not to frighten it away. Every flare of light threw the child into relief, only for it to be swallowed by fleeting darkness again. Yet with every step I became more confident of what I saw. I paused. If I had stretched my arm out, I could almost have touched it, but I didn't want to chance it. It was a girl – I was certain it was a girl – trembling in the corner. An old-fashioned dress hung from her frame. She seemed thin, malnourished. She didn't turn around, but I could feel her presence close in on me, her sadness filtering through my bones.

She whimpered – at least I thought I heard a smothered cry. She seemed to cower further into the corner, her body shuddering.

'It's all right,' I attempted to whisper, but my voice was hoarse. 'Please don't be afraid.' My words failed to carry through the air. She didn't move. It struck me then: was this another dream? I dug my fingernails into my palm.

The girl stopped crying; her body stopped shaking. She turned around, and I saw ... I staggered backwards. The light blinked on and off, rendering her an abstraction.

'Who are you?' I tried to shout, but no sound came from my mouth. All I could hear was the perpetual thump of my heart.

Before I could call out once more, the light came on again, bringing me back to the house, the cellar, the present. There was no sign of a child, of another human being. Save for my breathing all was quite still. I had seen someone. I was sure of it: a girl. And when she turned around ... I pinched my eyes; my hand was shaking. I glanced back to where I believed I'd seen her and approached the back wall. I touched the plaster, my fingers tracing her shape. I crouched down again to where I thought her body had lain. Although the chill lingered, the foul smell had disappeared and the corridor seemed quite empty. The change in air seeded doubt in my mind – that I had allowed my imagination to string me along, that I thought I had experienced something supernatural. As I returned to the stairwell, there was nothing, nothing that struck me as out of the ordinary – just dilapidated, forgotten rooms and a collection of junk.

The tremor in my hand persisted and I couldn't rid myself of the foreboding that unfolded at the back of my mind. My exhaustion, my bereavement, had started to pluck at the fringes of my sanity. *Enough*, I told myself over and over again as I walked back upstairs to the study. But the slightest sound made me jump and in the end it took longer than it should have done to sweep away the mess. Once I had finished, I wearily left the photograph in its glassless frame face down on the desk, along with the dustpan and brush.

The following day I wanted to leave as early as possible. Daylight brought a little calm, but my mind kept drifting back to what had happened that night and the night before. I told myself that if I got out of the house, I would feel better, more normal.

I quickly packed up. Before leaving my bedroom, I glanced at my old model cars again. They still had their bonnets pointing towards the room. I shook my head. I decided to do a quick run-through of the house, checking windows, closing doors, making sure everything was secure. I did it without thinking, or at least I attempted to. Such was my wish to leave that I hurried through the house, avoiding the cellar and without a second look at the Schiele on the wall in the drawing room.

As I was leaving I noticed smudges of dried blood dotting the marble floor in the hallway. Blood from the small gash in my foot no doubt, which I'd forgotten about in the whirl of events. I found a cloth to wipe them away, but the stains seemed to impregnate the stone. Getting rid of them proved more difficult than I thought, and, in turn, I wondered whether I had left a trail of blood on the floor of the study. So it was, with the drag of reluctance, that I went back into that room.

I saw the dustpan and brush, which I'd left in an untidy heap, intruding on the neat order of my mother's desk. Tiny remnants of glass stuck to the brush's bristles, catching the light coming through the gap in the curtains. I picked up the brush, intending to shake the splinters into the wastepaper basket under the desk, when my gaze strayed to the space next to the brush. The photograph wasn't there. I scouted around the room, catching sight of it propped back up on the bookshelf, sandwiched between two other ornaments. I stepped over to the photograph and just stared at it, wondering. I knew what I had done with it. I remembered trying to keep my actions mechanical. Then again, I had been certain of what I'd seen in the cellar, but that had been scrubbed away by my niggling doubt and the starkness of daylight. This hesitancy on my part, my inability to differentiate between what was real and what was not, what I did versus what I imagined, cut away at me. All I could think of was my grandmother's depression, her breakdown, her reported psychosis. Had it struck me? My hand went to the desk. I steadied myself, closed my eyes, tried to breathe. My grief, the realisation I had lost my mother: that was the root.

I didn't want to stay any longer. I abandoned the study there and then, grabbed my things and left the house. I walked along the driveway, gripping the handles of my holdall, my eyes fixed on the gate.

Don't look back.

Yet the more I told myself not to look back, the greater the temptation grew to do the opposite. As my hand went to the latch, I couldn't help it. I glanced over my shoulder. My gaze tracked over the front of the house, up towards the first floor, then to the window at the far right. I squinted, unsure of what I'd seen. But only tree branches were reflected in the glass, like thin, spindly silhouettes. I stumbled back, staring at the window, but there was nothing there, just glass and a glimpse of a curtain, plain and still. A knot tightened around my chest. My hand quivered as I slid the latch and yanked at the gate, wanting to get out. It slammed shut behind me. I didn't turn back a second time. The church spire peeping above the trees on Wolfrathplatz kept my focus. From there, Vivienne's house was a stone's throw away. Of all people, she was the one who could make everything right again.

I went through the small gate on Veitlissengasse and up the steps to the entrance of Vivienne's house. Painted bright primrose, it appeared out of place beside the towering Omani Embassy residence next door. Their juxtaposition would normally have brought out a smile in me; it didn't this time around. As I pressed the doorbell, I noticed the persistent tremor in my hands. I clenched my fists, digging my fingernails into my palms to bring it to a stop. When Vivienne opened the door I hugged her, almost unwilling to let go.

'Whatever's happened?' she asked, steering me through to her drawing room where I slumped down on the sofa.

Like my mother's place, Vivienne's home had retained the same look and feel I recalled from my childhood, despite the years. The faint rose scent, the furniture, the scatter of green velvet cushions on the armchairs and sofa were so much a part of her, as were the photographs and ornaments. Best of all was the fireplace that, during the winter months, lent the room an orange-hued comfort. While my mother's house carried the air of a stuffy museum, Vivienne's felt like a proper home, a space to be lived in rather than admired at arm's length. In all, it kindled nostalgia for my childhood years, when I was protected under the wing of my mother's closest friend.

Vivienne had made an apple strudel, a favourite of mine. It was as if she knew I needed that kind of comfort. She waved away my offers to help, so I simply watched her as she served me a slice along with some tea. She was quite sprightly despite her age, like my mother had been, and well dressed too. Even though Vivienne had lived unattached for as long as I could remember, I still had the occasional flicker of surprise that she had remained a spinster. I never really knew the reasons for the lack of men in her life. I knew she'd had her misfortunes, generalised in her own words as *small nuisances*. And as a result, she continued her life as if they had never happened, refusing to kowtow to bitterness or regret.

The sweetness of her dessert melted in my mouth. 'It's as good as ever,' I said, a grin breaking out on my face.

She nodded, but her eyes remained wary as she studied my face. 'Bad night?'

I didn't reply.

'And the smile vanishes again. Tell me, Max.'

I pushed around the remnants of pastry on my plate, unsure of what to say. 'The house – it's not the same. It's like she's there – I could smell her perfume.'

'It's only natural, Max. I felt the same too.' She dropped a slice of lemon into her teacup. 'It's hit you, hasn't it?'

'But I don't feel better for it.'

'It doesn't work like that.'

I put down my plate. 'I don't know how to put it. I can't concentrate, I'm forgetful, I feel exhausted almost all the time.

It's like it accentuates things I hear or see. Makes me think …'
I didn't know how much I should tell her. She nodded, so I
continued. 'There were doors and windows open that I'm sure
were shut. Objects seemed to have moved. Half the time it feels
as if my mind's on autopilot, like I'm elsewhere. God, I don't
know, Vivienne, it's like – with my grandmother and the way
she apparently went. What if the same thing's happening to
me?' I looked up at her. The softness in her eyes didn't hide her
worry.

Before I could go on, she said, 'You just need a proper
break.'

'Do you think Mama started to go that way too?' My
mother's desire to engage with Oskar Edelstein, this long-lost
acquaintance from her childhood – was it all just a fruitless
whim, I wondered.

'What nonsense,' Vivienne said. 'Annabel was perfectly fine.
She took her own life, yes. But it wasn't due to *madness*.' The
three grooves between her eyebrows deepened, then faded
away. 'Don't rush back into work. Stay here if you like, for as
long as you want.'

I said I'd think about it. Trying to change the subject, I turned
to what I'd do with the house. 'Perhaps I'll hold on to it for a
little while at least – maybe make some changes, then sell it.' A
few tea leaves had escaped from the pot into my cup. I swilled
them around with what remained of the liquid, thinking of the
cellar back at the house.

'Are you trying to read them?'

I let out a wisp of a laugh. Vivienne took the cup from my
hand and placed it back in its saucer on the coffee table. I told
her about my venture down into the cellar on the hunt for a
paltry dustpan and brush, but I didn't mention what I thought
I had seen.

'It's uninviting. Such a waste of space. Why did she keep it like that?' I asked.

'Annabel never liked it. She said something about a bad experience. When the house was left to her, she eventually ripped out everything below and just used the rooms for storage. She would send Ludmilla whenever she needed anything from down there.'

My heart thumped a little quicker. 'What do you mean, *a bad experience?*'

'Something about a game of hide-and-seek.' She shrugged. 'I don't know. I suppose those sort of things stay with us.'

Gently, I pressed her, but she just said, 'It's nothing, really. Your mother never went into detail and it didn't feel right to push. She would have told me if she'd wanted to.' Vivienne moved on to other things. 'I presume then you'll transform the cellar.'

I nodded. 'And I'm getting an alarm fitted.'

At this, Vivienne chuckled. I loved the sound of her laughter. *The babbling brook* was how her friends, my mother included, referred to it.

Seeing my furrowed brow, she said, 'Annabel used to joke that her presence would be enough to scare away any thief. But I suppose – just in case. There've been a few robberies in the last year or two. There's now a nightly police patrol – it's put people at ease.' She looked out the window, then squeezed my arm. 'The weather's still fair. Shall we go for a stroll? It'll do us both good.'

I patted my stomach. 'I should work off this cake.'

Vivienne shook her head, rolling her eyes. It was our usual act: her feeding me, my jokey protests. This time, they grounded me. She made me feel better about myself and her words helped to nudge my doubts away.

We left her house to enjoy the good weather. Adjusting her pale green shawl over her coat, she turned and smiled as she closed the latch on the gate before looping her arm through mine. There were only a few people out and about. One or two nodded to Vivienne as we walked past them and only a single car drove by as we headed towards the top of Ober St. Veit. She liked to play the local historian, pointing out the houses that belonged to old acquaintances and regaling me with tales of people long gone. I knew all of this, but I liked the way she wove her stories. No doubt that's why she went down well at the Albertina as she led groups from one exhibit to the next.

Later that afternoon I readied myself to leave for London, while Vivienne went about her domestic chores more quietly. The hallmark humming that normally accompanied her movements didn't waft through the house that day; no kind of music did for that matter. She had a love of opera, a passion she shared with my mother, and in Vivienne's home her favourites often played in the background throughout the day. I remembered during my mother's funeral how she had wept when two sopranos sang 'Agnus Dei' from Verdi's *Messa da Requiem*. Now it was as if the act of listening to an aria was too painful for her.

I found her in the kitchen staring absently out of the window. She almost jumped when I reached out to touch her on the shoulder. Her eyes were moist and I knew she'd been thinking of my mother again. I hoped my news would bring her a little cheer.

'I just got a call from the agency,' I said. 'They've found Oskar Edelstein.'

Vivienne didn't smile, she just nodded in response.

'Why is finding him so important to you?' I asked.

Plucking a loose thread from my sweater, she said, 'It's my way of remembering your mother.'

OBER ST. VEIT, VIENNA, 1938

'You've done nothing, absolutely nothing, when you said you would.' Mama's voice has gone all wobbly and it's too high pitched.

Annabel hesitates at the door before pushing it open: Mama had given strict instructions to Maria that Annabel was to go downstairs to say goodnight before they went out to dinner, and here she is. She bites her lip, then leans in closer, pressing her ear to the door.

Papa's pacing again. 'What am I supposed to do, mein Schatz?' he says. 'We're powerless. Hitler and his men are running all over the government. Besides, do you want to run the risk of them shutting the Trust down?'

'But the Zuckerkandls, Elias, the Edelsteins, others – they'll need our help,' Mama says.

'Bertha has her brother-in-law so she'll be fine. As for Elias – he's got people in London.'

'And the Edelsteins?'

'His money will buy them a ticket out.'

'Sometimes, Sebastian, you can be so …'

'Yes, mein Schatz?'

Mama and Papa have been arguing more often recently. Annabel doesn't like it. Normally they stop bickering when she comes into their room, but she heard Oskar's surname mentioned and now her curiosity is piqued.

'You know very well you have influence,' Mama says.

'And you know very well, given the men you sleep with, you have more.'

53

Annabel jumps at the sound of a sharp slap. Tears well in her eyes and she sinks down on to the floor, cuddling her knees.

She sees Eva trotting up the stairs and the maid that's like a sister to her crouches beside her.

'Fräulein Annabel, whatever's the matter?'

Annabel collapses into the young maid and hugs her, feeling Eva's arms wrap around her. She doesn't mind the smell of onions and starch mingling with the faint odour of something else on Eva's cotton dress. She could breathe it in forever.

The door to Mama and Papa's room opens. Mama steps out, dressed in a backless peacock-blue silk gown which Annabel would normally ooh and ahh at, but not today. The effect is lessened anyway, for Mama's graceful face is pinched, cool. The Snow Queen, Annabel thinks to herself.

'Why Annabel!' says Mama. Her fingers hover over her mouth, lingering there for a moment. Papa emerges, touching the splash of pink on his left cheek with his ungloved hand. It's Papa's comfort Annabel wants, but it's as if she's invisible to him. His gaze passes over and beyond her, and it's like he's hit her, just as Mama had struck him.

Before Annabel can go to him, Mama draws her away with great urgency and says, 'There's no need to cry. Come here, meine Maus.' Annabel doesn't want to have any of it. She shrugs away from her and runs upstairs to her bedroom, rubbing her tears away with the back of her hand. Wanted, but not wanted. Why does it have to be like this?

'Get back downstairs, Eva,' is the last thing Annabel hears. It's Papa's voice and it booms so loudly she thinks she feels the house shaking.

CHAPTER SIX

In all honesty, I was relieved to hear that Oskar Edelstein was still alive, and I hoped the discovery would close the loop on my mother's last request. The agency told me he lived in London. It had been quite easy to track him down, but they said that he came with a health warning. It became apparent during their research that he was known as a difficult character: he fought for what he believed in, sometimes going to extremes. When I pressed them, they said he had been locked in a few battles on behalf of his family, but they wouldn't divulge more. Everything I needed to know had been included in the report they would email me. In the meantime, they gave me a contact telephone number and wished me good luck. Difficult characters didn't faze me – there were plenty of them at work. And of course there was my mother; everyone else paled in comparison to her.

On my way to Vienna International Airport I called Mr Edelstein. He answered the phone just as I was about to hang up. My taxi went under a bridge and the reception cut out, fusing my name into a crackled abbreviation.

'Who is this?'

I repeated my name, then told him about my mother, her letter and the photograph. I didn't tell him about the words on the back.

'I don't remember any Albrecht, or photograph. And frankly, I have no idea what your mother could have wanted from me.' His impatience cut through his reply, throwing me off guard.

'She said it was important.' I tried to think of ways to prevent him from hanging up. Despite his impeccable English, I detected the slight accent edging his words, so I asked if we could speak in German. My request seemed to take him by surprise and his tone of voice softened. So I continued, joining strands of observations from Frederik Müller and Vivienne to embellish my story. 'She must have discovered the photograph shortly before her death. She said it had something to do with making amends.'

'Good Lord,' he said, 'I hope she wasn't seeking to atone for the sins of her forebears.' This time it was *his* language which caught me out.

'No – nothing like that at all. We – I mean my grandparents – distanced themselves from the Nazis, if that's what you mean.'

'Go on.' Although there was a touch of humour in his voice, in this situation I felt I was on the back foot. I had no idea what my mother wanted from him. Worse, I knew little of the man on the other end of the line. I decided to be open and told him about the words on the back of the photograph – the phrase, *You knew*.

There was a long pause before he spoke again. 'I have no idea. Sorry, my mind's a blank,' he said quickly, as if he were eager to end the call.

'Can I at least show you the photograph? I'm based in London. It's easy enough to …'

'I'm sorry for your loss, I really am, but I'm not sure …'

'Just this one meeting. After that, I won't bother you again. I give you my word.'

'I'm not sure it'll be of any use.'

'It's important. Not just to my mother, but to me.'

He sighed down the phone. 'Very well. Week days would be best, when my housekeeper's around.'

I sensed he wanted someone to be there; for all he knew, I might be a psychopath. I heard the rustle of pages. 'It'll have to be this week. Tomorrow.' Before I could utter a response, he said, 'Afternoon. Two p.m. I'm at 6 Keats Grove, Hampstead. Towards the Heath end of the road.' And that was it – no discussion, no room to negotiate a time and place – just a curt *thank-you-very-much-and-goodbye* before the click of the receiver.

With the conversation over, I slumped back into the seat of the taxi feeling quite deflated. My only consolation was that at least I had tried to reach out to the man. But that wasn't good enough and I wasn't sure if it would have been good enough for Vivienne.

Once more, I went through the possible explanations behind my mother's desire to trace him. He couldn't have been at the orphanage: the agency mentioned that both his parents had been alive when the family left Vienna in 1938. Too tired to consider it further, I rested my head against the window and closed my eyes. It did little good. Instead of Oskar, it was the house and my night-time experiences there that skittered back and forth and I found myself rationalising them away.

'Excuse me,' I said to the taxi driver. He glanced at me through his rear-view mirror. 'Can we make a slight detour – back to Ober St. Veit – Himmelhofgasse.' I still had plenty of time before my flight and I wanted to prove to myself that the house was normal, that I hadn't seen, heard or felt anything other than the tug of my wayward imagination.

'Now you tell me!' he said, his eyes darting back at me. We were close to the airport. 'My shift – it's almost done.'

'I'm sorry. I just want to see the house where my mother lived. Just one more time.' I noticed the mention of my mother awakened some empathy in him.

'Is she still alive – your mother?'

'She's dead.'

'I am very sorry. Don't worry, I take you there. No problem.'

I turned back to the window while the driver took out his mobile phone. Although I couldn't understand what he was saying I could tell by his hushed voice, and the repeated words, that the driver was placating the person on the other end. Then he held the phone away from his ear. I heard the crackle of a female voice above the thrum of the car.

'Your wife?' I asked when he put down his phone.

The driver rubbed his forehead. 'She is not happy.'

'I won't be long – I promise.'

As we pulled up to the house, the driver gazed up at the building. 'Take your time.'

I walked along the driveway, keeping my mind blank while my fingers felt for the house key inside the pocket of my jeans. I jogged up the steps. For a split second I hesitated, the to and fro of a debate about to begin in my head. I cut it short with a twist of the key and a push of the door. I glanced over my shoulder, catching the eye of my taxi driver. He had got out of the car and was standing by its bonnet. He smiled and said something I didn't quite catch as I entered the house.

Immediately, I switched on the chandelier in the hall, its crystalline light extinguishing the stretching shadows. Then I looked to the study. That's where I'd begin.

I went straight in. The photograph stood where I had seen it that morning, on the bookshelf. I walked right out. I did the same with each of the rooms on the ground floor: in, quick spot-check, then out, like a prison guard doing his rounds. As I came out of each room, my shoulders loosened, my doubts eased, my pulse slowed. I felt much better, even when I passed the cellar door.

I looked up to the first floor and then the second, before glancing through the side window by the entrance. I glimpsed the taxi driver, who had now opened up the bonnet of his car and had something like an oilcan in his hand. I still had a bit of time and I wanted to do a round of the rooms upstairs. I jogged up the staircase, then along the gallery towards my bedroom, my hand skimming the wooden banister. A song I'd heard on the taxi driver's radio buzzed around my head and I began to hum it out loud. But as I neared my old room, the chandelier lights flickered, then died out. I stopped humming.

Old wiring, that's all.

I recalled my conversation with Vivienne and let out a half-hearted laugh, calling myself an idiot, amongst other things. And so I carried on, checking the rest of the rooms, albeit with a bit more haste and a little less humming.

My bedroom was just how I left it. The others contained nothing untoward. Relief wafted through me. I shook my head, rueing my imagination and stupidity.

Since I hadn't ventured up there at all during my stay, I decided to check the second floor. It housed the door to the attic and three spare bedrooms. I went inside each one. Apart from the skeleton furniture, they lay quite empty and still. I approached the door that led to a steep, narrow staircase running up to the attic. As I reached for the doorknob I thought I heard something scurrying away. Looking up at the ceiling I frowned to myself before wrapping my hand around the metal handle, feeling its curve knead my palm as I twisted it. The door held fast. I was sure my mother had never locked it and I expected it to be no different now. I assumed it was just stuck, so I rattled the bulb of the handle this way, then that, but it didn't give. The door's stubbornness stoked my need to force it open. In a last attempt I kicked it, but still it refused to budge. I was about to kick it again when I heard footsteps. They seemed to come from downstairs. I cocked my head to one side.

'Who's there?' My shout rang hollow through the house.

'Hello? Sir?' The taxi driver's voice drifted up to the second floor. 'Hello?'

I brought my head to the door, laughing at myself. I took a moment then gave the attic door one last cursory look before hastening downstairs to find the driver in the hallway looking up at me. He had discarded his jacket and rolled up his shirtsleeves, revealing a straggle of dark hair on his forearms. 'We have a slight problem.' An air of apology hung around his smile. 'My car – it's broken down.'

I think my reaction must have been one of relief pitted with annoyance.

'But do not worry,' he continued, 'I fix it, but I need your help.'

After I locked up behind us, I felt the urge to look back at the windows, just like I had earlier that morning. But this time, I managed to ignore it, concentrating instead on helping the taxi driver fix his car.

For about an hour, the driver – his name was Zoran – tinkered with the engine. My job was to stay behind the wheel, testing the ignition when he gave me the nod. On the first three attempts, the engine emitted a strangled whine. On the fourth, I began to berate myself for bringing us back to Ober St. Veit. On the fifth, Zoran gave me a grin and a thumbs up when the engine let out a low rumble. I clambered out and gave him a pat on the back.

'This car – it gives me much trouble,' he said, waiting for me to climb into the back seat. 'You will still make your flight?' I nodded in reply. He scrambled behind the steering wheel,

revved the engine, then slowly rolled down Himmelhofgasse.
'It is hard – I mean – losing your mother?'

'Yes … and no,' I said, the relief of leaving the house feeling
like a welcome breeze on my face. In the rear-view mirror I
caught the question in his eyes. 'We didn't get along. At least, I
tried. She kept her distance. But it's strange without her.'

He didn't say anything until he pulled on to Hietzinger
Hauptstrasse. 'The house – it is very beautiful.' He tapped the
steering wheel. 'There is someone there?'

'Not at the moment.'

He scratched his forehead. 'Oh, I thought I see someone
upstairs. Well – I see curtains move.'

A chill ran through me.

'Sir?'

'It was probably me.' But I knew full well that I hadn't
looked out of any of the windows, that I hadn't touched any
curtains. Zoran frowned. He glanced at me again. His lips
moved as if he was about to say something else, but then he
appeared to change his mind.

I couldn't let myself dwell on what he'd said and I clung to
the idea that he'd probably imagined it, just as I had imagined
the figure. It *was* my imagination. I closed my eyes, willing away
the picture that my mind, in all its tiredness, had imprinted
there. As for the cellar, I was simply mistaken. I couldn't relax
during our drive to the airport. Before our chat, I had felt
reassured by my check through the house. But now, even with
my internal ripostes – both rational and logical – I struggled to
dismiss Zoran's observation.

In an attempt to push those seeds of doubt away, I steered
our conversation to other things – the weather, his family. A lot
of what he said washed over me as my mind slipped back to the
house. At the airport Zoran got out to fetch my bag from his

boot. I handed him a tip, larger than my usual, with the request that he get his car seen to properly. I moved to shake his hand, but he took my hand in both of his.

'God be with you.'

I nodded, wondering at his faith in this God of his.

At the door to the terminal I turned my head. Zoran was still standing by the car, watching me. He looked the way Vivienne did whenever she was concerned: his smile was there, but his eyes betrayed a fleeting apprehension which I caught before his smile turned into a beam as he waved goodbye.

I wandered over to the check-in desks, reflecting on what he had said, his show of paternal concern, the warmth of his goodbye, the way he'd wished me well. I tried not to think of it as anything more than old-fashioned politeness, but I couldn't help thinking that he was warning me.

OBER ST. VEIT, VIENNA, 1938

Fritz grabs Annabel and she shrieks with delight as he tickles and tickles her until she can't breathe anymore.

'Stop it,' she says through fitful giggles and tears. His fingers prod through her dress, digging into her ribs. 'That hurts!' she cries, wringing herself free. Brushing her blonde curls out of her face she shoots him a glare, then puts her hands on her hips.

'If you ask me again, I'll tickle you some more,' says Fritz, wagging his finger at her. His dark eyes sparkle like the light caught in a river, and his face, faintly lined, but still carrying a glow of youth, says everything about the love he has for the young girl of the house.

'She's been gone for the whole month of March and you've still to give me a proper answer,' Annabel says, narrowing her eyes and looking up at him in a way she knows will butter up his heart.

'You know you're for it if Maria catches you down here, Fräulein Annabel.'

'Why do you have to change the subject?' she says, watching Fritz limp over to the kitchen shelf where Elisabet's freshly made Linzer torte sits.

'Would you like a slice, Fräulein Annabel?' he says.

Annabel thinks for a moment. She really would love a piece, for she knows Maria won't give her any for her tea after she spilt milk down her new dress. Annabel doesn't like the dress, as it's teal and she simply hates teal, and Maria has tied the velvet bow at the back so tightly that she can barely breathe.

'No thank you, Fritz,' she says, summoning up willpower she never thought she had.

'I don't believe that for one moment, meine Prinzessin,' Fritz says, cake slice in one hand, plate in the other.

'Annabel?' Maria's voice floats down to the kitchens. Then Annabel hears her nanny's footsteps clump down the stairs.

Annabel's face pales because she knows she's in trouble. She turns on her heels and runs out the door, but comes back and pokes her head into the room: 'Please save me a slice for later.'

'Anything for my little special one,' Fritz says, a smile as broad as she has ever seen spreading across his face.

'I'm not little anymore.'

'Just special then.'

CHAPTER SEVEN

On my return to London that night I checked my emails: the agency's report on Oskar Edelstein was not amongst them. Not that I minded; it gave me less to think about. Lying in bed later, the constant rush of traffic down Wimpole Street took me away from my mother's house and my conversation with Zoran. I found that I had actually missed the sounds of the capital – from the rumble of refuse collection trucks on their late and early-bird rounds, to the clamour of London voices, the hollering of builders and children's cries. This felt normal; this was how my life should be. And for the first time in days I actually slept soundly.

Next morning, feeling refreshed, I went for a run around Regent's Park and up towards Primrose Hill. Autumn had well and truly arrived in England. The leaves had morphed from green to muddy orange, doing little to offset the sunless morning with its seeping dampness.

I hadn't been for a run for at least a couple of weeks and my legs and lungs felt the strain as I ran up the hill. I struggled more as I found I could neither put aside what I'd experienced at the house nor dismiss the taxi driver's claim that he had seen someone at one of the upstairs windows. It seemed sleep acted only as a temporary anaesthetic against the unsettling whir of my mind. As I quickened my step up the incline, his comment came back to me: *There is someone there.* Was it a question …

or a statement of fact? It needled away at me, as did the other incidents that plucked away at my threads of reason, leaving me with a creeping fear that my mind was unravelling. At the top of Primrose Hill, I stopped, unable to go on. Bent over, my breath coming in short rasps, I couldn't get enough air into my lungs. Grey spots floated before my eyes.

I needed to get home. I stood upright, still feeling unsteady in mind and body as I jogged back.

After showering I felt somewhat better, although the thought of my impending meeting with Oskar Edelstein dragged me down. While I clutched on to it with a persistent hope, part of me wondered if it would really draw a line under my mother's death.

The agency's report finally had arrived in my inbox earlier that morning. I printed it off and, armed with a cup of coffee, I sat down at my kitchen table and began to read. It comprised two pages of crisp reportage, starting with the basic facts: Oskar was Jewish, of Austrian origin, and had been married twice. As an art historian, he'd ascended the ranks of Sotheby's, the auction house, and despite his retirement, he remained quite well known in the art world. That was the first page. I turned to the second: he was a believer in justice; he'd fought hard on behalf of his family as well as other relatives of Jewish victims of Nazi persecution to reclaim what belonged to their families.

There was nothing wrong with that, I thought.

However, in one instance he had gone too far, the agency reported. He had near ruined an elderly couple who, he believed, were the wrongful owners of a Renoir. Even though they had sufficient documentation to prove its provenance, he continued to plague them with overriding evidence. It pushed the husband over the edge and he died of a heart attack. Later, it transpired that Oskar Edelstein had fabricated his evidence. Despite an apology and a swift retraction, a whiff of scandal followed him thereafter. For a while he wandered in the wilderness before getting another chance with a second marriage that lasted thirty years and a fortuitous position at Sotheby's.

The picture I now had of Oskar Edelstein was of someone as old as my mother, with a severity to match, forced into meeting a young man waving a photograph in his hand, like Neville Chamberlain post-Munich. I hadn't looked at the photograph since my mother's funeral, yet the image and words, *You knew* on its reverse remained fresh in my mind. That aside, I now wondered whether there was anything remotely insidious about it. By the time I jumped into the car on my way to Hampstead, my uncertainty was all the more entrenched.

Outside, the scene was quite different from that of the morning: rain had now come and a bitter wind buffeted the trees, forcing their branches to bow low as if in mourning for their lost leaves. With the rain came the chaos of traffic and I found myself weaving in and out of the throng of buses, cabs and cars along the Finchley Road. Time ticked by. The last thing I wanted was to arrive late. I had imposed myself on Oskar. What if he had a straightforward explanation for the photograph: something simple, like a kind of prank? He didn't seem the type to suffer fools gladly. I played out my potential embarrassment, almost jumping the red lights at the crossroads before the Royal Free Hospital. I clutched the steering wheel, cursing the weather, the traffic, myself for feeling the way I did.

The windscreen wipers' stuttered screech worsened my mood, and in my haste I missed the turning into Keats Grove. Performing a tight U-turn, I forced myself to slow down, and eventually parked outside Oskar's house at exactly two o'clock. I took a moment to pull myself together. This feeling – the *thought* of feeling out of control – was quite alien to me.

Oskar's home was one of those four-storey eighteenth-century townhouses that looked handsome no matter the time of year – the type that American tourists would call *quaint*. Oskar's was no exception, with its fiery red Virginia creeper enveloping part of the building. I walked through the gate and up the narrow path to the red door where a stout, middle-aged lady stood waiting.

'I'm Angela, Mr Edelstein's housekeeper,' she said, offering me her hand. 'Come in, won't you – the weather's just filthy.' It seemed the cushion of her Yorkshire accent could imbue any sentence with warmth, and in this case it lifted my mood.

'Mr Edelstein's in his living room – I'll take you through.'

I handed her my raincoat, remembering to take out the letter and photograph, then followed her to the room.

We found Oskar sitting in his armchair by the window overlooking part of his back garden. He looked up from his book and smiled. Shutting it, he put it down on the floor and rose to offer his hand, disturbing the golden retriever slumbering by his feet. The dog opened one eye to look at me, then promptly shut it.

'Don't mind Ripley – he seldom gives visitors the time of day.' Oskar nodded at his housekeeper. 'Just ask Angela.'

In person he was quite the opposite of what I imagined. His face, though lined, had a classical air about it, his mouth turned up naturally at the edges, and through the tortoiseshell frames of his glasses, his dark eyes appeared to read everything about me with one swift look. That's how I felt, at least, as he ushered me to the weathered Chesterfield.

'I don't entertain that much anymore, so I'm afraid you'll have to make do with this room,' he said, settling himself back in his chair.

I mentioned again that I appreciated him meeting me. He brushed it off, but I still expected a slew of sour words.

'I owe you an apology. I was quite abrupt. On occasion I get nuisance phone calls, and I must admit that I threw yours into the same bucket.'

'It doesn't matter – really.'

'When you requested to meet,' he went on, 'I wanted to gauge how serious you were. That's why I suggested we get together at such short notice. And, I suppose, your mention of the photograph and your mother's letter rather piqued my interest.' He watched me as I glanced around the room, taking in the books stacked on the table and floor and, more neatly, on the bookshelf behind him. On the walls were a number of watercolours and oils, their colours diminishing the austerity of the duck-egg blue decor. A drawing above the mantelpiece caught my eye: it was a side profile sketch of a nude, the sitter's face turned upwards with the crown of her head cut off at the edge of the paper.

'A gift from my late wife,' he said, following my gaze.

'Klimt?'

Oskar smiled. 'You know much about art?'

'Not really. My mother did,' I said, reluctant to elaborate. It didn't feel right, but Oskar stuck to the subject, pointing to a triptych of small floral watercolours behind me.

'Take these Noldes. Like a lot of the things in this house, they belonged to my parents. Thankfully, my father saw the writing on the wall, sending some pieces to an aunt in Switzerland. As for the ones we left behind in Vienna – we never found them.'

Angela returned carrying a tray laden with coffee and biscuits. She smiled, then swiftly left the room, leaving the door ajar.

'Please, help yourself,' Oskar said, waving his hand towards the coffee table.

I leaned forward for my mug of coffee, adding a drop of milk as I listened to the rest of Oskar's story. He told me in a rather efficient way that his family fled the Nazis shortly after the Anschluss in '38. Several detours later – he didn't give details – they eventually arrived in Britain, initially staying with some distant relatives in Tunbridge Wells.

'We never returned. I went back for a few months, toying with the idea of a career at the Dorotheum. I thought a position there could help trace some of the paintings.' He turned to the window before continuing. 'But restitution is such a difficult thing, you see. Memory alone is insufficient.'

I anticipated a story or two of his cases, perhaps even a mention of the infamous one which tainted his name. But he took a slightly different path.

'Overnight, I was thinking about our conversation.' He turned back to me. 'Perhaps your mother had some information on our lost works – is that it?' The lilt of hope lifted his question.

His comment put me on my guard. 'I don't think so.'

'What makes you so certain?'

'I'm sorry,' I said, 'I didn't mean to be so blunt. All I know is that my mother would've been very plain about that kind of thing. She helped people in the past with their claims, often criticising the government and its reams of red tape.'

His shoulders dropped and the flush of anticipation vanished from his face. In a show of empathy, Ripley rubbed his head against his master's shins.

'I see.' His gaze travelled back to the Klimt and then down to the photographs resting on the mantelpiece. 'You have a photograph you wanted to show me.'

I got up and gave him the black and white print and the letter. I held them a little too tightly, almost unwilling to hand them over.

His lips mouthed my mother's words in the letter. Then he switched his focus to the picture, turning it over, as I had done, to examine those two words. He put both of them down on his lap and took off his glasses, chewing on one of the curved ends. He didn't say anything. Not at first. But it was clear his mind was working away and I felt a little relieved. I tried to read his expression, watching the furrow of his brow, how his eyes trailed from the letter to the photograph. He sat back and closed his eyes.

'Of course, I remember our old home in Ober St. Veit. I noticed your mother's address, so I presume she lived there before the war?'

'Yes, that's right,' I said.

'I recall our house as a revolving door of people,' he went on, 'I can't remember who. But I think there were some people of note amongst them.' He opened his eyes. 'Albrecht.' He pronounced the name with the sharp syllables intoned in a German accent. 'I always tried ...'

'You knew my family?'

Oskar didn't answer me. He sat forward and put his glasses back on. 'There's the Trust – it was quite well known – is it still around?' he asked matter-of-factly.

'Very much so,' I said, wanting more. 'Do you remember much else?'

Again, he took his time to reply. He ruffled the fur on Ripley's head. 'Forgive me, it takes time for an old man to remember. Yes, I do recall: they *were* friends – your grandmother and my mother before we left – but they must have lost contact at some point. I'm not sure why.'

'My grandmother passed away,' was all I offered in return. 'And my grandfather? Do you remember much about him?'

He cleared his throat. 'My mother mentioned once or twice how your grandparents were highly regarded for the work they did.' He picked up the photograph. 'I vaguely recollect this picture. It was in the garden of their – your mother's – house.'

'It's changed a lot since.'

A crescent of a smile appeared on his face. 'We must have been playmates, your mother and I. I think your mother was older than me – at least, I look younger than her in this picture. I can imagine the games we …' He stopped short, frowned, then turned back to the window, his fingers playing with the edge of the photograph. The patter of rain on the windowpane punctuated his silence.

'Is it the words on the back?' I asked.

He still didn't reply. His lips were pinched and it seemed as if he was trying to remember something else. He looked again at the photograph.

'My face … I …' He turned the picture over again, rereading the words. 'It was just a game. I never saw …'

At least, that's what I thought he said – his voice was barely audible. Oskar looked up at me. His eyes were wide, with something like fear at their edges. Then he blinked and it was gone.

Handing back the photograph and letter, he pushed himself up and went over to the fireplace. 'My early years,' he said, regarding the other photographs sitting on the mantelpiece, 'are just a muddle, really. What I may remember – what it is that I'm supposed to *know* – may simply be fiction.'

Before I could coax more from him the telephone rang. Angela's dulcet tone echoed down the hallway as she answered it, soon followed by her footsteps and a knock on the door.

'That was the gallery again wanting to know if you'll accept their invitation.'

Oskar followed Angela out of the room. I glanced at Ripley. He returned my gaze, then got up, went to the door, pawed it open and trotted out to find his master.

While Oskar was gone I picked up the photograph. I searched for clues in the image, homing in on the young boy's face. Except for his expression, there was little else to go on. I was sure Oskar remembered something, something that seemed to unsettle him. In my view, his professed jumble of memories was merely an excuse. Yet how could I press him?

Frustrated with this apparent dead end, I set aside the print, finished my coffee and got up to take a look at the photographs on the mantelpiece under the Klimt. Many of them were black and white; two were of Oskar with a woman I assumed to be his second wife. One of them was from their wedding. For me, at least, it stood out from the rest; it reminded me of the lack of pictures of my mother and father. I imagined them to have been just like Oskar and his wife: always smiling, radiant, content. I would never really know. I studied the other photograph of the couple. It appeared to be more recent. In it his wife seemed quite frail and there was something odd about the left side of her body and face.

'The second stroke killed her.'

I hadn't heard Oskar slip back into the living room. 'I'm sorry. I had no idea,' I said.

'That's old age for you.' He blinked, as though to stem the threat of tears, then picked up the photograph of his late wife. 'We had a good life, Catharine and I. She kept me straight. No children. Perhaps that was my comeuppance. Not that it mattered in the end. But I have Angela to look after me – she's been with us for years now.'

Ripley padded in, turned his head to the window and, with his tail wagging, looked at Oskar.

'I think this one needs his afternoon walk,' he said, crouching down to stroke Ripley's head. 'Would you like to join us?'

I didn't want to overstay my welcome, but Oskar insisted, so I accepted, hoping that the walk would encourage him to open up more. Out in the hallway, I regarded Oskar as he readied himself.

His attire smacked of an Englishman through and through: tweed peaked cap, wax jacket and corduroys tucked into army-green wellington boots, garb which Angela gently poked fun at.

'Mr Edelstein always makes me laugh,' she said. 'If Ripley were a collie, Mr Edelstein would be right at home where I come from.'

'What nonsense,' said Oskar. 'What would I do on a farm all day!' He turned to me with a twinkle in his eye. 'Be careful. She's always joking, this one.'

We strode up Parliament Hill. The rain had since eased off, and a light drizzle hazed our surroundings, although it seemed to bother me more than Oskar.

'Doctor's orders,' he said, reining in Ripley's leash. 'My heart's not the same as it used to be, but walking does me good. Not that I mind it. I like the ruggedness of the Heath. In some respects it feels a world away from London.'

I tried to edge my way back to the subject of my mother. 'Have you been to Vienna recently?' I asked, dodging two oversized Labradors bounding towards me.

'Not for a year or so, but I'm due to go just before Christmas. I've got an invitation from a gallery to do a talk – they called just now.'

I took my chance. 'Perhaps if you do go, you could come by the house – have a look round, if …'

'If it would help?'

'Well, yes.'

'Help who exactly?' He bent down to unhook Ripley's leash and watched him run off towards the top of the hill.

'Both of us perhaps.'

'Tell me,' he said as we resumed our walk, 'why, at my age, I would want to look again at a photograph from a childhood friend – a photograph that on the face of it appears quite chilling?

Forgive my directness, but you appear out of the blue, chasing a demand from your mother to find me. And now you have. Isn't that enough?'

'I thought it would be too.' We had reached the top of Parliament Hill. Retrieving a blue cloth from his jacket pocket, he proceeded to wipe down one of the benches. 'But there's something more – I'm sure,' I said as we both sat down. 'Stopping by the house could help trigger a memory or two.'

Oskar turned to me. 'Why is it so important to you? Have you asked yourself that?'

'It was her last wish, that's all.' My knee-jerk reason – a shallow one, I admit – seemed to resonate with him.

'The dying and their wishes. Catharine made me promise not to wallow in my unhappiness. She impressed it upon our friends too. They've been on suicide watch for a while now,' he said with a touch of humour. 'But I've been trying.' He looked out towards the eastern reaches of the city and the sloth-like sway of the cranes in the distance. 'This skyline – ever changing, isn't it? I think that sums London up.'

'So you'll come visit the house?'

'I'll think about it.' Ripley rejoined us and sat by Oskar. 'I rarely give out advice,' he said, stroking the dog's coat. 'I dislike receiving it myself. But let me give you one small piece: chasing memories turns into an obsession.'

I looked at him, not sure how to respond.

'Tread with care – that's all.' His words seemed like an apology, more for his own misdemeanours than for anything else. I was just relieved that he'd consider seeing the house.

For the remainder of our time together he asked about my career in the City, my education in the US versus Austria. He didn't ask much about my mother, or, at least, the way he asked about her was through his questions about The Albrecht

Trust and her involvement in it. I noticed he spoke little about himself, and when we parted I was left none the wiser about the details of his life after his family's flight from Austria.

Later that evening, I called Vivienne to tell her about my meeting with Oskar. 'You could tell he was holding back, but he wouldn't share more – I don't know why. Claimed he couldn't remember,' I said. 'If it were me, I'd want to get it out in the open. Be done with the whole thing, you know?'

'Yes, but you're not Oskar, are you?'

She suggested that I could look for more information on the link between our two families. 'Something reflecting happier times before the Edelsteins' flight,' she said. 'Something that may prompt him to open up.'

Vivienne sounded happier now that I had finally met Oskar. I think it stirred up her curiosity as she asked me for details of what he looked like, his expressions and responses. She, too, seemed keen for him to visit the house.

'Tell me again why it matters so much? It's not just about keeping a candle burning is it?' I said. In this instance, she was quick to reply, ready with an explanation that rendered my own quite flippant.

'Your mother – well, she seemed troubled towards the end.'

'Isn't that normal? She was dying,' I said. 'Besides – why mention this now?'

'Because … well, it just didn't seem right to bring it up so soon after she died,' she said. 'And then with the funeral and so on … But now that you've met Oskar – it feels right to mention there were things that Annabel said about her family, things that can't have been true.'

'What things?'

'I'm not sure, Max. She didn't seem to be making much sense. She was taking strong medication to lessen the pain and she wasn't lucid at times. What was clear was that Oskar Edelstein held some sort of proof.'

Now Vivienne was talking in riddles. I pressed her for more.

'She would jump from one thing to the next. It was difficult to follow her, it really was. But what she did say – repeatedly – was that her family could never be trusted. *How will they ever forgive me*, she had said. I asked her who *they* were, but she just shook her head.'

I suddenly realised that, up until that point, I had never asked Vivienne about my mother's last days, about her illness and how it affected her. For me, it had been black and white: she was alive, and then in the blink of an eye she was dead. I didn't even know how long she'd been ill.

'She found out a month or so before,' Vivienne said when I asked her about it. 'The disease was quite far gone. As usual, she'd left it to the last minute to see her doctor. She felt that time was against her. She spent hours in the attic, sorting through boxes. She threw an awful lot out. It was as if she wanted to unburden herself of everything. And what she had to tell me – well, in the end, it came out in quite a jumble.'

'And you really think there was substance behind what she told you?'

'It was the way she looked. There was Annabel the actress and the real Annabel. I knew your mother inside out. Her mannerisms, the expression in her eyes, the subtle move of her lips or eyebrows always let me know what she really thought. She was ...' Her voice faltered. 'She was frightened, Max.'

Who was I to argue with Vivienne about whether or not my mother's words carried any significance? I was the estranged son with a mother who became more of a stranger to me as the years went by. But without anything more concrete from Vivienne, I found it hard to know what to read into my mother's desire to unburden herself. Perhaps I didn't *want* to.

In the week after our meeting, I didn't hear from Oskar. Holding out a faint hope that he would choose to share something with me, I was disappointed by his silence. On the other hand, what did I really expect? We barely knew each other. Whether I trusted him or not, I dare say he hardly trusted me. If I were in his shoes, I don't think I would have either. Despite the temptation to contact him again, I thought better of it. Rather than hound Oskar until I wore him down, I wanted to earn his confidence. I would wait a while for him to approach me before reaching out to him again, and perhaps return with a more pleasant keepsake to help jog his memory, as Vivienne had suggested.

During the month of October, I busied myself with researching suitable architects to renovate my mother's house. There were a few recommendations from friends and contacts that I explored. In the end I settled on a Vienna-based one – Matthias Ropach – whom I had also read about in some Austrian lifestyle magazines. He understood my brief: to modernise without compromising the house's period features. With a couple of projects already under his belt in Hietzing, he knew the area well.

'I want to change the cellar,' I said. 'That's my biggest priority – it's a rabbit warren down there. The space could be used better.' The chill, the stench and the child of my imagination floated back, triggering the tremor in my hands. This was the right decision.

'I'd need to see the house ahead of our meeting in December,' he said.

'Are you sure? I mean, of course – that makes sense.' I tried to bury the image of the child.

'It'll give us time to nail down the plans before we meet.'

I pictured him wandering around the empty house. 'Perhaps someone could go with you.'

Matthias sounded nonplussed. 'You should see some of the sites I see. It's not as if the house is falling apart. I'll be fine. Just some plans and the keys would be helpful.' He told me he had some free time in November to visit. I promised to arrange access and to send him the plans that Frederik Müller had given me.

The project gave me something to cling to: the focus on change, bringing the house into the present. Being back in London also helped to put me at ease. I couldn't say I felt altogether better, but being away from the house in Ober St. Veit brought some normality to my life. The cloud lifted from my mind; I could think more clearly, and the familiarity of my environment – of Marylebone, of my apartment – put things into perspective for me. I even toyed with the idea of returning to work following a conversation with my boss.

'If you're ready, you're ready. If you're not, you're not,' he had said, before going on to impress on me that neither he nor the firm had any intention of abandoning me. So I plunged back into work. I also read articles about bereavement and its different manifestations. Slowly, I began to see how my experiences at the house may have been part of the grieving process, and not as unique or disturbing as I had first thought. And with this understanding, the photograph's mystery also lessened. It was a kind of solace, but still I couldn't quite forget about Oskar. While I tried to see the man as a conduit to my family's history, there was something about him, the things he said and didn't say. And like an unshakeable fever, though I tried to fight thoughts of Oskar away, they always came back, plaguing my mind, holding me back from truly moving on from my mother's death.

OBER ST. VEIT, VIENNA, 1938

Annabel hasn't seen Oskar for days and with Eva gone almost two months, boredom finds her too easily. Mama said that they ought to do something about it.

Instructing Maria to get Annabel ready, Mama says, 'I can't bear it any longer.'

'Are we going to the orphanage, Mama?'

'No, my dear,' says Mama, taking Annabel's hand in hers as they walk a few steps down Himmelhofgasse and in through the Edelsteins' front gate. A large truck, its back wide open, fills most of the driveway, and Annabel can't help but peer into the cavernous space filled with furniture and paintings.

'Are they moving, Mama?'

Mama doesn't answer and Annabel tugs at Mama's sleeve, but still she doesn't get an answer. The Edelsteins' front door is also thrown open and Mama seems to have forgotten all formalities as she enters without knocking.

'Claudia?' calls out Mama, lines now scoring her forehead, which Annabel thinks makes Mama look older – and ugly too. They see Claudia Edelstein upstairs. She comes running down towards them. Annabel watches the two of them embrace.

'Where's Oskar?' asks Annabel.

As if by magic, his nanny appears from behind her, takes Annabel by the hand and leads her into the living room where there are more paintings shrouded in white sheets. One of the maids scuttles into the room after them and whispers in the ear of Oskar's nanny, who frowns

81

and whispers something back. Oskar's nanny makes Maria look like a teddy bear by comparison, and to tell the truth, Annabel's always relieved whenever Oskar and his mother visit them, rather than the other way round.

'Oskar's outside. Run along now. I'll be with you shortly,' she says.

So Annabel's left to make her own way to the garden. For a moment she's distracted by the objects hidden under their coverings and she really can't help it: she lifts up one of the sheets. Underneath is the picture of the phantom lady and her children that used to hang in the Edelsteins' hallway. Annabel always comes up in goosebumps whenever she sees it and today is no different. But she's not scared. Up close, there's something about the swirls of dark brown and black behind the woman that draw Annabel in. She reaches out to feel the bumps and lumps of the oil paint, reading the woman's expression with her fingertips, knowing full well she'd be on the receiving end of a slap if she were caught in the act. There's something funny about the picture too: something to do with the children sitting on the lady's knee. They look like two little harlequins, trying to make her laugh. Just as well, because she needs cheering up, Annabel thinks, turning to another shrouded painting, twice as big as her. Her curiosity stoked, she ducks under the sheet to take a good look. It's only when she moves her head back that she can see two bodies, nude, legs splayed out, hairy genitalia on display in all their raw frankness. She finds herself recoiling, thrust out from under the sheet.

There were many such paintings that used to hang shamelessly around the Edelsteins' home. Papa always expressed his disapproval. 'It's that Zuckerkandl woman,' Annabel had heard him say to Mama over breakfast one day, after Mama had given an impassioned defence of the Austrian Expressionists. (What they expressed, Annabel had no idea.) 'The hold she has over you and the Edelsteins makes me wonder.' In reply, Mama had simply dabbed her mouth with her napkin and walked out of the dining room, leaving Annabel to imagine the exotic wonders of Bertha Zuckerkandl's salon.

Annabel daren't look at the other paintings; who knows what else she'll discover.

'That'll teach me,' she says to herself as she runs through the living room and out into the garden where she finds Oskar brandishing a wooden sword.

'Take that!' he says, pointing its blunt tip at her.

CHAPTER EIGHT

A familiar noise rang out. I stirred for a moment before plunging back into my drunken sleep. The ringing stopped, only to resume minutes later, its harsh tone shrilling through my ears. I straddled limbo and the depths of a muddled dream. This time I was a school boy, sitting in an examination hall staring at a blank sheet of paper, unable to answer the essay question, *Discuss the key rights and implications of the 1955 Austrian Independence Treaty*. I couldn't recollect my history lessons and cursed myself for the scant attention I had paid in class. The prospect of failure worsened with the sound of a mobile phone ringing through the hall. Musical notes appeared on my answer sheet, first as faint shadows, before turning darker. Entrenched on the page, they danced to an unknown tune. The ringing was incessant as I tried to erase the notes, my despair increasing with each tick of the overlarge clock hanging on the wall. My heart skipped a beat and I hit something hard.

I had fallen out of bed.

I picked myself up and searched for my glasses in the neon-edged darkness. I found them on my pillow, thankfully intact.

Then I remembered: some friends from work had dragged me out. Lana, the girl I had met on the sailing holiday back in the summer, had also been there, which had given me further incentive to go. I hadn't returned to my flat on Wimpole Street until the early hours and must have fallen asleep fully clothed on my bed. My mouth felt as if it were stuffed full of cotton wool and the telltale signs of a hangover were beginning to reveal themselves. Stumbling over to the kitchen, I berated myself for staying out so long and for drinking too much. The ringing had since stopped and I didn't think to check my phone. All I wanted was to dilute the hangover poised to swallow my body whole.

I looked at the clock on the oven door. It was close to six – way too early in the morning to be harangued by phone calls. My mobile rang again. I went through to the hallway and found it on the table. Lana had sent a text message to say that she had left the keys to my apartment on the nightstand in my bedroom and that she looked forward to seeing me again soon, signing off with hopes that my head would feel better in the morning. Seeing her message gave me a momentary lift, until I saw several missed calls: two unknown, the rest from my mother's lawyer, Frederik Müller. I couldn't fathom why he would call me repeatedly, and at that time of day, unless it was something important. I called him back.

'Max – thank God.'

'What's happened?' My voice was nothing but a croak, and I struggled to hear Frederik over the din in the background. 'Where are you?'

'I'm at your mother's – your – house with the police and forensics. There's been an incident. A break-in.'

I blinked, trying to make sense of what Frederik was telling me. I stood quite motionless, unable to move. The house's contents, its works of art flashed through my mind … *The Schiele.* I suddenly realised how detached I'd felt about these things until now. To think it had taken a robbery to inject the responsibility of ownership into me.

'There was no alarm – Christ!' I had meant for one to be installed, but since my return to London, work and discussions with my architect had consumed all of my time and before I knew it, October had slipped by. It was a poor excuse. Thinking of the priceless work of art, the words *careless* and *stupid* came to mind, along with a slew of swear words.

'What's been taken?' I asked, bracing myself for the answer.

'Nothing.'

'You're kidding, right?' Thank God, I thought to myself.

'Around three a.m.,' said Frederik, 'the police came across a white transit van abandoned in front of the house with its back doors wide open. All the things that were taken from the house were still inside it. They saw the light switched on in the hallway. The front door was unlocked. They found ...'

'Frederik?'

'The place looks as though a hurricane ripped through it,' he said eventually.

My throat constricted; my mouth filled with saliva. Phone in hand I rushed to the bathroom and retched into the toilet.

'Max? Max? Are you all right?'

I slumped against the bathroom wall, pulling down a towel from the hook above my head to wipe my mouth. 'I'm okay.' For a moment I was lost for a response. 'What's the damage?'

Frederik spoke in short bursts. 'The art's fine. The banister on the first floor's damaged. It's as if someone fell through it or flung something against it.'

'Who's behind the break-in – do they know?'

'There's speculation, but nothing concrete.'

I laughed out loud. I couldn't help it. I just couldn't picture my mother's pristine house, ransacked. In fact, the whole conversation, with me sitting on the bathroom floor, had a surreal quality, like I had jumped from one bizarre dream to the next.

'They also found a book that had been taken from the library,' said Frederik.

'So they're after a thief with a literary bent?'

'Max ...'

'This isn't the time. I'm sorry.'

'There was something written inside.' He fell quiet.

'What exactly?'

He hesitated before answering. 'You really need to come and deal with this yourself.'

I sighed. 'I'll see what flights are available and get there as soon as I can.' Before hanging up, I said, 'I'm sorry it was you they called first. I appreciate you being there.'

'It's all right. It's hard for me to leave your mother behind.'

I couldn't tell whether it was tenderness or resignation that I heard in his voice, but there was something about the way he spoke that I'd never picked up on during past conversations. It wasn't implausible that he had been attracted to my mother – according to Vivienne a lot of men were – but my mother had seldom shown much interest in men after my father died.

I arrived at the house in the early afternoon. Frederik stood in the driveway with a man whom he introduced as Thomas Schmidt, the detective in charge. He had a haggard air about him: hunched shoulders, dishevelled hair and a face stained by a permanent five o'clock shadow. Frederik, too, looked far from his best with the dark smudge of fatigue under his eyes. Not that I was in any position to judge: on my way over, I had downed a combination of paracetamol and ibuprofen to stem the throb of my head, but my hangover still lingered, threatening to strike back. It was made worse by the realisation that I may have encouraged the break-in.

There was something about that taxi driver, Zoran, and his observations that had continued to eat away at me. But now … it all made sense. How could I have been so stupid? *There is someone there?* That's what he had asked. He claimed to have seen someone by one of the windows, but what if, *what if*, he had been fishing for information? So much for his sympathetic act, his innocent questions. *There is someone there?* Rattled by my state of mind, my exhaustion, I had told him the house lay empty, thinking he too had glimpsed a presence when he was merely establishing the facts.

'We just sent the third reporter away,' said Schmidt, his voice pulling me away from thoughts of Zoran. 'News in Vienna is quiet at the moment. The slightest sniff of a story gets them out like a pack of wolves.' His cigarette habit revealed itself in the rasp of his voice and nicotine-tinged breath. He nodded to a couple of police officers ambling by the gate. 'They'll stay until the fuss dies down.'

'We've given them a few facts to keep them happy,' said Frederik. 'Attempted break-in and so on.'

'Evidence in the van points to a Serbian gang. We think they're linked to three or four robberies,' said Schmidt.

I looked up at the house. I couldn't tell them about Zoran. Not just yet.

'Feel free to go in. Everyone's left. Just to warn you though – it's not pretty.'

Frederik put a hand on my back as we walked up the steps. 'We'll get it cleared up. Don't worry, Max,' he said.

The police and forensics team had finished their initial work and we were alone in the house. I surveyed the leftovers from the break-in and investigation: the white evidence signs, the powdery finger-printing marks on the walls and furniture. I gazed up to the first floor gallery with the banister ripped away. In its place was police crime-scene tape rippling in the draught from the open door.

'It's like they were possessed,' I said.

Frederik nodded. 'And if they really leapt down, they can't have escaped uninjured.'

I took in the remnants of a shattered Chinese vase, the walls, stripped of their works of art. Only the sculptures of the angel and saint remained intact, like silent witnesses to the scene.

I walked through to the drawing room. Broken glass and china ornaments littered the floor, and the back wall appeared vulnerable without the Schiele.

'Even though it's no longer my home – it feels …'

'It's a personal violation, I know,' said Frederik. 'You were lucky.'

A conflict played out in my mind: the violation, as Frederik put it, mixed with guilt for failing to oversee the property adequately and the information I had unknowingly slipped to Zoran. 'I hope they find the bas …' The expression in Frederik's eyes stopped me short. Just then, Schmidt came into the room.

'Frederik told me the thief had written in a book. Where is it?' I asked him.

'Let's go into the kitchen. The light's better there.'

Schmidt and I sat down at the table while Frederik busied himself finding glasses and a jug for water.

'There's something I need to tell you,' I said. They both looked at me. I told them about my conversation with Zoran, giving as best a description of the man as I could.

Schmidt pinched his lips together, scribbling a few notes in a notepad. 'When he spoke to his wife or whoever it was he was on the phone to, was he speaking Serb?' asked Schmidt.

'I've no idea,' I said. 'I just know his name was Zoran. He seemed like a decent guy. It never occurred to me that he was scoping the place out.' I glanced at Frederik and then Schmidt. 'I feel like an idiot.'

'You weren't to know, Max,' said Frederik.

'We'll track him down,' was the sum total of Schmidt's response, but I couldn't help thinking that what I'd told him had lowered his opinion of me. 'Now,' he said, fishing a clear plastic bag out of his coat pocket, 'perhaps you can help us with this.' He pulled on some plastic gloves and retrieved the book from inside the bag. My mouth went dry. It was Torberg's *Young Gerber*. Of all the books they could have chosen. Perhaps I had left it sticking out slightly when I returned it to the library, making it appear as if it were begging to be taken, just like the subtly nudged card in a magician's card trick.

'It's a first edition. I'm sorry,' said Frederik, sliding back a chair to join us. I wished the state of the book was my sole concern.

Schmidt opened the book at a page that was now marked with a red sticker, and swivelled the book around for me to see.

'We can't make head nor tail of it – nor why they chose to write in English,' he said.

A black felt tip pen had been used to scrawl across the two pages, completely defacing them. But what was far worse to my mind was the fact that the handwriting carried an unmistakable likeness to the handwriting on the back of the photograph my mother had left me. The childlike formations of each letter, paired with the deliberate aggression with which they were written spelt out: *O kneels, rats die*. Although the words were nonsensical, they jarred. I tried to pick through them to read the novel's text. I looked again to make sure, trying to ignore the anxiety unfurling in the pit of my stomach. The author of the message had chosen the page where I had stopped reading: at the death of one of Gerber's classmates.

I shifted in my seat. 'Where did you find it?'

'On the doorstep,' said Schmidt, his eyes darting from me to the book. 'We can't make sense of it. We want to hold on to it – get the handwriting analysed.'

Frederik touched my arm. 'I know a man who's good at restoring these kind of things. I'll get it seen to.'

I looked at him, failing to register his offer to help. I couldn't begin to tell them about the matching handwriting on the back of the photograph, nor could I tell them that I had been reading this book when I was last at the house and had stopped reading at the very spot where the message was penned. Had someone been watching me, or was it simply that the book had fallen open where I'd bent it back while reading? The rational part of me wanted to believe that an explanation could be found for everything. Yet it was the handwriting and the reference to rats that disturbed me.

The echo of voices, one of them belonging to Vivienne, came from the hallway. I had spoken to her before I boarded my flight to try to lessen the impact of the news. Despite my protestations, she had insisted on coming to Himmelhofgasse. A police officer showed her into the kitchen.

'I can't believe it,' she said, the shock blanched on her face. 'Whatever next?'

Frederik got up to leave. Patting my shoulder he said, 'I'll get this all cleaned up for you too – once the police are satisfied with their investigation.'

'Please – you don't need to do that.'

He brushed off my faint rebuttal. Admittedly, I was grateful for his assistance. In London I would have known what to do, where to go, who to speak to. Here, in Ober St. Veit, Vienna, I had no idea where to start, no contacts to call, and I was reluctant to burden Vivienne with requests for help.

'We'll be done in a few days or so,' said Schmidt. He returned the book to its plastic bag, then pushed back his chair. 'I'll be outside if you need me.'

Vivienne and I sat in silence for a while, both of us wondering over our own *what ifs* and *why*s. I tussled with the idea of confiding in her. 'There was a message written in a book from the library,' I said, pouring some water for her.

'What did it say?'

'*O kneels, rats die.*'

She looked at me, quite perplexed.

'It's not just the message. It's the handwriting.' I took a sip from my glass. 'I never showed you the photograph – but remember I told you about the writing on the back?'

'Like a child's, you said.'

'The writing in the book – it matches the handwriting on the back of that photo.'

Vivienne stared at me, creasing her brow.

'I'm almost certain.' Even though the photograph had been lying in my desk drawer undisturbed for a few weeks, the writing was imprinted on my mind. 'And the book ...'

A loud thud, like the sound of a box falling to the floor, interrupted me. I looked at Vivienne.

'Perhaps one of the officers is upstairs. I'll go and check,' I said, heading into the hallway. 'Is everything okay?' I called out. A few seconds passed without a response. I stepped outside, spotting Schmidt by the gate with one of the officers. He drew his cigarette from his mouth and dropped it to the floor, squashing it with his shoe. 'Is one of your men upstairs?'

He jogged up to me, shaking his head. 'What's wrong?'

'We heard something,' I said, stepping back inside. 'I'll take a look – it's probably nothing.'

I headed to the stairs. My hand went to the banister, but I couldn't bring myself to touch it. And when I took the first step, I hesitated. Doubt re-entered my head. I peered up to the gallery again. It was probably nothing, just as I had told Schmidt. I carried on, glancing ahead of me and over the edge of the banister.

On the first floor gallery I came to a halt, face to face with more of the thieves' destruction. Pictures hung askew, a vase lay half broken on the landing. I tracked their handiwork. The damaged banister looked like a dismembered body. I picked my way around the debris, moving from one room to the next, each one with its door flung wide open, the violation plain to see. The last room was my own, where the damage felt worse than an intrusion. My model cars, camera, books and other possessions had been strewn across the floor; drawers were cast out, a couple of them had been upended. My bedding, some of it ripped, muddied, soiled even, lay heaped on the carpet. I stood there with my back to the doorway, taking it in. And as I did so, a chill ran down my spine. I wheeled round, my joints stiff, almost unyielding. Only the vacant doorframe met my gaze. Yet I couldn't help feeling that someone was watching me.

I walked back out on to the gallery to find Schmidt and Vivienne looking up at me from the hall down below.

'Anything?' asked Schmidt.

It took me a few seconds to acknowledge his question. I shook my head.

'And the second floor?'

A crash resounded through the house.

Vivienne's hand went to her chest. We all stood stock-still, staring up at the second floor gallery. Silence enveloped the interior. Glancing at Schmidt, I moved towards the staircase. He silently motioned to me to stop, but I ignored him and carried on while he shuffled Vivienne away. I began to climb the stairs, my hand sweeping the wall, the noise loud enough to carry in the hush of the house. I was quite alone, and although I knew my solitude was momentary, I sensed a change in the air, the way it lingered about me. It had something to do with the house, its silence drifting through the interior, mirroring the stillness that had wrapped around me in the cellar. My resolve faltered. I stopped midway. I thought I heard something other than the brush of my hand against the wall. I tilted my head to the ceiling and took another step up. There it was again: travelling back and forth above me. It sounded like it came from the attic. And as I listened, it took on more force and speed, stuttering along the floor, east to west across the house. There was something else too, but I couldn't quite pinpoint it: a sound akin to murmurs, snatches of voices in the walls.

I continued up the stairs, fighting against the play of my imagination. With each tread, I pictured the attic as it should be: light pouring through its high window, boxes, shelves, old furniture my mother couldn't bear to dispose of, forgotten toys. An ordinary room: that was all it was. I came to the second floor. The doors to the three bedrooms were open, throwing funnels of light on to the landing. Each one had been left untouched.

I noticed, then, the sweeping to and fro above me had ceased.

The door to the attic stairs remained closed. I inched towards it, the floorboards creaking shamelessly under my shoes. I wavered in front of it for a moment, picturing someone hiding up there, a notion I couldn't shrug off. As if to confirm my suspicions, I thought I could hear the faint patter of footsteps; in my head, the image of a child flared up. A lost child. *That* child. Perhaps, then, it wasn't a trick of the light, or my state of mind. My hand gripped the handle.

It was locked like before. I leaned in, listening out for the faintest sound. But there was nothing. I twisted the handle to the left, then right, shaking it, forcing it to give way, yet it still held fast.

I banged on the door. 'Is there anyone there?' I called out. Silence.

I banged again. 'Is there anyone there?'

I stepped back, staring at the door, wanting a response. It came, or at least it seemed to, in the form of a muffled cry. I crouched down and put one eye to the keyhole. The figure of a child was edging its way down the stairs.

'You're not in trouble,' I whispered. 'Please don't cry.' I thought back to that night in the cellar. It could be the same child, the girl.

'Is everything all right?' asked Schmidt as he and one of the officers came up to the second floor landing.

I turned to them, my jaw set. 'There's someone in there.' I pointed to the door. 'It's a child. I heard her. We need to get her out.'

'Are you sure?'

'Certain. The door's jammed.'

Schmidt and the officer exchanged puzzled looks.

'What's wrong?'

'We had no problem getting in earlier,' said Schmidt. 'We had a quick look, but it seems no one's been in there for a while.'

'That can't be,' I said. To illustrate my case, I tried the door. It sprung open with little effort. Light teemed through the window at the back of the attic, flowing down the staircase. I stared at the door handle, then at my hand, then at the officers. 'How's that possible? I swear, it was stuck.'

A look of wariness stole across Schmidt's eyes. I turned my back on him and ran up the stairs into the attic, determined to find the child hiding away. But I found nothing out of the ordinary. To one side lay an old bed with an iron bedstead; on either side of it stood two armchairs shrouded in white sheets. A wardrobe and an old chest stood next to the window; the wardrobe doors were open, revealing nothing but a rusted metal rail. On the other side of the room was a crib, naked without its linen and muslin, and an old leather trunk, its chestnut patina faded and scratched. Perched on top was a forlorn-looking puppet theatre. A number of wooden crates with books, papers and photo albums peeping out of them and packed round with straw lay stacked against the wall closest to the door. In the centre of the room lay four or five similar boxes. One of them had fallen over, its contents spilling out on to the floor. Oblivious to Schmidt and the other police officer, I walked around the room, seeking out hiding places – behind the crates, under the bed, inside the wooden chest and wardrobe – disturbing the layer of dust that had lain dormant before my arrival.

My search was futile. There were no signs of a child, other than the old relics of nursery furniture and playthings. In all, there was little to suggest the presence of anybody living there, concealed or otherwise, past or present. And no indication of entry or escape.

I turned to the two men, who were watching me from the top of the staircase. Against Schmidt's advice, Vivienne had sought us out and squeezed her way between him and the police officer to join me. She looked about her, then put her arm around me.

'I swear I heard a child.' I turned to Vivienne. 'You heard her too.'

'I heard something.'

'You see!'

'I heard something fall. It was this box, that's all.' Her voice was quiet, almost faltering. 'I didn't hear a child, Max.' She lowered her eyes.

Schmidt cleared his throat. 'We'll be downstairs.'

I kept my back turned, wishing only to hide my embarrassment at having created a melodrama. Yet all the same I couldn't understand how the door could simply open without force when only moments before, it held fast. In the brief time I had been alone at the attic door, I was quite certain of what I heard: it wasn't just the travail back and forth, but the footsteps, the hushed weeping. Was this episode a by-product of my hangover? Or was it, when added to my other experiences, a symptom suggesting something far worse? As Schmidt and the officer thundered back down the stairs I kicked one of the crates.

'Max ...' Vivienne reached for my hand.

I shrugged it away. 'I'm fine.'

'It's me, Max. Remember? You can tell me.'

I crouched down beside the fallen wooden box and set it back upright. 'What's happening to me, Vivienne?' I hoped she didn't notice the tremor in my hands as she knelt beside me, her hand rubbing my back as she used to do when I was a child. I tried to keep my voice steady. 'It's like my ... What I see and hear ... It makes me think of what happened to my grandmother.'

'Enough, Max.' Her quiet response was as gentle as her hand on my back.

'I was starting to feel okay again and now ... now *this*.'

'When something happens – a death, an act of violence – it impresses itself upon us in different ways. Our senses are heightened: you smelled your mother's perfume when you returned. You said you felt and heard things. I still hear her chattering away. Do you see that?'

'I want to.'

She got to her feet. 'Would it help to ... see someone?' she asked, flipping through an old album she had plucked from one of the nearby boxes.

'Christ! No. No way.' The very act of seeking help felt like defeat, even though I knew I was being sabotaged by ill-feeling, self-doubt and the tail end of emotions that my mother's death had brought about.

She tucked the album back into the box again. 'Do you want a moment?'

I nodded and managed a half-smile. Her footsteps faded away as I tidied up the remaining things: news articles, photo albums. I had little desire to look through them. The faces and references, mostly anonymous, failed to stir my interest, until I came across a thick notebook. It had a piece of frayed red ribbon tied around its mottled deer-hide cover. I loosened it and flicked through the coarse pages: the book was filled with sketches and neat handwriting that matured towards the end. Tucked at the back were three newspaper clippings; browned and brittle, they carried a whiff of papery mould. While I didn't read them in full, I did notice circles drawn around three names with two digits written above them:

36
Elena Markovic

35
Christine Hintze

37
Josef Frank

'Max?' Vivienne's voice floated to the upper reaches of the house. I slipped the articles back into the notebook and re-tied the ribbon. Taking the notebook with me, I got up and made my way down the stairs, closing the attic door behind me. I paused for a second, deciding whether or not to try the door handle again. The door opened without effort. I tried again: it responded with no hint of it sticking. A test wouldn't be a valid test without trying a third time. The door opened as smoothly as before. I pushed it further back and glanced up the stairs again. Vivienne's laughter sailed up from the entrance hall, followed by Schmidt's laugh-cum-smoker's cough. For a moment I wondered whether the joke was on my account. I stopped myself there. Vivienne wouldn't do such a thing. I could only wonder at myself – the ease with which I paired seemingly innocent sounds with images in my head, making me overreact, making me look cartoonish in the eyes of Schmidt and his men.

But then there was *Young Gerber* and the writing inside. It was less the message and more the handwriting, the assault of the letters matching the writing of *You knew* on the photograph's reverse. I needed to lay out everything I had experienced, to map out each detail, sifting the elements that were fact from those that made little sense. A thread of explanation had to be found. It didn't require a therapist or medical treatment to figure it out.

What I still couldn't decide was whether to tell Vivienne about it all. I didn't want to worry her with my stories and theories, things that might lead her to believe I was disturbed. But still, she might be able to answer some of my questions. That would be the extent to which I'd let her in.

Annabel sits at her table in the nursery, scribbling in her notebook. The date, 15th April, is written at the top, followed by a couple of lines, but then she wobbles. Letting her pencil run free is her way of stemming her tears. After all, she promised Mama she'd be brave. Mama said that Oskar would be back in no time at all, but Annabel doesn't understand why he had to leave in the first place. She can't fathom why everyone's talking about the Edelsteins' trip. She's seen Mama cry. Papa hasn't been around for the last few days. If he were around, he would make things better, that's certain. Mama would stop crying, everyone would stop whispering and being all jittery, and she'd be allowed to go to the orphanage with Mama. She likes it there. She's been going more often now she has no one to play with. The house felt emptier without Eva, but at least Oskar had still been around then.

'And now he's gone too.' Her pencil stops. She presses the tip into the book and the lead crushes. Her lips tremble and Annabel can't help it now, as she grabs another pencil and knifes it through the paper soaked with her tears. Then she takes the page and rips it out of the notebook, and now she can't stop as she slashes out the next, and then the next, stopping at the one with her sketch of Eva. She takes one look at it and rips it away just as Maria walks in.

'Fräulein Annabel, you mustn't.' Maria moves the notebook away and brings Annabel into her arms, hugging her like Eva used to.

And more tears flow as Annabel's and Maria's bodies echo the sadness tolling around them.

CHAPTER NINE

Although Vivienne was doing her best to move on from my mother's death, she continued to mourn in her own way. That evening, back at her home, she put on Verdi's *Messa da Requiem* from beginning to end, insisting on listening to 'Agnus Dei' three times. Away from the backdrop of my mother's funeral, in the comfort of Vivienne's living room, I found it beautiful. Until then, I wasn't familiar with the piece. I had never really taken to classical music or opera, even though Vivienne had tried her best with me over the years. This movement, however, with the haunting rise and fall of its melody, the lullaby duet of the soprano and mezzo soprano, and the way in which the choir and orchestra floated towards its gentle end, for me at least, removed any sense of God or piety from the prayer, turning it instead into a piece of poetry. And for a while, it drew me away from everything that had happened.

Vivienne didn't raise the subject of *Young Gerber* and the words written inside the book, nor did she talk about what had happened in the attic. She probably wanted to have a few hours without thinking about the break-in and the wrecked state of the house. She skilfully avoided the topic, swiftly introducing another subject when the last one came to an end. As a result, our discussion spanned politics, authors, art and technology. She had bought herself a computer and decided to enrol on a course to learn to navigate the Internet. I admired her determination to constantly challenge herself, to shun the temptation to live in the past. She filled her calendar with social activities and her work at the Albertina, wanting to keep her life and mind active. Perhaps my mother's passing had reinforced that desire – to continue to seize every opportunity to live, and to push herself, spurred on by the thought that time was never on your side.

She told me about a tour she was giving for a class of seven-year-olds at the museum the following day. She enjoyed working with the young ones the most, taking care to select works of art that enabled her to tell the most colourful stories and histories.

'You should come along,' she said.

I laughed. 'You're kidding, right?'

'I'm being quite serious. It'll do you good to get out and about.'

'I'll think about it.' It was as if she wanted to look out for me, like a guardian angel. It wasn't that she was smothering me. She knew better than that. Perhaps she did sense something unsettling and wanted to stop me from wallowing.

Later that night I lay in Vivienne's spare bedroom thinking through everything that had happened thus far. The first night in my mother's house, the French windows thrown wide open: *fact*. The slip of shadows, the sensation of someone next to me, the reflection in the window: *fiction* – the stuff of Hollywood films. The second night in the house, the broken photograph: *fact*. The cellar, the lights flickering on and off: *fact* – the aged wiring was no doubt a factor, as attested by the lighting in the hallway. The image of the girl: *fiction* – a trick of the light, a product of my fatigue. Where I thought I had placed the photograph as opposed to where it ended up: *fiction* – exhaustion had fogged my mind. What the taxi driver had seen: *fiction* – doubtful. I really didn't want to think about how Zoran had played me. The attic, the footsteps, the crying, the image of the child: *fiction* – my senses were *simply heightened*, as Vivienne put it. I stopped. It struck me that I was fulfilling some sort of confirmation bias and I wondered whether it made sense to carry on. But then I had no other way to frame my experiences, so I continued.

I turned to the photograph. The words on the back: *fact*. That Oskar withheld something: *fact* – at least I thought so. The book, *Young Gerber*, and the pages selected to scrawl the message, the same page where I had left off: *fact*. The words, *O kneels, rats die*: *fact*. That the message carried a meaning I could only presume, but what exactly, I had no idea. Whether one of the thieves wrote it ... No, that was impossible. They couldn't have written it, just like they couldn't have written the message on the back of the photograph. I visualised the handwriting on the reverse of the image. The same. *Fact, fact, fact*. I wished I had it to hand. In frustration, I kicked back my quilt and got out of bed. Apart from the writing, everything else could be explained away. While I paced my room, I thought back to Oskar and the things he had said. He held the missing link to my own sanity and I needed a way to reach out to him without it appearing like I was haranguing him. My eyes fell on the notebook lying atop my clothes piled at the end of the bed. Maybe it contained something I could share with Oskar.

I sat back down on the bed and weighed it in my hands, considering the possible contents – the excerpts from my mother's childhood, the parts that were unknown to me. I wanted it to evoke a different image of my mother. I wanted to see glimmers of the person Vivienne knew and loved. I slid out the news articles and put them on the bedside table. Running my fingers along the notebook's edge, I opened it up.

Written in pencil, in careful sloping handwriting, was my mother's name in full, *Annabel Maria Konstantina Albrecht*, and the date: 1st January, 1938, followed by the words, *A Christmas gift from Papa*. A pencil drawing of a boy and a girl graced the first page. Above their heads, also written in pencil, was the inscription, *A&O*. I smiled to myself. There was an innocence to it, in the childlike lines, the faces, the stretched grins. This had to be a picture of my mother with Oskar. I could certainly show this to him. I flicked through the rest of the notebook. Much of it was intact, although a few pages had been torn out, the serrated edges at the spine the only evidence of their previous existence. I went back to the beginning and started again, more slowly this time. The subjects she had drawn ranged from people and faces to everyday objects – animals, trees and flowers. A melange of images and words peppered single pages, while standalone studies dominated others. On some pages there was just writing. On closer inspection, they were more like sporadic diary entries, short and to the point. Some entries followed in quick succession; others were separated by a gap of several weeks or, in some cases, months. All of them were written in 1938. In one, she made reference to a person called *E*:

18th March, 1938.

I went down to the kitchens. Fritz gave me a piece of cake and told me not to tell Maria. I asked him about E. I had asked him so many times before, but he never answered my questions. This time he told me Papa had found her a position in Salzburg. He said they needed her most urgently. I asked Mama about it too and she said that it was a good job – Papa had arranged it. She said that I should be happy for her. I try to be, but I wish we had said goodbye.

In another, she had referred to someone I could only assume was Oskar:

16th April, 1938.

O left in the middle of the night. I'm very sad. I told Mama that I was feeling quite poorly. She felt my forehead and told Maria to keep me in bed.

It appeared, then, that she and Oskar had been quite close as children. Had she later forgotten him, just as he had forgotten her?

Other entries hinted at her early involvement in The Albrecht Trust:

15th July, 1938.

Today I went on my weekly trip to the orphanage with Mama. I heard Mama tell Frau Werner that that little moustachioed Nazi would certainly not be shutting down the Trust. Afterwards we bought some cakes at Demel.

And some were quite amusing:

28th September, 1938.

Herr Adler came today. He insisted on embracing me. I told Mama that he smells. She became quite cross and told me that he was leaving too.

The drawings and diary entries from that first year continued in their haphazard way, the sketches evolving into something that one could apply the term 'talent' to. Maturity and confidence transcended her lines, shadings, proportions and angles. Vivienne had referred to this skill of my mother's, but I'd seen little evidence of it up until now. I studied her work, hovering my finger over her pencil and charcoal marks, and her drawings kindled my new-found respect for her.

After 1938, the diary entries ceased – perhaps my mother grew bored of recording her daily life, maybe she found other distractions, or possibly she simply misplaced the notebook and found it by chance in a forgotten place. Some of her later pictures were dated, others weren't. What was more notable, however, was the intensity of her sketches. One that stood out was dated 13th February, 1944. She had employed a darker pencil. Vertical and horizontal lines ran along the border of the page. Vicious in their strokes, the pressure of her pencil had penetrated the paper so that in places, rips appeared where she had forced her pencil to a halt. She had drawn a landscape, capturing the sky in a series of dark diagonal lines. A tree stood in the centre, naked without its leaves, its bark gnarled with knots. And beside it, the outline of a girl: a crude image, with the head and body drawn out of proportion. It seemed to rebel against her developing skill. Underneath my mother had written:

Run.
Away. Away.
Quietly now. Quietly.
Eyes closed. Mouth sealed.

I examined the picture, juxtaposed with my mother's words. Leafing through the notebook, I found similar drawings and musings of a girl entering the world of adolescence with all its insecurities, made worse by the hardships of war: smouldering

106

rubble, stick-men soldiers, weeping children, ragged Jews, a star of David with a swastika emblazoned in its centre.

Directly after this piece were two sketches of the same subject, each filling a single page. I recognised the image she had copied: it was the Schiele that hung in the drawing room. No month or year had been assigned to the first drawing. She had changed the faces of the three individuals and had drawn the child on the left as much older, still perched on her mother's lap, but with longer hair and wearing a dress, staring directly at the other child. I turned my attention to the picture of the mother: I recognised her as my own grandmother by the slope of her nose, that determined jaw I'd seen in photographs. Her eyes, like the original, were cast down, but looked directly at the infant she cradled. The baby in this drawing differed markedly from the original painting: his eyes were closed, as was his mouth; his head lolled back and his body lay limp in his mother's arms. Underneath his image was the word, *tot* – dead. It was quite a crude way for my mother to record the death of her brother, Thaddäus. Apparently he had died before he was six months old. As I understood it, the event had proved too much for my grandmother: it had tipped her into a breakdown from which she never recovered. My grandfather sent her to a sanatorium in Switzerland where she later passed away.

I then turned to the second rendition of the Schiele. The younger child remained unchanged from the first version. The image of the girl, however, was nothing more than a faint outline – an empty shell – positioned slightly behind and to the side of the matriarch. The mother's face was also just an outline. But by her feet, my mother had drawn the body of a man, his arms splayed out, one leg curled up under the other and his head contorted, twisting in the direction of the observer. His eyes were stretched wide, revealing nothing but their whites.

Underneath his body was the date, 10th July 1944: the day my grandfather passed away. At the bottom of the page, my mother had written:

Love, anger,
Shame.
Be gone.

I didn't know what to make of the picture – or the words for that matter. A few moments later, I returned to it, scanning the pages, the sketches. I wanted Vivienne's perspective of the time my grandfather passed away. All I knew was that he had died of a heart attack. And while I had a vague idea of who *Fritz* and *Maria* were, there were other things – like the reference to *E* – where I drew a blank.

I placed the notebook on the bedside table, disturbing the newspaper cut-outs. I picked one up. It reported the discovery of a murdered child, Elena Markovic. She was sixteen years old and had been under the care of the orphanage. Some railway workers discovered her body, barely clothed, alongside a disused section of railway. She had been strangled and her hands and feet had been bound. I looked at the number scribbled above her name in the article: *36*. I looked at the other two articles. They, too, reported the discovery of murdered children: Josef Frank, aged fifteen, and Christine Hintze, aged twelve. They were also said to have come from the orphanage, both alleged to have run away. A farm labourer came across Christine Hintze's body in grassland close to the border with Hungary. According to the article, he had been arrested and charged with her murder, but he had hanged himself while in police custody. Josef Frank's body was found in the woodland neighbouring my mother's house. I sat up. I had no idea that any of this had happened.

As I reread the newspaper clippings, I realised there was a pattern to the murders: all three had been strangled; all three were found in the same semi-undressed state; all three had been in the care of The Albrecht Trust. The news stories referenced my grandparents, their sorrow and their offer of a reward to find the culprit. In the article covering Elena Markovic, my grandparents' photograph shared centre stage with a grainy image of the girl.

I wondered if Vivienne knew anything about the disappearances, whether the *E* in my mother's diary referred to this Elena Markovic, and whether my grandparents had tried to protect their daughter by keeping the story hidden from her. I pictured my mother as a curious girl faced with the whirl of people leaving her life, people that she cared for. I tried to imagine how I would feel. I thought about the people that had left my life: my father, my brother, Chanoo, people that I barely remembered. Did I miss them for long, or did I just carry on with my life? That part was a blur, and I wondered if that was just a child's way of coping, of attempting to erase the past.

The following day I called my boss. I was due to travel to New York for a series of meetings. Given the most recent events at the house, I needed to take some time off again.

He laughed out loud. 'You've gotta be kidding me.'

'I know,' I said. 'I feel like a school kid explaining why I've bunked off.'

'The next thing you'll tell me,' he said, 'is that your house burnt down.' He laughed again. 'Don't worry.' He paused, and I knew what was coming. 'You're in line to make partner next year – you know that, don't you? You'll be one of the youngest.'

I'd heard this speech of his before and it had given me a boost. This time he ended it differently.

'So long as you don't fuck up, it'll be a shoo-in.' I should have been happy. But this message of his was more coded than anything else. I didn't want to let him down anymore.

I ended my call with him just as Vivienne was rushing out to give her tour to the group of school children. 'You're sure you won't join me?' she said, pulling on her coat.

I gave her a kiss on the cheek. 'I think I'll go for a run instead,' I said. 'Somehow, I don't think the chatter of children will clear my head.'

'You might learn some patience, Max.'

'I'm too young for all that.' I grinned, watching her shake her head as she closed the door behind her.

I had told Vivienne over breakfast about the notebook and articles. She was intrigued, and excited about looking through them with me on her return. I knew that if I stayed at home, I would simply brood over the material, so not long after she left, I went out for my run, heading off in the direction of the Schlosspark.

The sky had a wintry blue about it, with wisps of clouds milling in the distance. The coolness of the wind whipped around me as I jogged down Hietzinger Hauptstrasse, dodging the handful of pedestrians in my path. The quietude of the place displaced thoughts of the notebook. I lengthened my stride and my breathing relaxed as I entered Schlosspark. Whim dictated my route along the park's geometric paths, taking me around the Versaillesque Schloss Schönbrunn, uphill, downhill around the perimeter, the zoo and towards the cemetery at the south-west corner. From the crest of a hill, I could make out the bobbles of gravestones and memorials: they reminded me of a miniature army standing uniformly in their lines. I thought I could just make out the part of the graveyard where my mother's body lay along with the other members of our family.

The sight of a lone figure wandering through the cemetery caught my eye. A mere matchstick man from my viewpoint, I assumed he was a lone tourist searching out the resting place of Gustav Klimt or Engelbert Dollfuss or some other notable figure. I watched him with voyeuristic curiosity, waiting to see what he would do. Appearing to take his time, he stopped now and again at a few of the plots, spotting, I presumed, a headstone or memorial or vault of interest. I continued to track his movements. After about five minutes he came to a stop by my family's plot. At first I thought its golden relief of Christ had caught his attention, but he lingered there much longer. He reached out to touch the memorial, as I am sure others did too – that wasn't altogether unusual. But then he took a step back, bowed his head as if in prayer, and retrieving an object from a bag, crouched down and laid whatever it was at the foot of the memorial. He got up swiftly, looked about him and hurried towards the exit.

Picturing him as another anonymous admirer of my mother's, I wondered what he'd placed there. I jogged down to the cemetery, taking a short cut through the woodland lining one side of its perimeter. At the gates I glimpsed a vintage Mercedes R107 convertible pulling out. It looked just like the model of it that I had on my bedroom windowsill – it was silver too – and I experienced a momentary rush of excitement to see a real one in Vienna. Once the car had disappeared from view, I headed into the cemetery, trying to find the most direct route to my family's plot. After doubling back a couple of times, I arrived at the grave. Amongst some freshly cut flowers – probably left by Vivienne – was a small wooden plaque. I bent down to take a proper look at it.

It was a miniature coat of arms, comprising two majestic angels holding a shield between them. It was adorned with a silver key, a golden crucifix and a crown, all set against a chequered backdrop of red and white. Engraved at the bottom was the motto, *Quaecumque vera doce me* – teach me whatsoever is true. The coat of arms belonged to my mother's family. I regarded it as an odd offering to leave at her grave. For a brief, mad moment I thought I would take it with me, but common sense prevailed and I left it alone.

So I cast the thought to one side and turned around. Retracing my steps through the cemetery, I ran back into the Schlosspark. With the break in my run, I felt the sweat freeze against my skin, forcing me to push harder, my arms pumping in a bid to warm up. I tried to keep images of my mother, the cemetery and her grave at bay, willing myself to run faster. I picked out point after point: a gate here, a street sign there, the white plaque highlighting Egon Schiele's old studio on Hietzinger Hauptstrasse. Any meaningful object formed a marker on my race back up to Ober St. Veit. When I got to Vivienne's house, I checked my watch: I'd been out for just over an hour. Reinvigorated by the air and my speed, I also felt slightly euphoric that I had completed a run almost without the stray thoughts and self-doubt that had encumbered me before. I felt ready to tackle the puzzles of my mother's notebook and the riddle in *Young Gerber*, and I waited impatiently for Vivienne to come home.

'You know,' Mama says to Annabel, 'the way you hold your brother makes me think that you love him more than anything in the world.'

Annabel just smiles and continues to cradle four-week-old Thaddäus in her arms. Mama's still in bed, weakened by the birth, but Annabel thinks that with her dark hair flowing down her shoulders and her unmade-up face, Mama looks more beautiful than ever. She's like Mother Nature, and Annabel thinks she ought to sketch Mama when she can bear to put Thaddäus down.

Her baby brother grips Annabel's little finger. 'You're so strong, aren't you little man?' she whispers to him.

He's on and off sleeping, and for a moment he opens his eyes and she smiles down at him.

'You'll smile at me first, I just know it,' Annabel says, planting a kiss on one of his chubby cheeks.

He timed his arrival with the sunniest day in July, and just a few days before her own birthday. How his birth has shone a light in her home and in her heart! Dressed in white he reminds her of an angel.

'He's a little miracle, isn't he, Mama?' she says.

'Yes, he is,' Mama says, holding out her arms for her son.

'Just a bit longer,' says Annabel. 'Please?' And she vows to herself that no matter what, she'll always protect Thaddäus.

CHAPTER TEN

The scrabble of a key in the lock announced Vivienne's return. I went into the hall to meet her, making a play of her entrance. She gave me her coat and handbag, chuckling as I fussed around her. She even let me make her her afternoon cup of tea while she put on some music in the living room. From the kitchen I could hear the stir of Verdi's *Requiem* again. When I walked into the living room, my look must have said it all.

'Very well. What about *La Bohème*?' she asked.

I shrugged. 'Anything but this *Requiem* stuff.'

She narrowed her eyes. 'It's *music*, Max. Not *stuff*, as you put it. Has everything I taught you vanished from that head of yours?'

'Only the things I don't need.' I grinned.

She changed the CD in the player. 'You took me to see this in London for my birthday. I'm not sure you'd remember it though. You fell asleep.' She shook her head at me, a smile ghosting her lips.

She was right. I didn't recall the opera, but the music at least was far more playful than the *Requiem*, the thick molasses of the voices proving a welcome addition to the room, along with the fire I had lit. Vivienne pulled one of the armchairs closer to the hearth and sat down, taking her cup of tea and the slice of lemon I offered with it.

She took a sip. 'Just the way I like it,' she said, all the while watching the quiver of the fire. I asked her about her morning with the children at the Albertina. She laughed as she told me about a little girl called Gabriella with cascading curly black hair who had asked question after question on each piece. She had taken a liking to Vivienne and had clutched her hand as they walked through the museum. 'I have to say, though, my mind kept returning to Annabel's notebook,' she said. 'May I see it?'

I handed it to her. She put on her reading glasses, fiddling with their chain while she flicked through the book's pages. She had a smile on her face and let out little gasps of delight every now and again.

As she approached the later stages of the notebook, her smile faded. She eventually shut it, smoothing over the slight rifts in its binding. 'Quite dark in places, isn't it?' she said, removing her glasses. 'I wonder why she chose to copy that painting?'

I didn't dwell on her question, moving to the issue more pressing in my mind. 'You knew my mother at that time, didn't you?' I could never remember exactly when they struck up a friendship.

'Our mothers knew of each other, but they moved in different circles. After the war Annabel and I went to the same school; we were in the same class. We grew close quite quickly, and with no parents around, Annabel became one of the family. My mother ended up being her guardian, even though Annabel continued to live on Himmelhofgasse.'

'On her own?'

'Well, there was a skeleton staff. It wasn't the money – she'd been well looked after in that sense. It was more that she didn't care to have so many people around her.'

'And no relatives took her in?'

'They came and went. One aunt in particular would come to stay from time to time. She wanted Annabel to move to Graz with her, but Annabel wanted to stay in Vienna for her education.' Vivienne was quick to answer my unspoken question. 'Yes – even then, she knew what she wanted.'

'I seem to remember Mama mentioning Fritz and Maria. At least, I remember she talked *a lot* about Maria. She looked after Mama didn't she? But I don't recall her being around when I was born – right?'

'Maria was one of the ones that stayed behind – until she decided to find her family in Poland – sometime during the Sixties, I think it was. She never came back. I think your mother was quite heartbroken. Fritz I didn't know, but I presume he was your grandfather's valet or butler.'

I took the notebook from her, flipping to the last two pages where my mother's versions of the Schiele were depicted.

'What did my mother actually say when she talked about their deaths?'

'Your grandparents' deaths?'

'Well, my grandfather's, and her brother's too.'

'She was quite matter-of-fact – kept any emotion out of it,' Vivienne said. 'That was her way of coping.'

'But these pictures suggest something else, don't you see?'

'I think she was matter-of-fact about it because they were quite … well, horrifying.'

I struggled to comprehend what she was trying to say. Vivienne's expression changed again and her green eyes lost their sparkle.

'It was believed that Annabel's brother died of something similar to cot death, and that afterwards your grandmother became clinically depressed.'

'Believed?' I said.

'She …'

'My grandmother had something to do with his death?'

Vivienne looked away.

I pinched my eyes, unable to absorb this detail that Vivienne and my mother had kept buried.

'Your grandmother had what we'd now call severe post-natal depression. She suffered from delusions and paranoia. Back then, most people concealed or ignored things like that.' Vivienne spoke gently in that manner of hers, smoothing over confrontation. 'I'm the only person she told, and now you know, of course.'

My shock made me jump to the most extreme of conclusions. 'And did she kill my grandfather too?'

My question and tone took Vivienne by surprise. 'No, no, Max,' she said, sitting forward. 'She was the one who forced him to send her away to a sanatorium. Your mother never mentioned it, but perhaps they didn't want to send her to a place as harsh as a psychiatric hospital because your grandmother already recognised she was ill. She never came back – at least, as far as I know. Your mother told me how abandoned she felt.'

'So he died of a heart attack?'

She nodded, slowly.

'But?'

'There is no *but*, Max.'

'Then why draw him that way? And why did she write what she did?' I asked.

Vivienne sipped the remainder of her tea. 'She liked to write poetry from time to time. I did too. That was our age, I suppose.' She put down her cup. 'And the time we were living in.'

I glanced down at the page with its short verse. 'What about the word *shame*?'

She shrugged, then glanced away. *La Bohème* filled more of the room, accompanied by the stutter of the flames. 'He was a good man, your grandfather. What he and your grandmother built up,' she said a moment later, sounding quite determined, as if arming herself against a possible riposte from me. 'Through the orphanage, the Trust,' she continued, 'they saved a lot of young children – children left with nothing. One or two arrived on the Trust's doorstep barely a day old.'

But Vivienne's defensiveness puzzled me. I wasn't sure where this was leading, but I let her go on, not having the heart to interrupt her flow.

'They weren't like traditional benefactors. They rolled up their sleeves, got involved in the children's health and education. Some of the girls were sent to Eugenie Schwarzwald's school. The Anschluss changed all of that, of course.'

'And my mother was quite involved?'

'Yes. She told me stories of how she would go with your grandmother almost every week until … But she continued to go afterwards, on her own, making sure it was run properly, as far as she could. After the war, she wanted to expand it, but she was still young herself so she brought in expertise. And she stopped the apprenticeships, of course.'

'What apprenticeships?'

Vivienne looked at me, the disappointment quite visible on her face. 'Really, Max. You should be ashamed at how little you know about the Trust.'

I shrugged. 'I wanted to get involved a few years ago, but Mama … Never mind. Giving money was the alternative.'

'The *easier* alternative.'

Her words made me bristle. 'Well, maybe that'll change.' I didn't want to get into a discussion about my involvement in the Trust. 'So these apprenticeships?'

'Your grandparents would find positions of employment for some of the children, those that didn't have the aptitude for further education. I think one or two ended up at Himmelhofgasse.' Vivienne settled back into her armchair, seemingly comfortable with this journey down memory lane. 'I think your mother befriended them. She talked about those days as being quite lonely, with her parents in and out of the house, preoccupied with their projects and social circles. I expect that through the eyes of a child there were no boundaries. Everyone was a friend.'

I couldn't quite picture that, given the impatience I had sometimes seen in my mother's dealings with Ludmilla. But then perhaps she had just hardened over the years.

All this talk of the Trust and my mother's friendships reminded me of the newspaper articles. Vivienne seemed quite animated and at ease talking about the Trust and I debated whether I should show them to her, but she caught me glancing at them.

'I didn't want to change the subject,' I said, passing the clippings to her.

She put on her glasses, pursing her lips as she absorbed the stories.

'Did you know about them?' I asked.

'No. I was too young to remember. I suppose I only really knew of Josef Frank because of where he was found.'

'I had no idea about that until now,' I said.

'There's no reason why you would know,' she said, tucking some stray hairs behind her ear. 'I remember it vividly. We were forbidden to play outside on our own for a time. Rumour had it that your grandparents hired a private detective to find the culprit. All I know is that they never found who did it. And then came the Anschluss, and then the war. It turned calm into chaos.'

I took the articles from Vivienne and glanced through them again. 'But they were all similar – don't you see?'

'When you read them together, yes, I suppose so. I suspect at the time they were considered isolated cases.'

I went back to my mother's notebook, searching through some of the diary entries.

'Mama mentions an *E*. Do you think that *E* could've been Elena Markovic? Could she have worked for my grandparents? Were they friends?'

She drew a blank at my volley of questions. Then she reconsidered, her brow furrowing.

'I'm sure there wasn't an Elena.'

'Then who was it she spoke of – who was the friend, *E*?'

Vivienne shook her head, unable to remember.

I pushed a little further. 'But there was a girl who worked in the house?'

'No doubt, and I imagine Annabel befriended her,' she said. 'And then she must have gone away, and no one told Annabel until her conversation with this Fritz person.' She scrunched her forehead again as she scanned through the articles. 'These numbers – what are they?'

'I wondered the same thing.'

Her face brightened. 'Ah – they're years.' She tapped on the newspaper clippings. 'Josef Frank – his murder was in 1937. Hence the thirty-seven.'

'And the other two, murdered in 1935 and 1936,' I said. 'I'm sure it's easy to check.'

'So it can't have been Elena.'

At first I didn't hear her; I was too preoccupied trying to figure out why the articles had been kept aside all these years.

'*E* can't have been Elena,' she repeated, 'because she says in her notebook that *E* went away in 1938.' She seemed to be quite relieved by this, and rather pleased with her detective skills.

'The murders were never solved?' I asked.

'Josef Frank's wasn't. Perhaps the others turned cold too.' She scratched her forehead. 'Who would do such a thing to those poor children? I suppose too much time has passed for us to ever find out. But you never forget events like that.' She fell silent for a little while, then moved on with her thoughts, taking me with her. 'O kneels, rats die,' she said. 'I was mulling it over last night as I was falling asleep. What a curious thing to write.' She looked at me directly. 'You really think the handwriting's the same?'

'It wasn't there before.'

'What wasn't?'

Lost in the world of the notebook, my words had slipped out before I could stop them. 'Sorry, I'm not making sense,' I added quickly. 'I mean I don't think the writing's the same. It's hard to say really.'

Vivienne looked at me as if she were trying to open a door in my mind. I turned back to the notebook.

'Well, I suppose the police will have their own theories – if they ever find the culprits,' she said eventually.

I put on an air of agreement and steered our conversation back to the contents of my mother's notebook, hoping to learn more about my mother as a child. Reliving the highlights of my mother's happy-go-lucky childhood with Vivienne carried more weight. I saw them as small revelations, uncovering a side of my mother that made her seem warmer and more carefree.

Yet despite the stop-and-start nature of the notebook, the change in my mother was quite evident, her steps into adolescence painting her character with darker shades. I began to appreciate the impact of my grandmother's mental breakdown, her self-imposed exile coming at a time when my mother probably needed her most. And then I recalled how she dealt with my father's and brother's death.

'Her harsh exterior seems to make more sense now,' I told Vivienne.

She smiled. 'We all have faults and quirks. Sometimes there are reasons for them. Don't punish yourself over how you viewed your mother.' She stifled a yawn. 'And I think I need a nap. You don't mind, do you?'

I could see that, along with her tour at the Albertina, our foray into the past had made her tired. As I helped her move from the armchair to the sofa, I felt a pang of guilt.

'I'm sorry – for pushing you to remember things you probably don't want to recall.'

'No matter what you learn about your past or your family's past, you're your own person,' she said, squeezing my hand. She closed her eyes, the corners of her mouth edging downwards. I reached for the woollen throw and draped it over her legs, remaining by her side until she fell asleep.

Half an hour later, my mobile phone rang. It was the detective, Thomas Schmidt. I hadn't expected him to call me so soon after the break-in. He told me there was sufficient evidence in the abandoned van to track down the thieves and that they had been caught. They were indeed Serbian; the same gang was linked to a series of robberies in Vienna. It was a major coup he told me, good for the force, and so on.

'And Zoran?' I asked.

'We managed to track him down. Full name's Zoran Pavlović. We pulled him in for questioning. I'm sorry to say that your sympathetic taxi driver also had links to the group. Let's just say he supplemented his income by scouting out a property or two. He was also a courier for them, if you know what I mean.'

'Are you certain?'

'Believe me, we went through everything. After hours of denying his connection to the group he finally caved in, although he swore he had no involvement in the raid on your house. I had to laugh as it seemed you made quite a mark on him. He said he'd never forget a face like yours. I don't suppose you would know what he meant by that?'

'He startled me when he wandered into the house.' I said, recalling how I had been too mystified by the attic door to hear Zoran slipping into the hall downstairs.

'I guess that would explain it.' He coughed, then said, 'What's strange, though, is the stuff written in that book of yours. We analysed the thieves' and Zoran's handwriting but got nothing.' He broke off, barking orders to someone. 'Oh – and notwithstanding the fact that they're borderline illiterates – none of their fingerprints were on it either. We should've spotted that in the first instance.'

'Are you sure about that?'

'One hundred per cent.'

His verdict on the writing was bittersweet. I had hoped one of them had defaced those pages with that senseless message, disproving my theory about the matching handwriting. But the police findings vindicated my initial belief: that someone else had inscribed the message in the book, the same person who wrote *You knew* on the back of the photograph. It was this corroboration that needled me. These two samples of handwriting, with their spiking consonants and vowels, conveyed something quite malign, something all at once intangible, but nonetheless real.

'Odd message,' Schmidt said. '*O kneels, rats die,*' he mumbled slowly to himself.

'Perhaps someone wrote it long ago.' I pictured my mother as an adolescent, trying to convince myself as much as Schmidt of my fabricated theory. 'Maybe someone wrote it in a fit of teenage rage.'

He laughed and joked about his own teenage daughter, wishing those were the only things she got up to. 'It would make life easier – for her and her mother.' Schmidt rounded off the conversation by insisting he would drop off the book. He said he was at the local station in Hietzing and that he could easily call in.

When he arrived at Vivienne's home he declined my invitation to step inside, not wanting to disturb us. But though he didn't venture in, his short visit felt intrusive. It was the way he stood on the doorstep – his over-casual air, leaning against the wall, chewing gum – that annoyed me. He glanced over my shoulder, his eyes surveying the hall before he fixed them on me, appearing to analyse every move of my facial muscles and my body language as he handed over the novel. And I should have known better than to open up the book to those two pages while he was still standing there.

He cleared his throat. 'It's probably just me,' he said, scratching his nose, 'but you seem ... Have you seen ... do you recognise the handwriting?'

'I think it could be my mother's after all,' I said, doing my best to maintain eye contact with him.

Schmidt pressed his fist against his lips, giving me a hint of a nod.

'The Serbs – the two that were in the house – other than the shock of a few broken bones, it seems that something else got to them.' He checked for my response. 'But they're never going to be forthcoming, are they?'

I didn't offer a response.

'Couldn't tell us what made them abandon the robbery like that. There's always one who gives in the end, but in this instance, they clammed up. Funny, really.'

'What's so funny? They broke into my house.' It was the first time I had referred to the house as mine.

'No, I mean it's like they got a fright.' He laughed. 'I'm trying to picture it: two youths, built like bears with the customary tattoos, reduced to shivering shits.' He let out a splutter of laughter, then fixed his eyes on mine. 'Mind you, they'd ingested the usual chemicals. They probably caught sight of their own reflections and ran.'

His words triggered thoughts of the scare I'd given myself in the drawing room that first night. I forced a smile.

'But that message in the book,' he continued, 'got us all thinking.'

Not knowing whether to believe him, I told him it had also kept Vivienne awake at night. 'It probably doesn't mean anything,' I said.

Schmidt blinked twice in quick succession. Then he nudged up his jacket sleeve to look at his watch. 'I'd best be off.' He jogged down the steps. 'If you need anything, just give me a shout,' he said, closing the gate behind him.

As I shut the front door, Vivienne called out from the living room to ask who it was. 'Oh, you should've asked him to check the dates of those murders,' she said, after I relayed my discussion with Schmidt.

I gave her the novel so she could see the message for herself. She paled when she read the words. I felt like protecting her and I glossed over it with my theory of the writing being my mother's doing, just as I'd done with Thomas Schmidt. Vivienne knitted her brow, then put the book down, swapping it for the notebook that I had left on the coffee table. She opened it up to one of the pages where my mother's pencil had clawed at the paper. 'She had that streak. This seems to suggest it at least.'

She got up and I followed her into the kitchen where she started preparing dinner. 'It'll keep bothering me though,' she said, stopping in the middle of the room with two plates in her hands. Apart from the odd muttered phrase, she remained quiet as she cooked. No doubt, she was trying to work out the puzzle, and I did my best to steer Vivienne away from her prolonged attempts to solve it. It wasn't just the handwriting that unsettled me; the message did too. For me, it wasn't such an innocent thing, and I didn't want Vivienne or Schmidt – or anybody else for that matter – to decipher it.

I ended up spending a further four days in Vienna. I didn't have to. The police didn't really need me for their investigation. My reasons for staying veered between my wanting to see the house put back in order and wanting to spend more time with Vivienne. Aside from my daily news intake from the *Financial Times*, which, to my surprise, I found in the Tabak around the corner, I also bought the *Krone*, the *Kurier* and *Die Presse*. I buried myself in domestic Viennese news, observing the growing column inches devoted to the story of the robberies, their arrests, their links to one of the largest Serbian mafia factions, which led, in turn, to further arrests. It was indeed a coup for Schmidt and his men.

I managed to keep out of the spotlight until the news surge faded and the reporters, together with the odd member of the public lingering at the gates of the house, also tailed away. The house was left to its own devices again, no longer regarded as an object of curiosity for its role in a bungled theft.

With the house back in my possession, we were able to press on with returning it to its original state. In reality, it was Frederik who pressed on with everything. While I dealt with the insurance, he fulfilled his promise to oversee its clean-up. Yet he kept his distance from me. The warmth and concern he had shown at the time of the robbery had been replaced by a clipped business-as-usual attitude when we spoke on the telephone. It seemed like an imposition yoked around his neck, and there were a couple of instances when I detected his impatience. Perhaps he regretted his offer to help. In his place, maybe I would have felt the same. But when I suggested that he should charge for his efforts his response bordered on anger.

'Do you really think I would do such a thing?' he said.

I backtracked, fumbling with an apology for my mistake. He huffed down the telephone, then mentioned he needed to get to a meeting. The click of the receiver sounded before I could say goodbye, leaving my thanks hanging in the static of the phone line.

I didn't go by the house to check on the progress of the clean-up, although there were times when I wavered. I got into a habit, on my now daily runs, of continuing up to the church of St. Vitus, and then where I should have turned on to Himmelhofgasse, I stopped, the *should I, shouldn't I* oscillating in my head. Each time, I turned around and jogged back to Vivienne's house. It wasn't fear as such, but rather something akin to a misgiving, the discomfort of finding something else that would trigger more questions and underscore my unease.

So I eventually left for London without returning to the house. It was a wilful gesture on my part. I wanted to go back to it on my own terms: my next planned visit was scheduled for early December when I would meet Matthias Ropach, the architect. In the meantime, he intended to visit the house on his own and would collect the keys from Frederik's office. The timing of the architect's visit, given the break-in, was lucky to say the least. Vivienne offered to show the architect around the house, but I persuaded her not to, assuring her that Matthias would manage just fine on his own.

I wondered whether the house gave Vivienne the same sensation, whether it bore down on her like it bore down on

127

me in its on–off way. I wondered if she had really heard sounds emanating from the attic, or whether she had simply chosen to placate me. Before I left, there were a couple of times when I caught her studying me, watching my countenance, as if she was weighing the possibilities of a madness stirring inside me. She still hadn't mentioned the episode in the attic and I didn't volunteer to discuss it either. It was probably one of the few things she preferred to sweep under the carpet. I ensured that it stayed that way by maintaining a modicum of good humour, only speaking of my mother and the notebook in the most positive light, which I hoped would, in turn, draw her attention away from the message in the Torberg novel. What I wanted most was to forget about the whole thing, to throw the novel and the photograph – my entire family history for that matter – into the Danube or the Thames and watch the water suck them down.

OBER ST. VEIT, VIENNA, 1944

Mama's and Maria's whispers float into Annabel's room. Although Annabel has long since mastered the art of listening to hushed conversations, she can barely discern a word. Mama's been acting strangely of late, muttering to herself, walking around with barely a stain of rouge on her cheeks or lipstick on her lips. And now that Papa's gone away on some business or other, she's taken to sleeping on the second floor with them.

Annabel opens her door a little as quietly as she can, suppressing a shiver from the January chill that's seeped into the house. She's been caught too often recently, sneaking out of bed in the middle of the night to check if Thaddäus is quite all right in his white curtained crib. The last time Maria saw Annabel, she threatened to lock her in her room if she did it again. Annabel can't help it; if she could, she'd happily sleep in Thaddäus's room, and while Mama thinks it's ever so sweet that she would want to do such a thing, Maria decries Annabel's unhealthy obsession with her younger brother. The frustration wells in Annabel again and spurs her on to open the door a little wider with the gentle touch of a thief.

A small paraffin light stands on the chest of drawers, casting Mama and Maria as gilded silhouettes in Thaddäus's room. Yet it's clear enough what Annabel sees and it confuses her. While Mama's wearing her dressing gown, tied tight around her too thin body, Maria looks as though she's going out for a walk. Maria then embraces Mama, a thing that Annabel's never seen her do before, and the only explanation that Annabel can think of is that Maria is leaving. But what of Thaddäus? What of Mama? Annabel clenches her jaw to quell her cry. Through her tears she sees Mama take Thaddäus. Despite the twilight hour, he's wide awake, gurgling a melody of mellow highs and lows and stuffing his tiny fist into his soft mouth. He snuggles against Mama as she kisses his forehead and strokes his cheek before she hands him to Maria. The nanny cradles the six-month-old as if she's unwilling to let go and the muted light catches the sheen of Maria's tears, like snail tracks tracing down her cheeks. Mama looks as if she's weeping too; although her back's turned, Annabel can see her body shaking as if a jolt's running through it.

Mama removes something from her dressing-gown pocket. The rustle of paper seems to echo around the room. 'Here's your letter,' she says, her face shadowed by the lamp. It's a scene that Annabel can't take anymore and she runs to her bed, burying her face in the pillow to muffle her despair.

The next morning Annabel hears Maria's voice. Jumping out of bed, she runs into Thaddäus's room. Maria smiles at her, her face brighter than it's been in a long while, the melancholy from the previous night erased. Annabel's so happy to see that Maria didn't go away after all and Annabel can't help but hug her, almost toppling her over. And Maria laughs and Annabel laughs with her.

Annabel turns to the crib, filled with her usual longing to see her baby brother. 'Where's Thaddäus?' she asks.

Before Maria can answer, there's a commotion downstairs – her father shouting orders.

'Go back to your room,' whispers Maria, leading her charge to her bedroom. But Annabel won't be shooed away.

A torrent of footsteps sound before Mama rushes into the room, half dressed in a tweed jacket and skirt, but without shoes, without make-up, her hair uncombed, tangled and knotted like a woman gone mad.

'Sebastian,' she hisses, her face the pallor of a corpse's.

Annabel cannot stem the sickness mingling with the whirl of confusion in her stomach as she looks from Mama to Maria, their expressions mirroring each other's.

Mama just shakes her head, and mutters a constant no-no-no-no. *Annabel shrinks back against the wall, watching in part wonder, part horror, as Maria takes hold of Mama by the shoulders and mouths words that only Mama seems to understand.*

'I killed him,' Mama says.

The words fail to register with Annabel and she presses her temples because she can't bear what she has just heard. And it's her turn to deny, to ring out the word, No! *Just moments before, Maria's face had sparkled, exuding nothing but goodness, pure goodness, like those of the saint and the angel downstairs in the hall. And now this. It doesn't make sense. Annabel cannot believe it. She mustn't.*

'I killed him,' Mama says again and now she's looking directly at Maria. There's no waver of uncertainty on her face, no denial threatening to appear in her eyes or on her lips.

Then Mama turns to Annabel. Her jaw and mouth have hardened and she's not Mama anymore, but more like one of those SS officers Annabel has spied Papa with, bereft of a soul, devoid of clemency and in no mood to be crossed.

CHAPTER ELEVEN

I had been back in London for a couple of weeks. It wasn't even December, yet it felt that November had been nudged away by the Christmas lights and shop window decorations, which in only a matter of days had lost their sheen. Their cheerlessness made me long for the *proper* Christmas build-up of Vienna or Munich, with their winter markets and the accompanying aroma of Glühwein and cinnamon. I missed the ice-blue skies and biting cold – the cold that you could wrap up against, that invigorated you and put a smile on your face. Better than the inclement weather that arrived, uninvited, to England's shores, seeping through your clothes and leaving you feeling damp and miserable. This England I knew was a far cry from Blake's 'mountains green' and I craved a bit of sunshine.

The buzz of the office provided some respite. We were extremely busy, doing our best to keep pace with the accelerating treadmill of work. From time to time, I struggled to concentrate. My mind would wander back to the house, the message, the notebook, my mother. My only response was to dive further into work, or to exercise. While I knew I would be returning to the house with the architect, I felt that if I could hide everything away, I would be all right.

I even went on a few dates with Lana. Her law firm had transferred her back to London. After I had passed out on her the last time we'd been drunk together, I was sure she'd want to forget about me, but when I returned from Vienna, we saw more of each other. As a lawyer, she often worked long hours, and we took the view that we'd, in her words, go with the flow. There was something about her that distinguished her from other girls. Lana never took herself seriously. Her intelligence was a given; she was definitely more quick-witted than me. And then there were the freckles scattered across her face, adding to her English rose prettiness, something I never thought I'd be attracted to. The relationship, if I could call it that, felt uncomplicated and fuss free. Yet there were times when I sensed she wanted to know more about me – Vienna, the mystery of my mother – and each time I withdrew. I just didn't want to touch her with that part of my life.

Just as I was beginning to settle back into the everyday of my normal world, Oskar Edelstein called me. I was having brunch with Lana and a couple of friends who were in town for the weekend. I had taken them to a newly opened restaurant on the Marylebone High Street. It offered a refreshing change from the usual places, and its collection of Aussie and Kiwi staff filled the place with a breezy atmosphere. The general hubbub, clatter of crockery and music drowned out most things and it was only as we were leaving, when I checked my phone, that I discovered I'd missed two calls from Oskar.

I didn't manage to call him back until much later that day. While his tone was warm over the phone – how I imagined an elderly uncle might speak to his young niece or nephew – his voice seemed quieter, more conciliatory.

'I've something I'd like to show you,' he said. 'I really hope you don't mind,' he continued, 'I know you must be awfully busy, but I'd like it if we could meet again … soon.'

'Of course,' I said.

'Would tomorrow be all right?' It was as if he was unsure of himself, weaker even – quite unlike our first conversation.

'Is everything okay, Oskar?'

'I'm quite all right. But you'll come again? Tomorrow? I know it's an imposition, but it's quite important that we meet.'

To me, his urgency hinted at a quiet restlessness and something stopped me from insisting we meet at a time that suited me, not him. For all my wishes to distance myself from my mother's past, from the house as I knew it, the curiosity I'd felt when I first came across the photograph and my mother's notebook fidgeted at the back of my mind. So I found myself agreeing.

'There's something I'd like to show you too,' I said. The offer of the notebook was my quid pro quo.

On Sunday afternoon I arrived at Oskar's home, more relaxed this time around, though it was butterfly-edged with my ever-revolving speculation about what this next meeting might reveal.

Angela answered the door and showed me through to the living room. 'Mr Edelstein will be with you shortly. He's just had a nap,' she said. 'He's a bit under the weather. I've been staying overnight the last few days to keep an eye on him, although the doctor doesn't think it's anything to worry about. I think it's the time of year, to be honest.'

'I know the feeling,' I said. 'It's like a fist squeezing out daylight – I find it soul-destroying.'

'Gets us all down, doesn't it? I can't wait for spring to arrive.'

I struggled to imagine Angela ever being down. She had a pleasant smile on her face, and as she left the room, she hummed one of those Christmas songs which play non-stop at that time of year.

I put my mother's notebook on the coffee table next to a copy of *The Sunday Times Magazine*. While I waited for Oskar, I leafed through it, stopping at a black and white montage that captured the poverty of a favela. For a moment, I was drawn to the images of children peering out of doorways, or playing football in something akin to a large cage, blithe and at ease. Their innocence echoed the expression on my mother's face in the photograph with Oskar. It struck me then that childhood, that *feeling* of freedom, the ignorance of boundaries, was universal. This was far from a eureka moment, but it was a kind of realisation: childhood slips by without us noticing. It's only after the passage of time that we identify the point when we step from that innocent state to the first stage of adulthood, that something beyond our control moves us from one state to the next, like an invisible hand. Perhaps some refer to this as God; for others, it's fate, or a combination of both. I found myself wondering if my grandmother's decision to spend the rest of her days in a sanatorium had pulled my mother away from her own childhood. For Oskar, maybe it was his family's flight from Austria. For me, it was the death of my father and brother which put an end to that part of my life.

My reflection was put on pause as Angela pottered back in with a tray bearing a cup of coffee for me and some tea for Oskar. She had already added milk to my drink, remembering how I took it from my last visit. A few minutes later, Oskar walked in.

In spite of his smile and the geniality of his handshake, his movements were more laboured; he lowered himself into the seat as if he were afraid he would break. When I got up to help him, he stopped me.

'It's nothing,' he said. 'Just the cold getting to my bones. It takes a while for everything to wake up.'

The physical change in him, in just a matter of weeks, came as a shock to me. He appeared frail, thinner than before, attesting to a physical deterioration that I never would have expected. Only his eyes retained a glimmer of energy: at once incongruous with the fragility of his body, they seemed to reflect his fight against death.

'It should be me doing that,' he said as I poured him some tea. He watched me with a veiled look of amusement as I went about it. 'I was in Cornwall for a couple of weeks – Prussia Cove – do you know it?' he asked.

I shook my head. My only experience of England outside of London was a rainy four-day camping trip somewhere in the Lake District.

'Doctor's orders,' he said. 'I've had a bit of heart trouble. Seems to be getting worse. But that's old age for you.'

He accepted his cup of tea, taking a few sips, all the while regarding me. Then he looked towards the door. As if on cue, the pad of Ripley's paws could be heard along the hallway. The dog nosed the door wider, trotted in and sat by Oskar's feet to let his master ruffle his ears.

'Some friends have a cottage down there,' he went on. 'They persuaded me to stay with them. Air's good, managed to go for my walks ... I felt a great deal better, so I persuaded them to let me return to London.'

We continued to talk about Cornwall and when I admitted to my unwillingness to visit other parts of Britain, he laughed it off.

'You simply must visit Cornwall, at least Prussia Cove – you'll be surprised, you know. I certainly was.'

I said that I'd consider it one day and my response seemed to suffice. Our small talk helped us neatly sidestep the elephant in the room. He didn't even seem to notice my mother's notebook on the coffee table. I should have realised it was me doing most of the talking, regaling Oskar with tales of my miserable camping experience. Before I knew it, almost an hour had gone by without mention of Oskar's reason for his wish to meet. Our conversation eventually waned and we fell into a brief interlude of silence. I took the opportunity to observe Oskar more closely – his absent-minded stroking of Ripley's head, his slow blinks, his shallow breathing.

'You said you had something to show me,' I said after a few moments.

He nodded, then said, 'It's funny, isn't it? How you and I had never met before.' He turned to the window, with its view of his garden in the winter gloom. 'This photograph of your mother's …' He returned his attention to the room, to me. 'Much as Cornwall was a refuge, I couldn't stop thinking about that blessed photograph. You see, it's the image – of me, the young boy – the fact that I look startled to death. And then those words. I felt they accused me of some wrong-doing or other.'

I wondered whether the photograph and my request to meet had precipitated his ill health. My face must have been an open book.

'You mustn't blame yourself for my heart problems,' he said, smoothing down the fabric of his trousers.

I tried to believe him, but then I glimpsed the slight shake in his hand and my self-reproach trickled back.

'I wish I could forget about the photograph – let sleeping dogs lie, as Catharine would have said. But I can't. There are strands of memory here and there, but when I grasp at them they seem to fade.' He stretched out his legs, then pushed himself up. Ripley followed suit, his tail wagging in anticipation. 'You know, I haven't been out today. The sky's slate grey, but I think the weather will hold. What do you say we go for a walk?'

I readily agreed. My legs were also in need of a stretch. I had been running longer and harder most days, and the regular sparring I'd recently taken up had left my muscles the worse for wear.

'I have some letters to show you. I'll bring them with me,' he said.

A kind of hope skipped inside me, as I assumed the content of Oskar's letters would shed light on the *missing link* that my mother had referred to in hers.

I picked up the notebook and followed Oskar and Ripley out of the living room, listening to him call out to Angela to *kindly fetch those letters*. I noticed how Oskar struggled with his coat. He just stood there, his arms dangling in his coat sleeves, unable to shrug the garment over his shoulders. I jumped to help him, catching the disquiet in Angela's eyes as she came out of one of the other rooms.

'Don't be out too long, will you now, Mr Edelstein. They say it's going to rain.' She touched me on the shoulder as we stepped outside. Lowering her voice, she said, 'Make sure he doesn't overdo it.'

'I heard that,' Oskar shot back, looking over his shoulder with a grin on his face. 'As a matter of fact, the doctor said walking is good. And I'm not going to stop doing one of the things I still enjoy.'

Angela nodded, keeping that smile of hers pinned to her face. But I could see her worry as she watched Oskar and Ripley head over to the gate.

For all Angela's cautioning and Oskar's weakened demeanour, he adopted a brisk pace up Parliament Hill. Ripley, too, seemed to share Angela's concern, keeping at Oskar's side, even when his master bent down to unclip his leash.

We didn't talk, our own quiet mirroring the general stillness around us, save for the wind bustling through the trees and wild grass of the Heath, and the distant rattle and hum of traffic. I rubbed my thumb back and forth over the deer-hide cover of my mother's notebook. The feel of its slightly ridged surface made me feel closer to her again.

Once at the top, we settled on a bench away from the handful of people milling around. Pulling a slim bundle of letters from his pocket, Oskar said, 'When I returned from Prussia Cove, I went digging through the attic. I got Angela to help me. I think she rather enjoyed the whole exercise, likening it to a treasure hunt. My wife and I had cleared away a lot of things long ago, but a couple of boxes remained.' He glanced down at the letters cradled in his hands. 'I came across some correspondence between your grandmother and my mother. The two of them were indeed good friends. Then the letters stopped. I'm not sure whether it was on account of our house moves during the war.'

'My grandmother was sent to a sanatorium before the war ended. She died there,' I said.

He simply nodded before handing the letters to me. 'I don't know what it was that I was hoping to find. A clue, perhaps, to why I looked the way I did in that photograph of your mother's. There's mention of the picture – that was something at least. I thought you'd be interested, nonetheless.'

I loosened the coarse brown string that entwined them and flipped through the three envelopes. Peeling Nazi censor tape edged a couple of the letters; one had been left unadulterated. All were addressed to Oskar Edelstein's mother, Claudia, in an unrecognisable but elegant hand; two were blemished by a series of postage stamps with Hitler's glowering side profile.

'You remember what I said to you last time – about digging up the past?' asked Oskar.

I nodded.

He watched my fingers hesitate over the bundle. 'One of them … well, perhaps it's better if you read them in your own time,' he said.

It seemed as though sadness transcended his words, making me feel as if I'd perhaps gone a step too far, and the initial thrill of stumbling across items shedding further light on my family history quickly petered out. Other than the notebook, there was little I could offer to lift his mood.

'I wanted you to see this,' I said, passing it to him. 'I thought it would be nice to share it with you. The first few pages reflect on your friendship with my mother.' I hoped that something in her words or sketches would trigger more than a snatch of memory.

Oskar opened the book. Turning to the first page, he recognised himself as the young boy in my mother's first drawing. A smile edged its way across his face.

'She remembered me then,' he said.

He didn't stay on that page for long though, and continued to go through the book, page by page, reading extracts from my mother's short diary entries. I couldn't read much into his expression and as he reached the latter stages of the notebook, it seemed that my mother's teenage drawings and words bored him, until, that is, he arrived at her renditions of the Schiele. Examining them brought out an altogether different reaction. He traced the drawings with his fingers in the manner of the art historian he once was. Although his mouth twitched at the corners, he remained mute, the lines on his forehead deepening as he analysed her work. He tapped at the page as he read the words of my mother's verse, then shook his head impatiently, before snapping the notebook shut.

'Why choose that painting to copy?' he asked.

'I've no idea,' I said. 'It was a prominent feature in the house. It could well have fed her imagination.'

'I see.' Oskar didn't make eye contact as he handed the notebook back to me, his gaze resting on an anonymous point in the distance. Ripley, still sitting by his side, stood up, thinking it was time to go. He turned to Oskar, then looked towards the view, as if trying to fathom what it was his master was so entranced with. But once he realised we weren't going anywhere, he wandered off, leaving Oskar's side for the first time during our outing.

'Is there anything in here that jogs a memory or two?' I asked.

He turned to me. 'There doesn't seem to be.'

I wanted to believe Oskar, but his silence, the way he studied those pictures at the back of the notebook suggested otherwise. Nonetheless, it wasn't in me to push him. Perhaps I would have done if we had met under different circumstances. But here I was, seated next to a frail man, someone who was little more than a stranger to me, and I couldn't bring myself to challenge him. Despite his reticence, and the fact that we had only met twice, I liked him. It wasn't out of pity – Oskar wasn't someone you'd feel sorry for. His life, as far as I could tell, remained quite rich, and in spite of the dip in his health he had a get-on-with-it attitude that I admired. I wondered, then, that if young Oskar had been smiling in that photograph, would the message on its reverse have been seen as a joke? If my mother were still alive, the matter would have been resolved in a flash and we could all have moved on.

If.

A plane made its near silent descent below the clouds, its distance from us making it look like a small toy that I could cup in my hand. For an instant I wanted to do just that, to reach out and grab hold of it.

'I found a message in a book at my mother's house,' I said. '*O kneels, rats die.* The handwriting's the same as on the back of the photograph.' I offered up the bare facts – no made-up theories, no mention of the break-in.

Oskar nodded, all the while directing his gaze towards the financial district. His brow creased slightly and I thought I glimpsed a tease of a smile.

'Do you believe in ghosts?' he asked without looking at me. I couldn't tell whether there was a touch of humour in his voice. But when he turned to face me, his countenance was straight-faced, without a wrinkle of mirth or suchlike.

At first, my shock swallowed up any ability to speak. I glanced away from him, searching for the right words. Yet I could feel his gaze on me, as though he was studying my reaction.

'Do *you*?' I replied. It was all I could manage, not wanting to expand but wanting to buy time.

Oskar hesitated before answering. 'Perhaps. Sometimes I wish I could see the ghost of my wife, Catharine. To see her one last time. Dreams aren't quite the same, and even then, I feel she's slipping away.'

'You were together a long time, weren't you?' I already knew the answer but hoped to distract him from his original question.

'We were. Although looking back, our time together seems so fleeting.' He turned to me. 'Do you believe in them or not?' His tone was crisp and I felt like I had a spotlight shining on my face.

I removed my glasses and rubbed my eyes. I didn't dare answer him. At the same time, I couldn't skirt around the truth. I put my glasses back on, trying to sort out the various conflicts in my mind. 'I didn't ...'

'Until?'

'Until recently.' And there it was: my admission, my confession.

'Go on.'

'It goes against everything I believe ... But there've been things at the house. Things that I've heard and seen. I can explain some of them, or at least, I can explain them away.'

'And then there are others that you can't,' Oskar said.

The handwriting in *Young Gerber* sprang into my mind.

A young couple, dressed in trainers, jeans and hooded tops, ambled over towards our spot. Oblivious to the two of us sitting nearby, the boy kissed the girl on the cheek and gave her a gentle caress. It seemed their embrace triggered other memories for Oskar.

'Catharine used to admire this skyline,' he said. 'This was one of her favourite spots.' He watched the couple as they walked away, arms draped around each other's waists. 'When we mourn, we … I take it that it was your mother you saw?'

'No. A child, a young girl. At least I think it was a girl.' There was my next admission, sliding out as easily as the first.

'A young girl, you say?' His voice was quieter now.

My gaze returned to the view, to searching out that tiny plane again. I struggled with what else I should say. Luckily, Oskar didn't press for more details. Nevertheless, my brief words of disclosure couldn't be clawed back. My thoughts, doubts, now spoken out loud, were no longer the grainy visuals I tried to push away.

'There are times when I think it's me – my state of mind and so on.' I tried to sound relaxed, but my tone of voice let me down.

'You seem sane enough to me,' he said.

Part of me still wanted to believe that everything that had happened could be explained away, but with it now out in the open, my struggle to cling to a rational explanation became that much harder. It felt like I was teetering on the edge of a precipice, unable to look down for fear of falling.

'You kindly invited me to the house,' he said, taking off his glasses. He chewed one of the curved ends as he had done the first time we met. 'Is that invitation still open?'

I nodded slowly, wondering at his change of mind.

'Well then, perhaps I'll come just before Christmas. I hope that won't inconvenience you?'

143

'Not at all. I appreciate you agreeing to visit.' My reply sounded rehearsed, a mere platitude, and I hoped he hadn't noticed.

'I'm due to attend an event at a gallery in Vienna – I think I may have mentioned it to you – on the seventeenth of December. Perhaps you and I can meet the following day.' Oskar stood up and re-tied his scarf, nudging it up his neck. He indicated to the darkening clouds curtaining the distant reaches of Canary Wharf. 'The rain's coming in. Angela, as ever, was right.' He called out for Ripley, who promptly came bounding back, his tongue lolling out the side of his mouth, his tail wagging.

And so we headed back, walking at the same pace as before, despite the lean of the wind, which had since picked up. I tugged up my jacket collar and dug my hands into my coat pocket. Oskar chattered away, as if our discussion about ghosts had never happened. I remained silent, lost in my own world, my mind flipping through the different cards in this game of mine: the house, the photograph, the message, the notebook, the presence. I tried to think about the letters, now wedged inside the notebook, and the information they contained, but it proved difficult to focus on them. Oskar's sudden desire to visit the house left me unsettled. At our first meeting, Oskar had spoken of other doors that would beg to be opened. I didn't want to find any more doors. Oskar was right. But it was too late to turn back. I couldn't renege on my invitation to Oskar, not now that he'd accepted and we'd agreed on a date.

I wondered, then, whether this was Oskar's quest or mine. Up until that point, I had just thought he was assisting me. But now this journey seemed to be just as important to him as it was to me, if not more so. I glanced at him every now and again, questioning his motivation. It seemed our acquaintance made him agitated, wrestling him away from his quiet life of retirement. We both wanted a resolution – that was clear enough. With my admission of a presence, and Oskar's wish to see the house, my unease became deep-seated, a constant utterance in my head, faint, but audible. Whispering and whispering away.

OBER ST. VEIT, VIENNA, 1944

Annabel races down the stairs. She won't let Mama leave, she won't. Two men stand by Mama's side. Papa's nowhere to be seen, but Fritz is there, holding the door open, his face as grim as everyone else's, aged with the hardships of war which even the continued favours granted to the Albrecht name can't ameliorate. Something else sets him apart from the other staff though: it's the crumpled appearance of a man who no longer cares.

A grey Opel Olympia stands outside, a sheen of drizzle rippling over its body. The headlights are off, as is the engine. There are no bombs dropping tonight and the quiet seems alien, almost unwanted.

Fritz tries to stop Annabel from going to Mama, but she pushes him aside to be with her mother and is quickly enveloped in her arms. Annabel can't understand it. 'She's ill,' is all they say.

'I'm ill,' Mama says again. She sounds wooden and not like Mama at all, and Annabel, gripping the folds of her mother's raincoat in her fingers, won't believe it. Thaddäus is gone, and nobody in this household dares utter a word about it. Not even Maria who just falls quiet and fumbles with a rosary all the time, telling her young charge to pray for her brother's soul. But all Annabel wants is to hear those words, your brother is dead, *so she can grieve and cry out all the tears she's saved for him.*

Annabel clings to Mama. 'Please don't leave.'

Mama kisses her on the cheek and the forehead, brushing the tears away from her face with fingers that feel as rough as the bits of old tree bark that Annabel and Oskar used to collect just a few years before.

Caught in the limbo between childhood and adolescence she searches Mama's eyes, desperate to say something that will make her change her mind. 'They can treat you here, surely?'

One of the men goes to move Annabel away, but it only serves to make her hold on to Mama a few moments more before she's pulled away, her fingers unclasped from Mama's one by one. Their fingertips touch for the last time. Now Mama cries out and it's the mournful cry that makes most of the staff turn their heads away. Mama pulls at her hat. Strands of her hair come loose, hanging over her face, now stained with tears, and instead of wiping them away, Mama scratches her face, then tugs at her hair before the two men take each of her arms and drag her to the waiting car.

Never mind the chill in the air and her thin nightdress, Annabel runs out to Mama, but Maria catches her hand and pulls her into her body, wrapping her woollen shawl around Annabel's shoulders.

'Let her go, Annabel,' her nanny whispers. Annabel looks to Mama and then to Maria, and then she catches Maria mouth something to Mama, but she can't quite make out the words.

CHAPTER TWELVE

After seeing Oskar I stopped by the office, needing to review a presentation via conference call with colleagues in London and New York. I could easily have done it from home, but I just wanted a different backdrop. It partially worked, but I still found I drifted back to my conversation with Oskar. I stayed at the office longer than I intended, and by the time I returned home it was already past nine in the evening. On my way back I grabbed a burger and soon regretted it – the cheap meat and fries sat in my stomach, leaving a rancid aftertaste.

The sight of Oskar's bundle of letters lying on the table soon distracted me from my makeshift dinner. I settled on the sofa, untied the string and flipped through them, deciphering the smudged ink of the postage marks for dates. Feeling the thick cut of the envelopes between my fingers, I hesitated. I felt like a voyeur, intruding on the lives of others. After my mother's death, I could easily have rooted through her correspondence tucked away in the attic and study. But I didn't. For me, letters held secrets, sweet nothings, fears and hopes, to be shared only with their intended recipient. I would hate it if someone read through my personal emails or the odd letter I wrote to a girlfriend during my university years. I glanced down at the three letters once more, and picked up the first one.

Isabella Maria Josefina Albrecht
Himmelhofgasse 15, Ober St. Veit, Wien

14th May, 1938

My dearest Claudia,

I was so pleased to receive your letter and relieved to hear that you arrived safely in England. I cannot begin to comprehend the chaos and horror you witnessed during your journey. My heart goes out to you, to Pieter and of course to young Oskar. I think of you all daily, as does Annabel, who misses her friend most terribly. With our young maid Eva, and now Oskar gone she has become increasingly withdrawn of late and I put her despondency down to her loneliness, a void which neither I nor Sebastian can fill.

Life here in Vienna continues regardless, although the reminders of this farcical union are everywhere in the city – from the German soldiers on the streets, to the red, black and white of Nazi insignia draped outside government buildings and even residences on the Ringstrasse. And then there are the slogans. On the façade of the Loos Haus one reads, 'Those of the Same Blood Belong in the Same Reich!' It's quite horrifying how things have turned. The Ringstrasse plays constant host to either riots or parades, and at times it is impossible to go into the city. Thankfully, I still manage my visits to the orphanage. We're all quite afraid as to what will come next. So many have left – some have disappeared; rumours are rife. It was said that Viktor Ephrussi and his son were sent to Dachau. They returned, but they are now living in two rooms in that house of theirs on the Ringstrasse. To think of it – prisoners in their own home!

Our own place has undergone a bit of a transformation.

Sebastian decided to build a war bunker downstairs – he says the writing's on the wall. I've left him to it. Over the last month or so he's become quite restless. I suppose it's the political climate, the loss of sovereignty. The good news is that his old injury rules him out of being drafted.

At times I feel like I live in my own ivory tower, protected, but not protected. I feel outraged for what has happened and then a mute passiveness. Is that terrible of me? Our friends now seem to accept the status quo and many talk of support.

My dearest, I'm afraid to share my thoughts with others, share my fears of what may come, and I long for our tête-à-têtes. Just the other day, I had tea with Henriette von Hildenberg. As you well know she's quite a tiresome woman, but she's Sebastian's cousin, so I am obliged to endure her company. The only good thing about my visit was her selection of cakes from Demel. She began to espouse her view on the 'Jewish problem', as she phrased it, and even sullied your and Pieter's good name. Well, I couldn't just sit there. I argued back and as I did so, she looked at me with something bordering on shock and disdain. I stopped mid-sentence. In the end, I could bear to sit with her no longer, and feigned a headache to bring our engagement to an end …

The next few lines suggested some indiscretion by my grandmother, which made me feel like a reader of one of those celebrity magazines. I didn't want to read on. Until then, I'd had this picture of my grandparents as bastions of society with a perfect marriage, and this knowledge of my grandmother's infidelity felt like an immense let-down. Then I found myself wondering if my mother knew. Perhaps if my grandparents had lived for longer she would have found out. And I couldn't help but think about my own parents' marriage – had it been solid before my father died? I liked to think it was, and I didn't want that image shattered.

I returned to the letter. The mention of an Eva had caught my attention. I fetched the notebook and scanned the first few entries. The *E* in the notebook probably referred to this Eva. That piece of the jigsaw now fitted.

I turned to the next letter, dated five years later.

21st March, 1943

My dearest Claudia,

Too much time has gone by. I blame neither the war nor the post. I did receive your two letters and I'm sorry that I haven't written back to you until now. I don't have much of an excuse except that I am expecting another child. I'm sure that news will be as much of a shock to you as it was for me, given what the doctors had said. Sebastian is over the moon. And yes, my dear, there's no question that the child is his. In fact, I feel myself falling in love with him all over again. He has been quite attentive of late – the more so since I've been suffering from such terrible morning sickness which leaves me bedridden most days. The war isn't helping with the rations, and there's a shortage of basic medication. On the whole, I'm feeling quite depleted of energy and I'm unable to make my usual visits to the orphanage.

Despite all this, the baby is growing inside me and I think even now I can feel its little kicks. Annabel is ever so excited and likes to touch my tummy. Perhaps she's seen the others do it, but she likes to fuss around me and sits with me reading or drawing – her talent really is coming along quite nicely …

I tried to picture my mother's excitement at the prospect of a sibling's arrival, putting an end to her loneliness. I imagined her sitting with my grandmother, silently drawing or writing away. I looked back at the letter.

I do worry about her, and for our unborn child. I don't know when this will all end, what future they will have. Nowadays, Annabel seems to be quite content in her own company. Her studies are going well and her tutor seems to be pleased with her progress. Her father is less ambitious for her than I am, and I keep urging him to let her continue her studies at the university when the time comes. She seems determined enough and she certainly has a curious mind. I can imagine her travelling the world one day. I think Sebastian would like to keep her here for as long as he can, to have her accompany him on his walks through the woods until he's no longer able. She'll forever be special to him, I think.

And how is Oskar? I do hope things are getting better for him at school. You were quite right to take him out of that place – the boys and staff sound frightful. Perhaps home schooling will be better. You know, I came across a photograph of him with Annabel. It must have been taken just before you all left. It's quite endearing – the poor boy looks petrified though, as if he was quite afraid to have his picture taken. I had set it aside to send with this letter, but when I looked for it in my study this morning, I couldn't find it – goodness knows where it's got to …

The letter finished with a summary of society gossip and the *tiresome Fritz* and his drinking problem, which she had delegated to my grandfather to manage. I glanced through the excerpt about Oskar again. It piqued my sympathy. An image of a severe English boarding school tucked away somewhere in the countryside immediately came to mind. It made me root more for Oskar, and it seemed that my grandmother did too with her reference to the photograph. I wondered whether my grandmother had mislaid it, or whether someone had taken it. I noted that she hadn't mentioned the writing on the reverse. Presumably she would have said something if it had been there while she was alive. That was my assumption, at least.

I looked across to the third and final piece of correspondence, hopeful that its contents might reveal more. The postmark was smudged, but it seemed to be Swiss. Gone were the thoughtful sentences, the straight horizontal lines of my grandmother's impeccable hand. The handwriting was urgent, sloppy even; words had been crossed out making it difficult to decipher. In places, the ink had pooled, as if my grandmother wept as she wrote. There were half-formed phrases, muddled thoughts – in all, a stream of hysteria. Under other circumstances, this would have offered proof of my grandmother's breakdown, but the letter's rambling madness made it seem all the more authentic, and what I read horrified me; what it implied made my blood freeze.

I got up from the sofa, clutching the letter and walked over to one of the windows. My attention drifted to the building opposite, to a light in the window on the fourth floor. A boy sat at his desk, all hunched shoulders, his face lit up by the glow of his computer. He looked up, no doubt sensing someone watching him. I moved away and glanced down at the letter once more. I reread it – and read it again. *What if*, came to mind. *What if* it was true?

I slid out the articles tucked at the back of my mother's notebook. I reread these too, placing them alongside the letter. I looked at the way the numbers, or the years, as Vivienne had suggested, were written, and searched for numbers in my grandmother's letters, trying to compare them. Anyone could have circled those names and noted those figures. Had she searched out these news reports, circled the names and written the years in which these children had died after learning what she did? But then again, how could she if she was in the place she really claimed she was?

My mind went to Oskar. I hadn't thought to ask him about what he had taken from the letters. I just presumed that the content was more for my interest than his. I glanced at my watch. The late hour didn't stop me from picking up the phone to ring him. But no one answered, not even Angela. I left a message, asking him to call me back. I waited all of five minutes before I called him again. Still there was no answer. So I tried again after another few minutes. In the end, I left a second message, unable to mask the urgency in my voice.

OBER ST. VEIT, VIENNA, 1944

Annabel runs straight to her bedroom, ignoring Maria's calls. She shuts the door and locks it. Catching her breath, she wipes her mouth with the back of her hand. It's shaking, and then she realises she's quaking all over. The skirt she's wearing is torn at the bottom where she caught it as she tried to run away, and the button at the top has been ripped off. There's a stain, too, that Maria will notice straight away. There'll be questions, and then what? Annabel's petrified. Her mind blanks and she feels the caustic taste of bile in her mouth. She wants to retch, but she mustn't be sick, she mustn't. Slumping against the door, Annabel prays no one will come knocking. The wood steadies her. She takes off her skirt, shakes it down her legs and tries to step out of it, but losing her balance she collapses to the floor like a limp puppet.

She pokes the pink and blue bruises smudging her thighs. There must be marks on her neck too, where his large hands had gripped her and pinned her down. Tears sting at her eyes.

From the beginning there was something disquieting about that outing of theirs. His mood was as dark as the soil peeking through the snow beneath their boots: his strange muteness, his need for Annabel to hold his hand, the way he stroked the back of it, his thumb smoothing her skin, massaging it before he placed her hand on him.

'You'll always be special to me. Let me show you how much,' he had said to her. Yet what he did next only served to confuse and repulse her. She had tried to run from him, but he was too quick – or she was too slow. She must have done something to deserve this, she

thinks, but it's no good, as her head still rings from the blow she took when he knocked her to the ground.

She retches again, her hand straying subconsciously to her mouth before she quails, remembering. She drags herself over to the washstand, rubbing at her hands, at her face, inside her mouth. Then she pulls down her underwear and holding a cloth in her trembling hand, she wipes herself. A smell, reminding her of cleaning fluid clings to her, and no matter how much she scrubs, she feels stained.

She goes to her bed and climbs in, curling up underneath the bed covers, and cuddles her old doll, Esther.

There's a knock on the door. The sporadic three taps mean it can only be Maria.

'Annabel, your tea's ready.'

Annabel pulls the bedcovers tightly over her. I wish I were invisible, I wish I were gone.

'Annabel?'

The door handle rattles.

And with all the will Annabel can muster, in a small, strained voice she says, 'I'm really not feeling well.'

If only Mama were here. She'd wrap her arms around Annabel and somehow make the fear go away.

CHAPTER THIRTEEN

I tried to get hold of Oskar the following day, and again a couple of days after that. I didn't hear back from him. Meetings, conference calls, a day-trip to Frankfurt, followed by a day and a night in New York left me little time for anything, let alone trying to call him once more. If we had spoken, my shock might have lessened, but Oskar's silence and the lack of an explanation made me feel much worse, and I found myself venting my frustration on my more junior colleagues.

I did manage a couple of calls with my architect, Matthias Ropach, who seemed to work 24/7. He had since sent me finalised plans for his renovations and couldn't stop telling me how he loved the house, understanding *immediately* what I had in mind when he set foot inside.

'What did you make of the cellar?' I asked.

'Just as you described it,' Matthias said. 'There's something about it, though. I'll show you when we meet.'

I felt the jump of my heart. 'What do you mean?'

'It'll be easier to explain when I show you – but don't worry. Could be something interesting.' Matthias's eagerness only augmented my disquiet and made me question again whether everything I had experienced there had taken place only inside my own head. He wouldn't let me probe more, and he quickly jumped to discussing subcontractors. He said he had a couple in mind and hoped he could get some quotes before we met.

'Choose whoever you think's best,' I told him. 'And I want them to start before Christmas.' I just wanted to get the work done. For me, doing away with the staid grandeur of my mother's era wasn't just any old building project, it was like an exorcism – a dual one: to banish the presence that lingered in the house, and to ease the disturbance in my mind.

During my flight to Vienna I glanced over Matthias's proposals again, but I was so exhausted I struggled to keep my eyes open. I fell asleep with images of Oskar, the letters from my grandmother and the house carouselling around in my head, only to wake up with a jolt when we landed.

As usual I stayed with Vivienne. She seemed to sense I was preoccupied – at least she steered clear of questions about work and Oskar – and over an early dinner she chattered away about other things, telling me how she had completed her computer course.

'Don't let it go to waste,' I said.

'As if I would! You know, I'm using the Internet a lot these days. I even tried to look up the dates those children died,' she said. 'But I didn't have any luck.'

My fork slipped from my hand and clattered on to my plate. 'Oh, really?' I mumbled.

After dinner, Vivienne and I sat in her living room. Despite the warmth of the fire, she had draped a blanket over her legs. Orchestral music played in the background and a newspaper lay on her lap. She had turned on a couple of lamps and their muted light made it seem later in the evening than it was. I needed to review a presentation for my team before the end of the weekend, but my concentration lapsed and the only things I noticed were two glaring mistakes within the first two pages. I tossed the document on the coffee table and picked up my mobile, leaving a terse voicemail for the analyst and associate who had put it together. My voice rose as my message went on, prompting Vivienne to peer at me over her reading glasses. After I had finished my message, she put her book to one side.

'Now,' she said, 'about these letters.'

I had brought only the last one with me, but it wasn't difficult to recall the contents of the other two. I gave her a brief rundown, omitting mention of my grandmother's extramarital affairs. She nodded now and again as she stoked the fire, and said little other than a muttered *of course* when I revealed *E*'s identity.

I went upstairs to fetch the letter. When I got back, Vivienne was sitting down, her eyes lit with such excited expectation that I held back from giving it to her.

'Perhaps it's better I read it out to you first,' I said.

She looked at me, her eyes smiling, then said, 'Oh very well, have it your way – but don't keep me waiting.'

'Are you sure you want to hear it?' I asked. 'It's just …'

'Max, don't treat me like a child,' she chided, settling further into her chair, before nodding at me to begin.

11th April, 1944

Claudia, my dearest Claudia.

I need you – I need your help – my sweetest, dearest friend.

My children – I need to save them – it's S – he's a paedophile – a mdre a murderer.

I wanted to tell you – I really did. But I didn't have time –

and wretched things got in the way you see and time – time just
ran out – just like my own.

*I've got to think straight – <u>THINK STRAIGHT</u>. It's so
hard – they strap me down – shock everything out of me leaving
me a shell – and then I remember and that's the most horrific
shock of all. ~~I must~~
——I will try to explain – forgive me for spilling it out – it's the
only way I can.*

*It began with Fritz's drunken tirade – no sign of S – this
time I'm the one who goes downstairs. But then I hear S – the
bear as they're wont to call him. WHAT? WHAT DID YOU
SAY? And Fritz demands more money for his silence. S growls
NO – so many <u>strings pulled</u> – a telephone call – that's all it
takes – and the fairy tale's over. Fritz shouts back – predilection
– YOUR PREDILECTION for the young ones isn't that
right sir – got us into trouble – near got us into trouble with the
Frank boy didn't it? DIDN'T IT? To think all the lies I told,
the risks I took – for you SIR. ~~All this these ptify~~
Oh but there's proof Fritz – S now – his voice so quiet – I can
pin the blame on you – for all of them. There's screaming – on
it goes until I realise it comes from me. His slap to my face shows
the monster inside the man – my HUSBAND.*

*S leaves – away on business he says – gone a week he says.
There's a whisper in my ear – don't do anything silly will you
– who will believe you Schatzi – in your head anything goes.*

*How heavenly is that week! So much to do – we need to
leave – me, Annabel, Thaddäus – and heaven's in the form of
sweet Maria – she takes Thaddäus away. Just in time – you see
– S comes home before the week is done.*

*WHERE'S THADDÄUS? He'll never touch my son –
oh but what to do? CALM DOWN – Maria tells me. And I
am ~~d~~ calm when I tell them I killed him – I tossed his body in the*

river – a lie to protect my son. Oh his face – that monster's face – to see it fold and ~~crmple~~ crumple. But it doesn't last you see.

Touché – S whispers a game of I won't tell if you won't tell – you'll do as I say – you'll say you need help – no police – our secret. Money makes everything go around and around and around.

I'm to go away – paints a truer picture S says – trust me – you'll be in Davos – ~~Schalp~~ Schatzalp Sanatorium – choice name don't you think? When you return you're free to leave – just make sure you keep your silence – like I'll keep mine.

What choice was there but to go along with this game? Trust him? My heart knows he plays by his own rules.

I'm not in Davos – not in a sanatorium. I'm locked in an ASYLUM – Dante's HELL. There is no return. Days pass when I want to kill myself but then I cannot – I must live – for the sake of my children – you see I still get letters – from Annabel – from Maria.

And I write to them – but God only knows whether they reach – whether they're tampered with – Oh I <u>mustn't think</u> like that.

THINK.

I need to find my ~~presion~~ precious son – to know he's safe. I thought Annabel was safe for she has dear Maria. Yet now – oh God – what have I done? I left her in that house with HIM. And I think – I think he has touched her – her letters before pleaded – now they chill – they chill Claudia! I can barely repeat her words for fear of it being more true. Papa she writes – ~~touches me~~ Papa touches me ~~hurts~~ – I'm afraid Mama. He has touched my daughter – tainted her – and Oh God – Oh God she maybe next! I have lost my son. I will lose my daughter.

Is this my just deserts – my comeuppance for all I have done? If it is – then God forgive me.

Claudia – please – believe everything I've told you. You're the only one. Help me – save Annabel – find Thaddäus – help me get out before they KILL MY MIND – before they take EVERYTHING away from me. YOU CARRY MY ~~Hope~~ HOPE.

When I had finished, I looked to Vivienne for her response. Although her lips were pursed, she showed no sign of shock or surprise.

'Can I see for myself?' she asked.

I got up and handed her the letter, perching on the arm of her chair to reread the contents over her shoulder.

'What do you think?' I got up and went over to the window, wanting to put physical distance between me and my grandmother's words.

'Could it be – really – that your grandfather did such a thing?' Vivienne said. 'To ... that ... he could have touched those children, touched ...' Her fingers went to her mouth. 'It ... everything ... it doesn't bear thinking about.'

I dug my hands into my pockets, fidgeting with some loose change.

Vivienne turned to me. 'He was such an honourable man, but ...'

'But what, Vivienne? You never knew him,' I snapped.

'There's no need to lash out, Max. I'm just as disturbed as you are, but you need to calm down.'

'I'm sorry. It's just this letter,' I said. 'On its own, it reads like textbook hysteria, like she was some sort of paranoid schizophrenic, exercising delusions that her husband – my grandfather – was a paedophile, a murderer, that he threatened her children. Perhaps she was in constant denial about what she did to Thaddäus because she was so ill. Maybe my grandfather covered up the real place she was sent to to keep up appearances.' I shook my head. 'But then when you put it next to the notebook, with those newspaper articles – and then I can't stop thinking that if what he did was true and if he did it to Mama …'

The look on Vivienne's face disrupted my train of thought. It wasn't that she appeared visibly upset. It was just her stance, the way she sat back in her armchair. She had removed her glasses and her fingers teased at the chain.

'It makes more sense now.' I couldn't tell whether she was talking to herself or addressing me.

'What do you mean?'

'Perhaps it's better if you sit down, Max,' she said.

I did as she suggested.

'You remember I mentioned that your mother talked about a lot of things towards the end of her life.'

I nodded.

'Some things she said were quite puzzling, and some … disturbing.' She pressed her lips together. 'I wanted to forget them and I didn't want to burden you with things that I couldn't fathom myself.'

She spoke slowly as she attempted to pull together threads of various conversations she had had with my mother, the three grooves between her eyebrows becoming more pronounced.

'One day, Annabel called me. It was quite early in the morning. She told me she'd been up all night, in the attic, *tidying things up*, as she put it. She needed to see me. By the time I arrived at the house, she was lying in the drawing room, drowsy from the painkillers she'd just taken. I offered to come back later, but she pressed me to stay, telling me it was important. She began to describe how she had stumbled across a few things from her childhood.' Vivienne glanced at the notebook by my side. 'She said they'd stirred up memories of happier times before the war. She mentioned Oskar Edelstein and then began reminiscing about their friendship, reeling out stories one after another. They all seemed to blur into one and I couldn't tell when one anecdote ended and the next began.' A brief smile edged on to her face. 'And then she started talking about the cellar, how she was loath to go down there, ever since … *Ever since what?* I asked her. She spoke about a game of hide-and-seek with Oskar and how it had gone quite wrong. Then Annabel mentioned a photograph, which I assume is the one she sent you of her and Oskar as children. But after that, much as I tried to understand what she was getting at, it sounded like she was throwing out a jumble of memories. All I know is that she wanted you to find out more. That's why I didn't want you to give up so quickly on Oskar.'

'Did she ever mention the words on the back of the photograph?'

Vivienne shook her head. 'She could well have done, but it probably got lost in the rush of everything she said and I just missed it. It was as if she was trying to offload everything before she passed away. The only thing that was clear to me was that the subject made her very restless. She said she'd written you a letter asking you to contact her. I told her it would be better to call you, but she was quite sure you'd refuse to speak to her.'

I chewed my lip.

'Don't feel guilty for not getting in touch. The things she said to you the last time you saw each other were disgraceful. I even told her so myself, and I think that day Annabel regretted them.'

After a moment or two, Vivienne returned to her story. 'The effort of telling me about Oskar had exhausted your mother and she rested for a while after taking another painkiller. She wanted me to sit by her side, which I did. After an hour or so, she woke up quite confused and far from her lucid self.'

Vivienne glanced at the hearth. She stretched over for the poker and began to prod at the logs with little effect. I got up and finished the job for her while she continued, her eyes watching the lick of flames.

'Your mother had her eyes closed while she talked. At times her words trailed off and it was difficult to follow her. But what came through loud and clear was how everything went wrong during the war. And then she said that she only had herself to blame and that she had been an utter coward for hiding too much. I said something like, *Don't be silly, Annabel*, and at that she became quite angry. *How would you know?* she'd said.' Vivienne looked up at me. 'And then she laughed, Max. She laughed. She frightened me. It was as if she were a different woman ... I didn't know what to say. In the end, I had to leave the room. I put it down to the painkillers, but ...'

'Did Mama mention anything about my grandfather, about him ...' I couldn't say it out loud. I felt sick. The words, *Papa she writes – Papa touches me*, soughed in my ear.

'No, she didn't, Max.' Tears welled in Vivienne's eyes. 'Not once. Not then. Not before.'

'Perhaps she knew all along, about my grandfather, about all of this.'

She stared back at me, shaking her head.

Inside, I couldn't let it go. I thought of the notebook and its contents, which by now I could visualise well. The words accompanying my mother's crude image of the girl came to mind:

Run.
Away. Away.
Quietly now. Quietly.
Eyes closed. Mouth sealed.

The gentle skip of the music and the occasional spit of flames filled the silence between us, as if cajoling us to speak. Vivienne blinked her tears away. She picked up her tale where she left off, stopping once or twice when her voice faltered.

'I had a cup of tea with Ludmilla in the kitchen. When I came back to the drawing room, Annabel had fallen asleep again. I stayed by her side. Her sleep was quite disturbed and she drifted in and out of consciousness. Every now and again, she would mutter a word or say someone's name – she mentioned you, Max, just once.' At that, Vivienne threw me a fleeting smile. 'On and off she mumbled another name, someone I didn't know, but now after what you've told me, I'm certain it sounded like Eva … That's it. Eva. Over and over again. And then she said something like, *Being there when Papa died. My life began when I saw him dead.*'

'Do you think Mama murdered my grandfather?' I asked. 'Because of what he did to her?'

'I can't believe she'd do such a thing,' Vivienne said. 'And to keep it hidden like that. She confided in me. But this? The drawing she made in that notebook shows his death. She was still so young … We've both seen pictures of your grandfather. He would have overpowered her … I didn't know her then. Only afterwards …' Pain flickered on Vivienne's face.

'So if my grandfather really locked up my grandmother to keep her quiet, then is it possible that Thaddäus may be alive?' Nothing could stop the theories multiplying in my head, each born from a word or a phrase in my grandmother's final letter.

'With the notebook you discovered, and now this letter, you can read something into everything. But we're still none the wiser,' said Vivienne, her voice almost a whisper.

'Did Mama say anything else?'

'No. But she began to weep, saying that *she knew* and *how sorry* she was, but *sorry wasn't good enough for Eva* – she mentioned

166

that same name again. *I must find him,* she'd said, *because he knew too.* She must have been talking about Oskar Edelstein,' she said. 'Then your mother woke and stood up, shaking off my efforts to help her. She looked at me and said, *They'll never trust this family again.*'

Vivienne stared at her hands, now resting in her lap. She summoned up a smile, trying to look brighter than she obviously felt. 'That night she took her life.'

Vivienne put the letter and her glasses to one side and got up to switch on the main light by the door. 'It's too much, isn't it?' she said, squeezing my shoulder.

I put my hand over hers, wanting her to keep it there, but she soon moved it away and went upstairs to her bedroom.

I remained on my own in the living room until the fire burned out, reflecting on the things I had learned. They were like stars thrown randomly together, except when you stood back, they formed a constellation that was clear enough.

So this was the conclusion that formed in my mind: my grandfather, Sebastian Alexander Albrecht, was a paedophile and murderer. He was a father, a husband and a philanthropist who abused his position of responsibility, who abused my mother and who imprisoned my grandmother. Revulsion wound its way through me, tightening around my chest. A part of me hoped that this tale I had pieced together was like a Chinese whisper, the story growing taller as the years went by. Yet a mosaic of facts had come to light that made it all the less fanciful. Other things, too, rubbed away at the sheen of my family name: the mysterious death of my mother's brother, Thaddäus; the chilling ambiguity of my grandmother's last letter to Claudia Edelstein; the photograph of Oskar and my mother; the words *You knew* on its reverse, and then the scrawled riddle in *Young Gerber.*

As for Eva, I considered the words that Vivienne told me my mother had spoken in her fitful sleep. If they were true, and I believed they were, then something must have happened to Eva to have plagued my mother's conscience. I just sat there, unable to stop the reel of events. I wondered, then, if it had been my mother – not my grandmother – who had written the years above the names of the victims in those articles; I wondered if she had found something else that pointed to my grandfather's involvement in their deaths, if she had worked it all out, if she had connected Eva with the things that my grandfather had done. As I recalled from my mother's diary entries, Eva – this *E* that she referred to – had gone away to Salzburg. Maybe she was one of the lucky ones who had escaped. Maybe she had run away, far from the clutches of my grandfather. And maybe, just maybe, my mother had worked that one out too and wanted to find Eva, the girl she had once been close to, to tell her how sorry she was.

OBER ST. VEIT, VIENNA, 1944

Papa's back. The front door's just slammed and there's an exchange of terse words with Fritz, which Annabel can't make out from her bedroom. She's been reading a letter from Mama – at least, it's signed by Mama – but there's so little of Mama in it, and the handwriting's different. There isn't even an I love you, my dearest heart, which was the way Mama always used to end her letters.

Annabel hears the door handle turn. Her body trembles. The door opens and Papa is silhouetted in the doorway. She knows there's little she can do, of course. She can't scream; she can't run. This is how it feels when an animal's snared. All she sees is him drawing closer. His lips are open and if words slide out of his mouth, she doesn't hear them.

But then he stops. He's staring over her shoulder at the wall behind her bed. He tries to say something, but his words choke in his throat and he clutches at his collar, tugging at the starched strip of white. Beads of sweat dot his forehead as he stumbles backwards, grasping the doorframe.

'Help me,' he says to Annabel. But Annabel remains on the bed, watching him. He staggers out of the room. There's a clatter of footsteps, then silence, then a shout and a crash. Annabel rushes out and peers over the broken banister to see Papa's body sprawled on the floor below, his open eyes staring up at the atrium.

Then she feels it: a chill in the air that wasn't there before. Instinct prompts her to look over her shoulder, back towards her bedroom. Someone is standing in the doorway.

CHAPTER FOURTEEN

As we left for Himmelhofgasse the following morning, Vivienne gave my arm a friendly squeeze, but it made me feel worse rather than better. While neither of us mentioned my grandmother's letter, it hung between us. Tension dug into my shoulders, and the food in my stomach churned, a sensation that only grew worse as we neared my mother's house. The proximity of the place compounded everything I felt, the revolving questions and doubts, and the admission I had made to Oskar Edelstein about the existence of a presence. As we walked uphill, this thought and others whispered in the breeze. At one point, I tried to laugh them away. Vivienne turned to me with concern in her eyes.

'It's nothing,' I said.

She gave a small shake of her head, then adjusted her pale green shawl about her shoulders.

I hadn't noticed the cold until then. I fastened the top button of my coat, and drove my hands into my pockets. The sky was almost cloudless, the crisp December air brushed against my skin. It should have felt good, but it didn't.

Turning into Himmelhofgasse, she said, 'When it's like this, the cold doesn't matter so much.' She made it feel like we were taking one of our normal strolls together, with her casual chatter and questions about Matthias Ropach, his background, his growing recognition. I found her talk helped me relax a bit.

When we reached the house, we both fell silent. As we walked through the gate, a flock of birds appeared above us, their swirling synchronisation briefly captivating Vivienne.

'Like a wave floating to and fro in the sky,' she said. 'Quite marvellous, isn't it, how they do that. Which one's the leader, do you think?' She shielded her eyes as she tracked their motion.

I left her side and headed over to the entrance, in a hurry to get the visit over and done with.

'What a contrast!' said Vivienne, her voice echoing in the stillness of the house, as did the click of our shoes on the marble floor. No trace of the break-in remained. A smell of cleaning fluid hung in the air. The walls had been wiped down and all of the artwork had been returned to its rightful place. The new banister above us looked as though it had always been there, carefully crafted to match the original. Damaged frames had been replaced or restored; broken china, ornaments, where possible, had been repaired. Even the saint and the angel in the hallway had a polish to them. The blacks of their eyes now gleamed; the despondent gaze that I remembered had vanished. Frederik had gone beyond the call of duty and I realised my tactlessness in failing to acknowledge the extent of his friendship with my mother. I would call him to say thank you – it was the least I could do.

Yet as I walked about, it struck me that the house had disappeared into itself. The creaks, the stretch and contraction of the wooden eaves, the stammering pipes – all the familiar noises had vanished. This silence was altogether different. It wasn't the silence that spoke of anticipation or of secrets; it was as if the clean-up had sanitised it. What's more, part of me missed it. The house felt dead – that was it – and to think of it like that took me by surprise. I glanced across at Vivienne as we walked back from the living room to the hallway.

'She's well and truly gone,' she said, sitting down on the bench. 'This – it's sealed her passing for me.' Her eyes remained dry; there was no sadness written on her face. In fact, she showed little emotion at all.

The chime of the doorbell announced Matthias Ropach's arrival. He walked in, long and lanky with an ear-to-ear grin, laden with a bag and laptop, his easy air putting a halt to our own brooding. He looked about him, glancing this way, then that, the delight evident in the dance of his eyes. I imagined him envisioning his plans, stripping the house bare. It triggered a surreal tug of war in my head: a radical overhaul versus rekindling the soul of the house.

Even though Matthias had seen the house before, he wanted to take another look with us to, in his words, *bring his ideas to life*. Such was the transformation of the place since the break-in that I led the way upstairs to the second floor without the slightest bit of hesitation. All the rooms up there felt quite normal, and I was so absorbed with identifying what was now missing about the house that I only half listened to Matthias and his patchwork of comments. Everything had been tidied up, even the attic, which had been swept clean. The wooden crates that had been in the centre were now stacked against the wall. They all looked the same and I couldn't identify the one in which I had found the notebook. And as for the relics of furniture – the cradle, the wardrobe, the trunk, and puppet theatre – they all carried a shine and looked nearly useable again.

The same could be said of the first floor. All appeared neat and orderly. The bedrooms looked like refurbished hotel rooms, ready for their first guests. I smiled to myself. The combination of cleaned surfaces, starched linen, the way the furniture had been put back, all polished, positioned to perfection was such that, if she were still alive, my mother would find little to fault.

We stepped into my bedroom, except it no longer felt like the room of my childhood. My model cars had disappeared from the windowsill, the bookshelf lay half empty and the desk was bare, apart from my Pentax camera sitting on top. Noticing a crack in the lens, I picked it up. Its broken state stung a bit. I turned it over in my hands. The compartment for the film was also damaged. Its sorry state made me feel like it was well and truly the end of a long companionship. Thinking of the moments I'd captured with this camera pushed me down. It was like it had recorded a more carefree life, one that lay far away from the one I was leading now. I tried not to think of it by paying more attention to Matthias, and soon, both Vivienne and I were salting the discussion with our own views, pronouncing our shared passion to ensure that he retained the library. Fortunately for all three of us, Matthias had left that untouched in his plans.

Back downstairs, the architect indicated to the cellar. 'Shall we take a look?'

I turned to Vivienne. 'You don't have to come.'

She didn't put up a fuss and I didn't blame her. There was little for her to see and she was quite content to wait for us in the drawing room. So it was just Matthias and I.

This time, he took the lead, jogging down the stairs. I paused at first, watching the bob of his head as he made his way to the stairwell. My stomach lurched. He looked up, waiting for me. I forced a smile and nodded, before going down to join him.

It seemed I had nothing to be afraid of. Frederik's restoration had extended to the cellar. The naked light bulb in the stairwell shined brighter, throwing more light into the corridor. If it wasn't for the chill, I would have gone almost so far as to say that the new light gave a bit of life to the space. Even so, I hovered at the foot of the stairs.

'Each time I'm down here, the more sure I am that this has to change,' I said, cursing myself for sounding too cheery.

Matthias just nodded before disappearing from view, his footsteps growing fainter. I hesitated again before seeking him out, hurrying over to join him at the far end of the cellar where the corridor narrowed. He had his back to me, and for a moment, his stance reminded me of the child, its image inching its way from the back to the front of my mind. Matthias eventually turned around, just as I remembered the child had done ... I blinked the picture of her away. A frown replaced his grin as he told me the extent of the work required. Then he turned to face the wall again.

'Is there another room behind here?' he called out.

'Not that I know of,' I said, watching him run his hands around the edges of the wall, knocking in various places. 'My mother never mentioned anything.' I went over to him, my curiosity nudging me on.

'Funny, there seem to be tiny gaps – here, and here.' He indicated various places. I struggled to see what he was talking about. Matthias shook his head at me, as if I were playing dumb. 'This wall's thin and hollow. If you touch here, there's a draught. Can you feel it?'

I put my hand where he pointed and felt the tickle of air against the edge of my palm. I hadn't noticed it before, at least I didn't think I had. I remembered how, that night I thought I saw the child down here, I'd felt along that very same wall after the presence had gone. Perhaps the cold was such that I hadn't noticed any difference.

Matthias turned to me. 'Are there any other plans of the house?'

'Just the ones I gave you.'

'When were they drawn up?'

I shrugged. 'I've no idea. I suspect when my mother remodelled the place.'

'Is there anyone you could ask?'

My thoughts went to Frederik. After he had overseen the clean-up of the house, I didn't want to bother him again. I was certain he wanted to move on, yet here I was, doing my best to prevent him from doing that.

'It's no big deal. We'll find out soon enough,' he said, glancing up and down the length of the corridor.

'I better go back and check on Vivienne,' I said, eager to return to the light of the ground floor.

'Go ahead. I just want to have a look at something else. I won't be long.'

I rounded up the stairs before Matthias could ask another question. As I passed along the hallway I looked up at the atrium: a veil of grey cloud now obscured the crisp blue sky of earlier. The dim light transformed the mood of the house. But there was something else. I noticed that all the doors to the rooms were shut when I was sure that almost all of them had been left open. Worse, it seemed the sterile silence had been replaced by an altogether different stillness that was at once familiar. It was like the house, the air, were closing in on me. And as I approached the drawing room, I had the distinct sensation that I was being followed.

Before entering, I became aware of Vivienne's voice. It sounded like she was on the phone, yet her words seemed slurred and thick with sleep. Then I heard her laugh tinkle through the closed door, and a smile broke out on my face. I slipped inside, careful not to disturb her.

The closed curtains censored the daylight, throwing a shroud of honeyed darkness over the room. There was a chill too, which floated in and around me, sending a faint shiver down my spine. Once my eyes had adjusted to the changed light, I saw Vivienne perched on the edge of the sofa. She had shed her coat, which now lay draped over the armrest. Her shawl hung from her shoulders and her back was slumped. She looked as if she had been drugged.

She was smiling, but it was a smile that didn't belong to her, making her look as though she'd had her memory erased. Her vacant gaze was transfixed on the corner of the room. I followed her line of sight to the curtains. I was about to draw closer when they seemed to move. I froze. I thought I saw a hint of a small body crouched behind them, tugging the material tighter around itself. The child, the girl I'd seen down in the cellar flickered through my mind. My stomach knotted.

No, it can't be.

I strained to see exactly what it was, fighting against the part of me that didn't want to know, when a small pale hand snuck out. I blinked. It was still there, its fingers clasping the curtain. It looked quite real, and even in the weak light I could make out a wound scored black around its wrist.

Vivienne spoke – not to me, I quickly realised. 'Why don't you come closer so I can see you better?' She wrinkled her brow. 'There's no need to be afraid.' Her voice teased, like a child at play.

I glanced back to the curtains. They shifted in response. Vivienne chuckled, but like her smile, her laugh wasn't hers. 'You want to show me something? Very well, I'll come to you.'

I felt sick. *No, Vivienne*, I wanted to shout.

She pushed herself up from the sofa, her shawl slipping from her shoulders to the floor. She looked like a marionette: at first her body was loose, then it pulled taut with every step she took. Only her eyes remained focused, trained on the corner of the room.

'And where will you take me?' She tilted her head to one side, waiting for an answer as she moved forward.

I looked again to the curtains. This time they appeared to move only slightly.

'Where? Down there?' Vivienne giggled.

I tried to call out to her but her name choked in my throat. I tried again; the words came out as a whisper that only I could hear. Fear coiled around me. Vivienne was only a few metres away, but I felt as though I had been paralysed. I fought against it, my alarm growing as I watched the presence behind the curtain play puppet-master to someone I loved.

Vivienne tripped forward. The alien smile, still fixed on her face, broke. 'You don't have to be alone any more,' she said.

I reached out to touch her on the shoulder just as the doorbell rang but she didn't respond and her lurch forward continued. It seemed that something in the house gripped us both. Vivienne was being propelled in her world, while I was trapped in mine.

The doorbell rang again, seemingly louder, its echo bouncing off the walls.

Vivienne turned around. Suddenly her eyes were wide open, fully conscious. Her mouth opened, as if she was about to say something, only for confusion to cloud her face. She looked at me, then at the sofa, then back at me. We both turned towards the corner of the room, to the curtains. They hung as they should, no bump or bulge otherwise disturbing their form.

'Why on earth are you looking at me like that?' she said, her gaze wandering from me to the sofa, then back to me. The familiar facial expressions had returned and she was back to the Vivienne I knew.

Images and words tumbled over in my mind. I attempted to explain, but my voice wouldn't work. I just stood there, blinking at her.

She scratched her head and frowned. 'I must have nodded off. But how ... Was I sleepwalking?'

I found myself nodding, and her concern didn't seem to last long. She showed no recollection of having had a conversation, nor of being coaxed towards the French windows.

'Old age – some things continue to surprise me,' she said, sitting down on the sofa.

The only thing I could do in response was to hug her. I didn't realise until then that my whole body was shaking.

'Max, there's no need to worry.' She rubbed my back, then gently pulled away from me and looked at me with eyes betraying an inkling of vulnerability.

'It's just the house. Even with Mama gone, and that letter, I still feel this grief steeping inside me. And seeing you, just now ...' I couldn't tell her.

'I'll be quite all right. And so will you.'

Just then, Matthias walked into the drawing room, scratching his forehead.

'Weird,' he said, 'I popped out to grab something from my car but when I got back, the front door was locked. I rang the doorbell a couple of times, and when no one came, I tried the door again and it opened – just like that.' He looked at me, then at Vivienne. 'Is everything all right?'

'Just a funny spell, that's all,' said Vivienne.

I summoned up a smile. 'Perhaps it would be better to do this at Vivienne's.' I turned to her. 'You can rest there.'

I led the way out, keen to leave the place where I'd witnessed the spirit's latest turn. I noticed that all the doors on the ground floor were now open again, just as they had been before Matthias and I had headed to the cellar. The atmosphere had changed too – clearer, lighter, as though a blast of fresh air had been let in. But it did little to lessen my fear.

Back at Vivienne's place, we congregated in the warmth of her kitchen. Even though I relaxed a bit in the security of her home, when Matthias rolled the house plans out on the table, my mind flicked back to Vivienne and the glimpse of the childlike hand. I forced myself to ask questions about the project, but it was clear my interjections made little sense. While Matthias politely answered my muddled queries, Vivienne glanced at me now and again, her face lined with worry. I got up to make some coffee, yet I still couldn't focus. Matthias's drawings seemed to hover off the page and I didn't absorb much more about the redesign. It was only when he mentioned *ambitious transformation* that I realised he was referring to his plans for the cellar. I looked up at him.

'Is there anything wrong, Max?'

I cleared my throat. 'It's fine. All fine.' I could barely string a sentence together. 'Oh, there was something else I forgot.' I took off my glasses and rubbed my eyes. 'How much will all this cost? You know, approximately?'

I didn't hear what he said, but I heard Vivienne stifle a gasp.

'Let's just go ahead,' I said.

She stared at me. 'Are you sure? Don't you want to think it over?'

'No.' I fixed my eyes on Matthias. 'I've made up my mind.'

'Any changes you want to make to my plans?' he asked.

'No. None.' I gripped my coffee cup to stem the tremor in my hand. 'Any news on the contractors?'

'One can start before Christmas – at least with the cellar. I'll get a structural engineer in too.'

'Very good.' Relief flooded me with the comfort of the hot drink I sipped down. Seeing my old home play its tricks again made me regret my nostalgia for the house of old.

While we were tidying up in the kitchen, Vivienne said, 'You just want to forget, don't you?'

'Something like that.'

'I want to forget too. I've been trying. But it's a little bit too much, even though I hate dwelling on things – so did your mother, at least she did, until the end.' She patted my arm. 'Are you all right?'

'I'm fine. Just tired. Maybe I'll have a nap.'

'It'll do you good.' Then she said, 'It's funny. When I saw the Schiele again, it brought back memories of when your mother bought the piece – it was quite a steal at the time.'

'I thought it belonged to my grandparents?' As I thought about it, I realised I'd never really explored the provenance of many of the things in my mother's house. 'I assumed it'd always been in the family?'

'She bought it from a gallery desperate to get rid of it,' Vivienne said. 'It was just before you were born. Schiele and others were out of favour for a while. That's why I thought it strange that she chose to copy that painting in her notebook. And now – well, it's astonishing to see their value. I don't think we could ever have imagined it. Your mother regretted not buying more.'

Her comment prompted thoughts of storage before the renovation began.

'Do you really think it's necessary to put the paintings in storage?' she said.

Her reaction struck me as a little offhand and I said as much, trying my best to mask my irritation.

'Well,' she said, 'I suppose after the break-in it makes sense. I'll call the Dorotheum and arrange it for you. Now – why don't you go upstairs and get some rest.'

I put Vivienne's nonchalance down to her age. She was of a different generation, when doors could be left unlocked and trust was more commonplace. Still, given her earlier remark about the Schiele, I couldn't work out why removing it and the others seemed so unimportant to her. But I couldn't stay annoyed. The scene in the drawing room continued to play on my mind.

Up until then, the things I had experienced left me feeling unsure of myself. But what I felt when I saw Vivienne in that state in the living room pierced me with a fear that I had never felt before: pure, cold fear. It was the presence, threatening someone I loved dearly, and the horror of being utterly powerless to do anything to protect her that caused it. I thought back to the cellar, the figure – the child. Was it really a girl I had seen, as I had told Oskar? I remembered hearing the child's cries in the attic. At least, I *thought* that's what I heard. Was she good or evil? I didn't know, but from what I had seen earlier that day, the ghost seemed to have morphed into something else, something altogether malevolent. Picturing Vivienne again, what I saw … I blinked the image away – or tried to. Fear wrestled in my stomach and my hands trembled. The words my grandmother had written in that final letter of hers, my mother's apparent restlessness, her guilt, her sorrow in her final days, followed by what I had witnessed earlier on – everything I had seen and heard – seemed more than just figments of my imagination brought on by the emotional chaos of mourning and exhaustion. And then there was the glimpse of the tiny hand, too. It made me think that the presence in the drawing room and the child I had seen that night in the cellar were related.

If that was the case, I needed more information to cement this link. I wanted to know *why* there was a presence. And if it did in fact take on the guise of a young child – a girl – as I now believed, then I needed to know more.

The following morning I called Thomas Schmidt, the detective. It was a rather stunted conversation and a bit awkward to say the least.

I cut straight to the chase and told him about the three murders. 'I want to get more involved in The Albrecht Trust, like my mother would've wanted, and I came across these incidents. I just want to know when they happened and why they went cold.'

Schmidt's pause hung between us down the phone. 'Do you know how long that would take? It's not as if I or anybody else here has time on our hands.' He broke into a hacking cough. 'Those cases would've been closed long ago. Why's it so important? Is one of the deceased's relatives asking?'

'No. But I am,' I said, chopping at his reluctance. 'I think they're connected. I think ...'

'Yes?'

'I think I know who did it.'

He cleared his throat. I pictured him processing what I'd just said.

'You do realise, don't you, the seriousness of this?'

'Yes, it had crossed my mind.'

'You have evidence, I presume?'

I knew that the proof I had would amount to nothing in his eyes. 'Yes and no.'

He laughed. 'Can you be more specific?' I told him about my grandmother's letter, revealing only that she had identified someone who could have committed the crimes, and how she was wrongfully locked up in an asylum after the death of her son. I couldn't bring myself to mention my grandfather.

'Is the murderer still alive?'

'To be honest, I'm still unsure how much, if any of it, is true, given what happened to my grandmother.'

'I'd need to see the letter,' he said. 'And anything else you've got.'

'There's somebody else – he's still alive – who could help too.'

'Who's that? When can I see him?' The abruptness in his voice put me off. So far it had been just Oskar and I travelling along this path.

'It's taken me a while to find him,' I said. 'It hasn't been easy for him. He's only just agreed to meet me.' I'd told so many white lies so far that this one slipped out without any effort.

'This is a police matter.'

'Yes, but he's an old friend of the family's. It's a bit delicate,' I said. 'He's due to visit soon. I'll mention you want to meet him then, if that's okay?'

He puffed down the phone. 'Give me a name, at least.'

So I relented and told him about Oskar, and about my mother's desire to reach out to him before she died.

'I'd need that letter of your mother's too. When's this Oskar Edelstein coming again?'

I gave him the date. I could hear the scratch of pen on paper.

'By the way,' he said, 'that book – *Young* ...'

'*Gerber.* What about it?' I said, wishing the casual inflection in my voice didn't sound so forced.

'The message ... Has that got anything to do with this?'

I told him I still had no idea, sticking to the pretext that my mother had done it.

'You know, none of us can work it out still – we even have a wager on it. I reckon it's ...' I could hear the scratch of his pen again.

'So you'll help me – on the other stuff?'

'Let me see what I can do,' he said. It felt like he was indulging a spoilt child. 'But I'll need the letters and anything else – and I'll need to speak to Oskar Edelstein. I'll make sure I'm around.' After I put the phone down, I wondered whether it was the right thing to do, to loop in Schmidt. I didn't want him to confront Oskar unexpectedly with rounds of questions, so I thought it best to warn him.

That said, I'd still been struggling to reach Oskar. When I eventually tried again, it was Angela who picked up.

'He got all your messages, Max,' she said. 'He's away at the moment but he'll be in touch when he returns. Is there anything else you want me to pass on to him?'

'No. It's okay, Angela. It would be good to talk to him. That's all.' My urgent need to speak to him was ever-present; to compound it, there were other things that were pressing.

I had noticed that Vivienne had become withdrawn and I was worried about her. It was as if she was mourning again. She did her best to hide it. She still played music, but it was back to the *Requiem* again. Later that day, as I watched her from the doorway of the living room, she seemed lost in her own thoughts, and her eyes, while directed at the novel she was reading, didn't appear to absorb a single word on the page. When I went in to join her, she erased the look from her face. She closed the book, removed her glasses and mustered up the semblance of an apologetic smile.

'I thought I knew your mother inside out,' she said.

'Would you have done anything differently if you knew everything about her? From the moment you met you were such a good friend to her – there when she needed you. What more could she have asked for?'

Vivienne shrugged her shoulders, then turned to sorting through the newspapers on the coffee table, as if she needed something else to focus on.

'I don't want to leave you,' I said.

She sat back down on the sofa and patted the seat next to her. 'It's you I worry about.'

I joined her, fiddling with the tassels on one of her velvet cushions. 'Why don't you come back to London with me?' I suggested.

'And after I'd been to all the museums and galleries, what would I do, with you in the office from morning until night?'

She had a point. I dropped the idea. Lana and I had talked about getting away for a week during Christmas, but nothing was set in stone and much as I wanted to spend time with her, in this instance, it didn't feel right.

'How about after my visit with Oskar, I'll stay on with you over Christmas?'

'Weren't you meant to go away with your new girlfriend?'

'She's not exactly my girlfriend …'

Vivienne shook her head at me, but I could see the cheer unfold on her face. 'Are you quite sure?' She clapped her hands and the sparkle returned to her eyes. 'That's simply the best news. I thought Lana and work would keep you in London.'

Her delight partially made up for the knowledge that Lana would be less than pleased at my decision to stay with Vivienne, and it made me realise that I should have opened up to her about what was going on; she was more of a girlfriend than I admitted, even to myself. Before the Christmas break: that would be when I'd try to explain a few things to Lana. I made a promise to myself.

For the rest of the day, Vivienne maintained her good humour, chatting about her plans for the holiday period. Not wanting to alter her mood, I didn't mention my conversation with Schmidt, nor my intention to drop by the house on my way to the airport.

When my taxi arrived, I asked the driver to take a slight detour towards Himmelhofgasse. He didn't seem to mind either way, uttering a grunt in response. Once at the house, I told him I'd be less than half an hour. He grudgingly agreed to a fixed price, but judging by the look in his narrow eyes, I couldn't be sure whether he'd honour our arrangement. With a loud sigh, he switched off his engine, tapped open his packet of cigarettes and drew one out.

I went inside, swallowing down the lingering fear. I didn't think about the *what ifs*. I didn't want any thoughts to crawl into my mind at all.

I went first to the study. I looked at the photographs on the bookshelf. The one I had left lying in its broken frame all those weeks before had been put into a new frame – all thanks, I assumed, to Frederik. I took it down from the shelf and had a closer look at it. My grandparents sat in the centre. Next to them, on either side, sat some children, the smaller ones sitting cross-legged on the ground in front of them. A rather severe-looking lady, her hair pulled into a neat bun, stood to the side of the group. I assumed this was the Frau Werner that my mother referred to in her notebook. I studied the children: they all wore white shirts; the boys were in dark shorts, the girls in dark pleated pinafores. None of them resembled the children in the articles – there seemed to be no Josef Frank, no Christine Hintze, no Elena Markovic. All of them looked anonymous, their faces made up of smiles or straight lips, wide or narrow eyes, their heads half-cocked or held high.

I homed in on the image of my grandfather. He was sitting very straight-backed, a little removed from my grandmother. He looked like a giant of a man. I examined his eyes. They were bright, soft, less piercing than my own. Were they the eyes of a monster? I felt the knot tighten around my chest again. I wrested my eyes away from his. Then I noticed something else. One of his hands rested loosely on his lap while the other lay by his side, his little finger and ring finger appearing to touch the girl sitting next to him. I scrutinised it further, concerned that my new knowledge of him was prejudicing my interpretation of his body language. Turning the frame over, I slid open its back and removed the photograph. On the reverse was a month and year: July 1937. Written in pencil, in the handwriting I now recognised as my grandmother's, were the names of the children: *Henriette Bertelsmann, Gretel Moser, Jakob Hass* ... Seated next to my grandfather was *Eva. Eva Schwartz*. I flipped over the photograph. There she was, a dark-haired girl with an awkward smile on her face, her eyes staring at the camera. She couldn't have been more than thirteen years old, and although she sat with the same straight back of her peers, the subtle twist of her shoulder away from my grandfather's body screamed louder than anything else in the picture.

I took the photograph with me, leaving the empty frame on the bookshelf and headed out to the hallway. Outside, the winter sun was fading, so I switched on the light, the soft sparkle from the chandelier banishing the gloom indoors. I felt better with the additional light, less wary about my next task as I jogged up both flights of stairs to the attic door, which, in turn, opened effortlessly. It all seemed so easy, something that I was glad about, and any remaining anxiety I had fizzled away.

I went straight to the pile of boxes and tugged down the first one. I should have taken more care rummaging through it, but

I was aware of the taxi driver waiting and I didn't want to waste much time. I leafed through letters and loose photographs hoping to find something, but everything seemed to date back to the 1960s. There were letters from Vivienne, notes from my father, images of my mother wearing thick black eyeliner and short dresses, and one of a man sporting a chalk-white face, with dark paint oozing down his head and the length of his white suit. I put them back and pushed the crate to one side. Just as I reached up for the next one, the attic door at the foot of the stairs slammed shut behind me.

My breath caught in my throat; my fingers gripped the box's edge. I couldn't stem the tremble in my hands as I wrestled to open it up. While this one contained more old letters and photo albums of one sort or another, at first glance, they appeared to date back to the early 1900s. There was nothing amongst those things that seemed to be of any use to me and I quickly moved on.

After rooting aimlessly through three crates, despair set in. Outside, rain began to fall, each minuscule drop tap-dancing on the slate roof and window. The happy-go-lucky rhythm goaded me, as though it were clear that I'd little chance of finding anything significant. My search felt all the more futile as I'd little idea of what it was I should be looking for. I hurried through the fourth box, throwing old books and even more letters to one side. Doubt nagged at me and I couldn't shake it off. And neither could I ignore the silence of the house, the way it seemed to bear down on me, like a pillow pressed upon my face. I had to get out, but I couldn't leave empty-handed. My fingers, now clammy, stumbled through pages of old magazines and yet more damned photo albums. What was I doing? What did I think I'd achieve rifling through old possessions? I looked to the fifth box, hoping that I would find something.

In desperation I raked through endless paper straw, accidentally ripping useless newspaper cuttings, finding nothing. Until, that is, I felt the tough leather binding of another photo album. I pulled it out, my hands now shaking uncontrollably.

Please. Please let this be the one.

I dusted it with my sleeve and looked inside.

It contained photographs that appeared to commemorate my grandparents' patronage of The Albrecht Trust. There were prize-givings, sideways profiles with stiff handshakes, sports days, a vee of skinny boys in vests and shorts sprinting towards a finish line, children in uniform, standing with matriculation certificates in their hands, grins pinned on their faces. Names and dates were written underneath. I scanned them, looking for the names now ensconced in my head: *Josef*, *Christine, Elena.*

The faint rumble of the car engine outside put a halt to my search. I wedged the photograph from the study into the album, snapped it shut, and ran down the attic stairs to the door. I turned the handle. It was stuck. Panic fluttered through me. I tried again, yanking it with such force that it flung wide open, slamming against the wall. Just as it was about to swing closed, I slipped through the gap and ran out on to the landing. My heart skipped a beat. All the lights in the house had gone out. I flew down the stairs and into the hall, hearing the slow crunch of the taxi's wheels on the gravel as it pulled out of the driveway. I raced out of the house towards the car and banged on the boot. The vehicle screeched to a halt, throwing me off kilter.

I stumbled around to the driver's window. 'What the hell are you doing?' I yelled.

He stared back at me, shrugging his shoulders. I ran back to the entrance, jamming the key around in the lock until I heard the click. Spotting my bag dumped at the foot of the steps, I grabbed it and got into the car.

'Christ, why did you drive off?'

The driver blinked at me through the rear-view mirror. 'I saw the lights in the house go off. I rang the doorbell several times. Then I tried the door, but it was locked.'

I closed my eyes, not wanting to hear more. I dropped my head back against the headrest, thankful that he hadn't left me behind. My heart took a while to settle. Only the knot in my chest and stomach remained, tightening then loosening, tightening then loosening.

Under the bright lights of the airport departure lounge, I returned to the photograph album, my eyes skipping from one image to the next, scanning the handwritten captions squashed under each picture.

I found Elena Markovic midway through. She was wearing a maid's uniform, almost lost inside her grey dress and white apron. I searched for Josef and Christine among the brunettes and blondes, the dark and pale-eyed, and eventually found them. Christine was dressed in what seemed to be a school uniform and young Josef was pictured receiving a small trophy for coming first in three races. The common denominator in all three photographs was my grandfather: standing too close to Elena, his hand hovering somewhere behind her back; his arm extended tightly around Christine's shoulder, his eyes directed not at the camera but at a point on her chest; his giant hand enveloping Josef's, his fingers digging into the boy's flesh. None of the children were smiling, their faces like masks that concealed their terror. I dug out the picture I had taken from the study. I compared the other children's images with Eva's. The expression on her face mirrored theirs. So now I had evidence. Of course, it wouldn't stand up in a court of law, but for me it was sufficient.

Yet even with this so-called evidence, I still had little to identify the presence. While the conviction that I had seen a young girl was there, I remained none the wiser about her identity. Was she Elena or Christine? I forced myself to conjure up the image of the girl in the cellar – her face, her eyes – then tried to blink them away. I looked at the pictures of Elena and Christine: they were both light-haired. I was sure the child I had seen had dark hair. But then again, my sighting of the girl had been fleeting. There was something stirring at the back of my mind that I wanted to ignore, but I couldn't. I revisited the photographs of Elena, Christine and Jacob, and the group photograph with Eva seated next to my grandfather. There was something about her, an air of familiarity. The presence flickered back into my mind, and I wondered if it was the distance of time that further distorted her appearance ... I didn't have it in me to conjure up her image again. I put the things away, willing myself not to touch them.

Still, my disgust for my grandfather fermented inside me. I thought of my mother. I felt for her. In what I'd discovered, I'd found another piece of the puzzle that probably explained her behaviour. It went a long way towards bridging the gap between us. All I could feel now was a strange mixture of sorrow and admiration: sorrow for the events that had blighted her life, and admiration for her ability to carry on regardless. Now I understood her cast-iron exterior, her determination to protect herself. I still didn't understand her need to push me away, but at least that didn't hurt quite as much any more.

Perhaps I could close the loop with Oskar and assuage my feelings of guilt and regret.

But what about Oskar? The man remained a mystery with his unexplained silence, his distance. The words *You knew* turned over in my head and it left me thinking that he and my mother were inextricably linked.

FIRST DISTRICT, VIENNA, 1965

'I'm going to take you to Demel,' says Annabel, her arm looped through Vivienne's as they walk through Heldenplatz.

Vivienne nods and presses her handkerchief, streaked with mascara and face powder, to her eyes. Her head rests for a moment on Annabel's shoulder. Annabel kisses it, breathing in her friend's familiar rose scent.

Annabel has taken a break from her work at The Albrecht Trust to spend time with Vivienne, whose relationship with the love of her life lies in tatters, thanks to the mesmeric beauty of a local girl who stole his heart in Lima. Only yesterday, Annabel toyed with the idea of getting on a plane just to scream at him for hurting her dearest friend. She was quite serious, but Vivienne's horror at the idea and her pleas to stay put, anchored Annabel to Vienna and her friend's side.

Morning rain slicks the statue of Archduke Charles sitting astride his leaping horse, and both man and steed glisten in the sun's rays, now peeping from between the clouds. Only a few people wander around the opulent Hofburg Palace, mostly po-faced officials and a straggle of tourists.

Annabel unbuttons her mackintosh, and the crimson wool and silk of her dress flares out. She cares about neither the unfashionable hemline nor the cut. What mattered, when she discovered it a few days ago, was its lack of moth holes and its fit. In it, she feels like Mama.

Just then, a commotion breaks out close to the entrance of the Hofburg Palace.

'Will you look at that,' says Vivienne staring at a blue duck – a Citroën 2CV – that had arrived from out of nowhere.

Annabel looks over and laughs as a suited man, painted white from head to toe, steps out of the car. A black bolt of lightning zigzags down his back and front. He walks through the open courtyard of the Hofburg Palace followed eagerly by a group of men and women younger than Annabel and Vivienne, their clothes, their manner, their attitude, rebellious against the status quo. Two or three onlookers – tourists, perhaps – charmed by the pop-up entertainment, tag along.

Annabel and Vivienne look at one another.

'We might as well,' says Annabel, grinning.

For the first time in days, Vivienne smiles and the two hurry after the one-man show, giggling like schoolgirls at the double takes of passers-by, the whispering behind cupped hands, the pointing fingers, the clicking cameras. But the parade only makes it as far as Michaelerplatz, where the white man is stopped by a huge double-chinned policeman bedecked in a shapeless raincoat. There's a terse conversation, a lot of nodding, some gesticulating. The scene draws an even larger crowd, people jostling for position in front of the Roman ruins. But there's little to see: no shouts, no scuffling, no handcuffs. Five minutes later, they shake hands. A taxi pulls up, hailed as if by magic, and the white man gets in. Sighs ripple through the crowd, the weight of collective disappointment as heavy as the muggy air. Within seconds, everyone has dispersed.

As Annabel and Vivienne pick their way along the cobbles, a man brushes Annabel's elbow.

'Oh, I do apologise,' he says with a cut-glass English accent.

He can't even be bothered to say it in German, Annabel thinks. Offering a brief nod, Annabel walks on with Vivienne in the direction of Kohlmarkt and her precious Demel, but annoyingly, the man sticks by her side.

'You see, I'm a little lost. Would you mind pointing me in the direction of Albertinaplatz?'

Annabel stops. She eyes him with the severity of one of her old school teachers, yet it only makes him break into a lopsided grin. If Vivienne wasn't with her, she would pause for longer. Instead, she rattles off directions in English that's almost as perfect as his, leaving him open-mouthed and flustered. Then she turns her back on him and quickly walks away, clutching Vivienne's arm for dear life.

After four cups of strong coffee, much talking and more tears from Vivienne, Annabel spies the same Englishman in Demel. He's tucked away in a corner pretending to read a copy of Die Presse. *He catches her eye and gives her that lopsided grin of his again.*

CHAPTER FIFTEEN

Back in London, I struggled to keep my unease at bay. When work began on the house, I thought I'd feel better, but instead, my anxiety worsened, making a show of itself in my on–off hand tremor and my short fuse with people at the office.

The smallest remark would ignite my temper. After a heated conference call with colleagues in New York, I ripped out my telephone and hurled it against the wall of my office. Suffice to say, my uncharacteristic display caused ripples of alarm across the floor. Seeing the heads of the others bob up above their cubicles reminded me of some meerkats I'd seen in a wildlife documentary, and in that moment I couldn't help but laugh out loud, which, in turn, caused my assistant's face to pale.

Matthias Ropach and his project manager kept me updated on the house. The initial structural work seemed to be progressing well, and in spite of my misgivings regarding the house and the cellar, neither of them mentioned anything untoward. Hearing of their unhindered progress was a small consolation, but it did little to settle the whispers in my head.

I had been clinging to the belief that work kept me sane, and I purposely spent more time at the office to avoid going home to dwell on my family's secrets. But work felt like an uphill trudge. Such was my schedule that I went from meeting to meeting, country to country, client to client as though I were a robot with flagging batteries. Our efforts were paying off though. The firm was doing well, and while *the-powers-that-be* spoke of the need for humility, no one paid much attention as they awaited their bonuses, greedy-eyed and salivating with inflated expectations.

In the bathroom at the office, I got into an argument with a colleague over a passing remark he'd made about linking female staff bonuses with their looks.

'Lighten up, will you?' he said. 'I'd be careful. People say you're losing it.'

I couldn't swallow my rising anger. I grabbed him by his collar and tie and shoved him against the wall. I wanted to punch him, to throttle him, and I found my hand edging around his neck, my grip tightening. I could smell his fear, feel his shuddering breath on my face, see the panic flaring in his eyes. If someone hadn't walked in, I would have continued. I let him go. He straightened his shirt and tie and threw me a look that spoke of unfinished business. I went into one of the cubicles and slumped against the door, unsure of what I'd done in those few seconds, shocked by the side of me I'd just glimpsed.

A week before I left for Vienna my boss summoned me into his office. 'What's up?' he asked, tipping back in his chair as he waited for an answer.

'I'm tired, that's all.'

'No you're not.'

I took my time, trying to weigh up what I should and shouldn't say. 'What would you do,' I said eventually, 'if you learned something that undermined everything you believed?' I cringed at my question.

'Are we about to get into an existential debate here?' He fixed his eyes on me.

I glanced away.

'What's wrong?'

I shifted in my seat. Two or three times I opened my mouth to speak and couldn't find the right words. But there was no way my boss was going to let me leave his office without a plausible explanation.

'I learned things recently about my family,' I eventually said. 'Shocking things.' I still couldn't look him in the eye.

'Care to elaborate?'

I shook my head.

'Something to do with the whole Nazi thing?'

'No! Nothing like that! I mean … no.'

My boss rubbed his temples, then rested his chin on his hand. I couldn't share what I'd learned. It felt like everything my grandfather had done had tainted me and I didn't want the stain to seep deeper by telling others. 'Just things I wish I'd never found out. I don't know … I don't want to talk about it,' I said, stuffing my trembling hands in my pockets.

He nodded. I'm not sure he understood, but he had the sensitivity to avoid asking for more details. As I got up to leave, he said, 'There's something else.'

I sat back down.

'I can't keep defending you the whole fucking time.'

I looked up at him.

'You're not making it easy for me.' He shrugged. 'The co-heads in New York want you to go.'

'What?'

'I tried to persuade them to change their minds. You'll get your bonus, your gardening leave.' He looked out the office window. 'They'll let you resign, Max. So long as you leave quietly.'

My mouth felt like a river run dry. 'I worked so hard for this firm. I've never let you down. I've …'

He turned back to me again. His face had hardened; it was

smooth, still. 'You're unsettling too many people. What if it's a client you lash out at next?'

'Out of everyone, it was you I looked up to, you I trusted.' I said, watching him copy a number from his computer screen onto a scrap of paper. It was like I was a spectator in someone else's life.

'Here,' he said, sliding the paper across his desk towards me. 'It's a counselling helpline number. There're people you can talk to. Professionals.'

'I see,' I said, barely swallowing all the things I wanted to hurl at him and the firm.

'I'm sorry, Max.'

I left the piece of paper where it lay, and quit his office and the building without a word or a glance at the others.

Three days after my unceremonious dismissal from my firm, Oskar called me. He apologised for taking so long to get in touch but kept his reasons vague. He wanted to confirm our visit to the house and told me that he would be staying at the Hotel Bristol in Vienna.

I said that I would rent a car for the day and offered to collect him from his hotel. 'We could perhaps drive around Hietzing – I thought you might like that.'

'I would, very much.' Then Oskar appeared to hang back, to pause for breath. 'There's something else – but on reflection, perhaps it would be better to talk it over when we see each other.'

'Actually, there's something I want to ask you,' I said, but before I could get my question out, I saw another call come through on my mobile. 'I'm sorry, Oskar. I've another call that I need to take.' I frowned at the phone.

Oskar glossed over my apologies for ending our conversation prematurely. He didn't sound disconcerted at all. Indeed, I thought I could hear a wisp of relief in his voice. 'I'm looking forward to seeing the house – and you, of course. The time feels right this time around,' he said. He sounded firm down the phone and his tone was brighter, as if he had well and truly recovered from his ill health.

The other call was from a lawyer renowned for winning tough unfair dismissal cases, and notoriously hard to get hold of. It was only on account of Lana's connections that he agreed to take me on. I didn't pay much attention to his untrammelled thoughts on the way the firm had acted, catching only his mention of *discombobulation*, probably because of the merry-go-round playing out in my own mind. I was too mired in my own frustration at not being able to probe Oskar further, at not getting the opportunity to raise the subject of the letters. I even considered making up an excuse to cut short the conversation to try to call Oskar back, but I didn't. So I made a mental note to call Oskar again later that day. Petty administrative battles between myself and the firm's human resources team, however, thwarted my attempts to find time to pick up the phone. The only person I really wanted to talk to was Lana, who let me rail against the firm's injustices. I could have confided in her then, told her about my mother and the things I'd discovered, but in my head they seemed like a loony set of excuses for the way things had turned out at work. In the end, although I tried to call Oskar several times in the days that followed, we only got to play a frustrating game of phone tag.

On the seventeenth, the day before I left for Vienna, I got a call from Matthias Ropach.

'There's a room down there after all,' he said. 'Two doors – one steel, the other wood – leading to a tunnel.'

I sat forward. *Was it possible?*

Matthias carried on talking. 'It looks like a reinforced room. Could be an old war bunker – it's difficult to say.'

My grandmother's letters drifted into my mind. I felt sick.

'You didn't have any luck, did you?' he asked.

'With what?'

'With the plans.'

'I tried.' I had spoken to Frederik but I hadn't mentioned the plans. I had thanked him for restoring my mother's house after the break-in, but his tone did little to encourage me to ask another favour of him.

'It's important that you have some title deeds, boundary documentation or whatever,' Matthias said. 'There's no physical marker. I'm not an expert, but …'

The rest of his words faded out as I vaguely recalled my grandmother's words: *Sebastian decided to build a war bunker …* With my grandfather's name attached to this thing, it seemed polluted with ulterior motives. To call it a war bunker seemed too neat, too innocuous.

'But do make sure you call your lawyer,' Matthias urged, keen to impress that point on me. He ended the phone call by saying that I should feel free to take a look since I'd be in town that weekend.

'I will, it's just …'

'It's all okay down there. Just be careful where you step.'

I was curious about the room. Part of me wanted to explore what they'd uncovered. Yet even when I tried to reason away any ulterior motive for the hidden room, I couldn't stem the sickness in my stomach. I decided to call Frederik, hoping a conversation with him would plug further thought of it.

'I'll have someone look around for older documentation,' he said. 'How urgent is it?'

I told him about the renovation work and the discovery of a room and a tunnel in the cellar.

'Interesting ... I never believed it.' His voice was almost a whisper.

'You've seen some other plans?' I asked, my hopes rising a notch.

'No. What you have is the sum total of what I've seen,' he said. 'Either myself or one of the others will get back to you, but it won't be today.' The call was over within five minutes. There was no further discussion, no speculation about the house. It seemed to me that Frederik was distancing himself from us, from my mother in particular.

For the rest of the day, news of the room and tunnel stirred up the murmuring voices in my head, feeding my sickness. This latest discovery made the upcoming trip to my mother's house feel like I was being sent to the bleakest prison imaginable. Thinking of it as one last hurdle before the Christmas break didn't do much to ease my anxiety. Each time I caught sight of my watch or the clock, time seemed to be slipping away.

That night, I couldn't help taking another look at the paraphernalia connected to the house's unsavoury past. I'd kept it all in a drawer in the spare room, along with the paperwork that Frederik had given me the day I learned of my inheritance. Sitting on the floor, I began to sift through it. There were a couple of formal envelopes from two banks and a third from the Dorotheum, which I assumed dealt with my mother's art collection. Much as I expected, there were no plans or title deeds evidencing the existence of the room or the property boundary. Catching sight of my grandmother's correspondence lying in the open drawer, I put the official papers to one side. I reread her letters several times over. They sucked me back in time and I felt like a shadow following my grandmother. I wanted to bring her and the children to the present where no one could hurt them and where Thaddäus would still be alive.

The ring of my mobile phone from the hallway interrupted my pointless daydreaming. It was Lana. She had been at a work dinner and planned to swing by before she and I went our separate ways for the holidays. I wanted to see her, I really did, but in that moment my head was elsewhere.

'I've been held up.'

'Where?' she asked.

'Just … some place.' My excuse was so paper-thin, I might as well have held up a sign saying, *I am lying.*

'Some place?' she said. 'Your lights are on at home – did you know that?'

I glanced out of my living room window. The boy on the fourth floor in the building opposite was at his computer again. Down below was Lana, standing by a cab, her phone pressed against her ear as she looked up in my direction.

'First you cancel our trip and then … after everything … Oh, just forget it.'

'Wait! I can explain …' The line had gone dead. All I could do was watch her get back into the taxi. I tried to call her but it went straight to voicemail. I dropped my mobile and sank to the floor. My firm had just fired me. My so-called attempt at a relationship now hung in the balance, and here I was, sifting through papers and mementos which had unearthed so many dark secrets that it felt as though I were bearing the guilt of them all. I raced out of my apartment, jumped into my car and drove to Lana's home. I'd explain everything. No dancing around, no more secrets.

Yet as I weaved in and out of the night-time crawl of
traffic on Park Lane, doubts pecked away at me. How could
I even begin to tell her about everything without her thinking
I was deranged? Her rationality was more clinical than mine.
She'd laugh me out of her home if I mentioned a presence,
strange writing, strange photographs. And if I told her about
my grandfather, then along with these things, she'd see me as
someone forever broken. I was sure she'd want to run as far
away from me as possible. It was no use. I circled Hyde Park
Corner and drove back home.

I wanted to let these secrets drift off into the ether, pretend
they'd never existed, but I couldn't. Back in my apartment, I
picked up the photo album, along with my grandmother's last
letter to Claudia Edelstein, Torberg's *Young Gerber*, my mother's
notebook and the photograph of Oskar and my mother. I
wandered into the kitchen and placed them in a row on the
table in the order in which they had come into my hands: to the
left was the photograph, then the copy of *Young Gerber*; next to
that was my mother's notebook, followed by my grandmother's
last letter; to the far right was the old photo album. I took a step
back. My grandfather played a role in the notebook, the letter
and the photo album; he was quite absent from the photograph
and the message scrawled in the novel. I opened the book to
those two pages. The words *O kneels, rats die* glared back at me.
Then I turned over the photograph where *You knew* was written
on the back. Without question the handwriting was identical –
something I had never really doubted. Oskar knew something
– that at least seemed obvious – but *what* he knew I would have
to wait until the next morning to find out.

The message in the book made no sense at all. It had been
a long time since I had looked at it: *O kneels, rats die.* I recalled
my conversation with Thomas Schmidt. Before I had cut him

off, he had been in the middle of making a remark about it. I grabbed a pen and paper and pulled a chair up to the kitchen table, sat down and wrote out the letters of the message in alphabetical order:

A D E E E I K L N O R S S T

I began to play around with them, struggling to form words that made sense. I looked at the message on the photograph's reverse, then flipped it over.

Of course!

I turned over my page and started again. It didn't seem possible at first, but I thought I'd give it a try. I wrote out the forename and surname, crossing off each letter as I went along.

O S K A R E D E L S T E I N

That's why Oskar had smiled when he saw it.

I picked up the phone to call the Hotel Bristol. A female voice answered.

'I need to speak to Herr Edelstein,' I said.

'I'm sorry, but Herr Edelstein has kindly requested not to be disturbed.'

'But it's urgent. Tell him that Max Gissing is calling. We're due to meet tomorrow. He'll understand. Please?'

'I'm sorry, Herr Gissing. There's nothing more I can do.' It sounded as if she were reading from a script.

That night I tried to sleep, but couldn't. The whispering inside my head persisted, urging me not to go. My stomach twisted. Time didn't stretch out as it should have done. Before I knew it, my alarm was ringing, herding me out of bed. I regretted the 6 a.m. flight I had booked. I hoped for Heathrow's usual delays, but there was barely a queue at security, my flight was on time, and we arrived into Vienna just after nine. Despite my deliberately slow pace I still arrived first at passport control. At the rental car desk, I tried to stall my pen as I filled out the forms, but my hand rushed across the blanks in an act of rebellion. And when I pulled out of the airport and on to the motorway, there were only a few cars cruising its three lanes.

No one seemed to be in a hurry, yet I pressed my foot down on the accelerator, hurtling towards the lorry in front of me, drawing closer and closer. If it braked, I'd career into it, no problem. I'd nothing to lose. I drew closer, wanting to feel the impact ...

But flashes of memories – the scatter of freckles on Lana's face, Vivienne's tinkling laugh – pulled me back from the edge. I slowed right down and pulled into the recovery lane, trying to slow my heartbeat, searching for that precious piece of calm, wanting to return to my old self.

After that, I deliberately drove in the slow lane, trying to focus on the smoking steel chimneys of the OMV and Borealis plants. They soon gave way to the snaking canal of the Danube and I slowed the car to a crawl. Within moments, the spire of St. Stephen's Cathedral came into view above the heart of the First District, agitating the sickness in my stomach once more. I didn't want to collect Oskar; I didn't want to drive to Ober St. Veit. Yet I couldn't disregard my mother's house. It felt as if the house had me on a thread, gently tugging at me to return. Perhaps, I thought, Oskar felt the same.

I pulled up at the Hotel Bristol, parking the car opposite the entrance on Kärntner Ring. Snow had fallen over the last couple of days. The cold was such that tiny ice particles floated in the air, their doily edges caught in the sun's rays. I blew on my fingers as I locked the car door, then jogged to the hotel entrance, which welcomed me in with a blast of warm air. The man behind reception informed me that Oskar was in the dining room having breakfast and that he expected me to join him.

I found him towards the back, tucked a little way from the pink marble buffet wall. He was half hidden by a copy of *The Times* and when I greeted him, he peeked at me over the top.

'I still can't bring myself to read an Austrian newspaper,' he said, folding the paper and placing his glasses on top. The remains of his breakfast lay to one side, next to a postcard of the Donnerbrunnen.

'It's for Angela,' he explained, seeing me glance at it. 'She always insists that I bring back a postcard from wherever I've been.'

I sat opposite him, turning down the offer of a tea or coffee from the waiter. Despite his thick jumper and tweed jacket, Oskar still looked frail – maybe even thinner than the last time I had seen him. I noticed a blister pack of pills lying by a glass of water.

'Ahhh, I've been caught,' he said, putting them in the breast pocket of his jacket. 'It's the real reason you haven't been able to get hold of me for a while. I had a bit of heart trouble again, that's all.' He went on to explain that he had been in hospital for several days. 'You must have thought me rude for not getting back to you.'

'It's me that was rude with my persistent calling. If I'd known …'

'Quite understandable,' he said, a flash of amusement in his eyes. 'They told me you phoned last night. At first I thought you were cancelling on me.'

'I worked it out – the anagram, I mean. You knew it was your name all along, didn't you?'

Oskar gave a small shrug of the shoulders. 'It was a fun way of learning English, trying to form words from our names. I think it was your mother who came up with that one. She was smarter than me.'

His attempt to make light of the situation didn't make me feel any better. 'I just don't ...'

'You don't think it's a good idea to go to the house.' He leaned back in his chair, his fingers fiddling with the top edge of the newspaper. 'You told me you believe in ghosts.'

I nodded, feeling my heart lurch.

'We've been presented with a number of things – the photograph, the messages, your mother's notebook, the letters written by your grandmother.' I wanted to interject, to ask him if he believed the claim she had made in that final desperate note, but he shook his head, determined to continue. 'I think the last letter may have arrived too late for my mother to have done anything. The contents shocked me, just as much as I'm sure they shocked you. And that's my point: the correspondence and everything else you've discovered resonated with us, although perhaps in different ways. I believe ...' He coughed, bringing his handkerchief to his mouth. 'Like you, I didn't believe in ghosts, but as time's gone by, things have happened, or items I've come across have made me believe otherwise. And I rather think there's a reason – something left unresolved, unspoken, or hidden.' He took a sip of water, then put the glass back down on the table and traced the rim with his finger. 'You don't want to return to the house. But I do. If I don't, I think I'll come to regret it. And when my time comes, I don't want to have any regrets.' His eyes fixed upon mine and I nodded as if to say I understood. But I didn't. Not really.

We said very little during the drive out to Hietzing. Oskar spent most of it regarding the grand boulevards and the smaller residential streets that lay beyond the First District. I took my time, making a detour around the perimeter of the Schönbrunn, partly to give Oskar a chance to revisit the places he had left behind, but mostly to put off our arrival at Himmelhofgasse. Once or twice he glanced at me, as if questioning my choice of route, but then I think he understood my intention and left me to it. On Elisabethalle I slowed down further. The road ran alongside the ash-stained walls of the cemetery. I briefly toyed with the idea of going in, but decided against it and accelerated again. As I glanced in the rear-view mirror, I saw a vintage silver Mercedes R107 convertible pull out of the cemetery entrance. I was sure it was the same car I had seen the time I went for a run around Schlosspark, but the red Fiesta behind me blocked my view and when I checked again, the car was turning to travel in the opposite direction.

Eventually I headed towards Hietzinger Hauptstrasse, this time eschewing the side roads and diversions. Children wrapped up against the cold milled alongside parents on the streets, pulling sledges up towards the open fields to take advantage of the snowfall.

'Care to join them?' Oskar said.

I forced a smile. 'Tempted.'

At the junction of Erzbischofgasse and Himmelhofgasse, I gripped the steering wheel all the more tightly and took a deep breath. Some other words of cheer came to mind, but they felt contrived so I remained silent as we pulled up in front of my mother's house.

Oskar got out of the car and immediately walked down towards the neighbouring building, where he and his family used to live.

'Has it changed – from what you remember?' I asked.

'Perhaps. But it's the same overall, I think.'

I followed as he ventured towards the gated entrance of his old house to peek through the railings. A short-haired Weimaraner appeared at a window on the ground floor. It barked at us, prompting us to return to my mother's house.

I went into her driveway, eyeing the winter remnants of the honeysuckle laced across the house's walls, the weave of its branches like arteries, keeping the house alive. It was an effort to stop myself from surveying the windows. I looked at Oskar, wondering what he thought of the place, what memories it evoked, or whether my mother's home and the time he spent there remained blurred.

'May we see the garden?' he asked.

His question put an end to my speculation and I led the way around the side of the house, bringing us out to the middle of the lawn. The white carpet of snow set against the pale blue sky diminished the harshness of the place, which, together with the soft crunch of our footsteps, helped me to relax a little. I left him to explore the grounds for himself, watching how he stepped back to look at the house, then how he glanced behind him, before heading further down the garden. Despite the thick covering of snow, he moved with a kind of grace, and even though his coat hung shapelessly from his shoulders, there was strength in his movements as he came striding towards me, his cheeks glowing pink from the frosty air.

He pointed behind him. 'I can remember it quite vividly,' he said. 'We used to run down there to play our games, pretending we ruled over the whole of Vienna. And this' – he cast his arms wide – 'was our palace.' His voice was buoyed by excitement as he recalled that time. 'I can almost hear our laughter, far from the ears of adults.'

I tried to picture the scene too: my mother and Oskar playing, their whoops and screams. I watched him take a few paces back.

He stopped, then glanced again at the house. 'I'd like to go inside, if that's all right with you?'

I fought the urge to say no.

As we retraced our steps to the front, I talked about the renovation, the plans for the cellar.

'The workmen found a … hidden room,' I explained. I still couldn't bring myself to call it a *war bunker*, yet my avoidance of the term felt like an admission of guilt.

'Hidden, you say?'

I nodded, expecting him to ask more questions, but he drifted back into his own world, keeping his eyes trained on the ground in front of him, oblivious to my internal conflict.

'It's a bit of a mess,' I said as I unlocked the door, swallowing my unease, before letting Oskar in first. With its bare walls, the cardboard covering the marble floor, the absence of furniture and the sentry-like figurines of the angel and saint, the house appeared even more sterile. Oskar took a step back just as he had done in the garden, his eyes sweeping the walls, exploring the atrium, naked without its chandelier.

'Beautiful feature – the atrium, I mean,' he said. 'But I don't remember it. Not really. Interesting, isn't it – what the brain chooses to retain and discard?' His voice bounced off the walls, the acoustics carrying his words up to the ceiling.

'I think your memory's better than mine,' I said. 'I can't remember much about my childhood years. Now and then things come back, but I find it difficult to hold on to them.'

'Perhaps our brains determine what's important,' Oskar said. 'The more I think about it, the more certain I am that memories are kept in storage, as it were, then dusted off when needed.'

I wondered, then, if this trip to the house was simply an exercise for Oskar to test his ability to recollect. 'Is there anything in particular you want to see?'

He took off his gloves and tapped them against the palm of his hand. 'I'd like to see the Schiele, if that's all right with you.'

'Unfortunately it's in storage,' I said, catching the disappointment in his eyes. 'But I'll take you to the drawing room, so you can see where it hung,' I added, as if that made up for the painting's absence.

Oskar followed me, somewhat reluctantly. I sensed the futility of my offer, but I didn't know what else to do.

'When everything's done you'd be more than welcome to come back,' I said, opening the door.

When we entered, I felt quite foolish. While the room was as stark as the hall, the Schiele and a couple of other paintings were hanging where they'd always been, appearing all the more striking in their solitude.

'Why on earth would they do that?' I said, frowning to myself. I got out my mobile to call the Dorotheum, readying myself for a heated exchange, but I put my phone away when I saw how Oskar was mesmerised by the Schiele. I couldn't quite see his expression, but I noticed him touching its edges. His hesitation lingered in the air. He turned to me, his eyes lowered, then he glanced back to the painting.

'There's something that's been weighing on my mind,' he said. 'That day we went for a walk on the Heath, you showed me your mother's notebook.' He turned and looked at me, then shrugged. 'I think we both know I wasn't exactly forthcoming.'

I let him continue, hoping to hear some revelation that might bring this strange hunt of ours to an end.

'The sketches at the back – the renditions of the Schiele that your mother made. They had the strangest effect on me. I've no idea why she drew them – that's not what I mean – but when I saw them I could visualise the Schiele in my head. I could see the brushstrokes, the colours, smell the linseed in the oil paint even. Have you ever had that sensation? Something jogging your senses like that?'

I nodded, remembering the remnants of my mother's jasmine perfume in the air.

'So it made me think. Why should a sketch – those pencil copies of your mother's – make me feel that way?'

Confounded by his renewed interest in the Schiele, I couldn't think of anything reasonable to say.

'I think I told you of the things my family salvaged and the things we lost at the hands of the Nazis,' he went on. 'And then I saw your mother's drawings.' He turned back to the Schiele. 'It's just a faded memory, a hunch, but that painting, you see ...'

Oskar turned to look me in the eye. 'Forgive me, Max. But I think this painting belonged to us.'

Any hope I'd had of resolving this family mystery transformed into plain disappointment, falling upon me like a leaden cloak. Two factors entwined with one another: the possibility that the painting didn't belong to me, and the possibility that seeing the Schiele in the flesh was the sole purpose of Oskar's trip to the house. Given his past efforts to recover lost or stolen art, I shouldn't have been surprised. That must have been the reason why my mother wanted to find Oskar. The provenance of the Schiele was the *missing link* she had referred to.

'I'd need proof,' I said.

Oskar patted my shoulder. 'If I were in your shoes, I'd feel the same,' he said. 'I did try to find some paperwork, references in letters and so on ...'

I attempted to smile, but I think it was more like a compression of my lips. I didn't want to stand in front of the Schiele any longer. I knew the process to contest Oskar's claim would be a lengthy one, one that he wouldn't give up on. But a part of me didn't want to oppose him. If he were someone else, it would be a different story – I'd be willing to roll up my sleeves and enter the fray. But fighting Oskar … I just couldn't. Although our interactions had been few and far between, his ties to my mother, his humour and self-deprecation now made me consider him a friend.

It was Oskar who changed the subject. 'You mentioned the cellar and the discovery of a room down there,' he said, turning to leave. 'It sounds intriguing. I'd like to see it, if I may?' His casual reference to the hidden room reawakened the ice-cold fear inside me.

'Yes, I was going to take a look. I'll be a few minutes, that's all.' It slipped out before I could think of anything else to say. I hadn't intended to go downstairs, but the pull was there.

'I'd like to come down too, if you …'

'It's a mess, and the dust – I wouldn't want you to injure yourself.'

'Nonsense.' Oskar was already at the drawing room door. 'I'll be quite all right, I promise you.'

I took one last look at the Schiele and went after him. He was standing in the hallway looking about him. After a moment, he got his bearings and made his way to the cellar door. The whispers in my head grew louder, more urgent.

Don't. Don't. Don't.

Much as I didn't want to go, I couldn't let an elderly man venture down there alone.

SCHÖNBRUNN PALACE, HIETZING, VIENNA, 1966

Annabel packs plates, cutlery, the leftover bread, cheese and Linzer torte back into the picnic hamper Christopher Gissing had brought with him.

She loves the colonnaded Gloriette, the way it overlooks Schönbrunn and its gardens. It's as close as she's taken him to Ober St. Veit. For now at least. That's not to say she hasn't opened up. Christopher's been picking away at the locks to her secrets with a tenacity she can only put down to his so-called profession, and he's done quite well so far. Certainly she'd tried hard to fend off his questions at first, but it was the way he'd asked them – the gentleness with which he'd guided her down avenues she'd rather not tread – that made her let go of her caution. Yes, she was afraid of what he'd think, that he'd run away from her, but when she got to the final chapter, he just folded her in his arms and told her he loved her.

'No one will hurt you now,' he said.

She looks over to where he's standing with his back to her, gazing at the views across Vienna. He cuts a lean figure, straight-backed, though the crumple of his linen trousers and his rolled-up shirt sleeves soften his edges.

He turns around and she smiles at him. With the lowering sun, a shadow purdahs half his body and she can't make out the lopsided grin that she knows has appeared on his face. Annabel goes over to him and he wraps his arm around her shoulders. As she interlaces her fingers with his, she feels something pressed into her palm. It's hard, cold, sharp. He closes her hand around it.

215

Delight flutters through Annabel. With all the wine she's drunk she feels giddy, weak at the knees, and she sinks down on to the grass. Christopher kneels down next to her. Save for a soft breeze ruffling the leaves on the trees, silence lingers between them.

Annabel regards the ring, its floral-shaped sapphires catching remnants of light that freckle her skin. She glances up at him, shyness taking hold of her for a moment as if they were meeting for the first time.

'Yes,' she says. 'With all my heart, yes.'

CHAPTER SIXTEEN

With every step down into the cellar, the knot tightened in my chest. My hand shook as I flicked on the light in the stairwell, revealing a canopy of dust particles suspended in the freezing air. 'Are you sure about this?' I asked, a question for myself as much as for Oskar.

A thin smile was impressed on his face as he nodded. He regarded the puffs of our clouded breath and I assumed he thought it all part of the experience.

The scene was quite different from my last visit – more chaotic than I had imagined, more like an excavation. Walls had been knocked down, creating a cavernous, anthracitic hole. Loose wires hung down from the ceiling or lay exposed in the walls, and tools and equipment of varying sizes were scattered about on the floor. Oskar knocked over a can of Coke that had been balancing on the edge of a box. It clattered to the floor, the sound reverberating through the quiet of the cellar. I glanced at Oskar to check if he was all right, but he simply waved me on.

As we walked further, it was impossible to ignore the seeping damp in the atmosphere. It penetrated my clothes right through to my skin, and once or twice I shivered. What was more, a putrid odour lapped the air in gentle waves. I tried to imagine the cellar as it would be once the work was done, to think beyond the here and now, but I couldn't.

'Are you all right, Oskar?'

'Yes, yes,' he said, his voice muffled by the handkerchief pressed over his nose.

From somewhere at the far end, I heard a solitary drip. Given the drop in temperature in the cellar, I thought it strange. Not wanting to show the fear now rising with every thump of my heart, I relented and walked over to its source. A couple of makeshift lights had been strung up overhead and I searched for the switch. After an uncertain flicker, their white light spilled out, highlighting the carcasses of rooms, and at the very back was the door Matthias had referred to, left slightly ajar. Just as he had told me, it was a steel affair, at least ten centimetres thick with knots of rust scattered across its length and breadth. Nothing could have penetrated it.

Oskar joined me. 'Is this it?'

I nodded, trying to muster up a smile in response. I ran my hands across the door. Ice cold to the touch, the metal's roughness scoured my palms and I couldn't help but wonder how it had lain hidden for so many years. Oskar turned to me, one eyebrow raised, as if asking what we should do next. There were a couple of torches lying on top of a box beside the door. I handed one to Oskar and took one for myself, fully aware of my curiosity locking horns with my unease. I pushed the door wide open, its hinges letting out a yawning creak as though they had awoken from a deep sleep. Oskar put a hand on my shoulder. It felt like a prompt and a reassurance all in one. We went inside, leaving the stench behind us.

Flashing my torch around, I took stock. The room was large with exposed concrete walls and floor. A pile of wood and rags lay in one corner, together with what looked like a couple of small cans of fuel. They were relics from another era and when I picked them up I was surprised to discover that both cans were full. What surprised me more was the sight of an electric blue cigarette lighter and a half-full packet of Marlboros lying on a wooden bench in the opposite corner. Contrary to Matthias's claims, the builders hadn't exactly left behind a tidy site and I planned to call him to complain about the mess. But when I placed the torch on the bench, I received an altogether different shock. It was clear that the ceiling was much lower than the one running through the rest of the cellar. I stretched up to touch it, feeling the claustrophobia creep through my body, threatening to take me hostage.

I glanced over at Oskar. Something at the back of the room had caught his eye. I followed his gaze and saw the second door, exactly as Matthias had described. Oskar walked up to it, slowly at first. He tugged the door open, then shone his torch into the blackness of what looked like a tunnel.

'It was here,' he said.

Even in the torch's blanching light I could see that the colour in his face had drained away. Behind his glasses, his eyes – wider, their whites more exposed – betrayed a mix of sorrow and fear. He looked like a fragile deer, trapped by its own terror.

'Oskar, what is it? Are you all right?'

'I suppose I've never *really* forgotten.' He glanced around the room, then stared into the entrance to the tunnel. 'It was a game of hide-and-seek. I came down to the kitchens to hide. There was nothing special about that – we always gravitated here. That day, there weren't so many people around, so I scurried further down the corridor, forgoing my usual hiding places where I knew Annabel would find me.' He glanced at the doorway leading back to the cellar, where I was now standing. 'A large wooden cupboard stood in front of that door. It had been moved forward, creating a small gap between it and what I thought was the wall.'

'So you went to hide there?'

'Just like any child would,' Oskar said. 'Hearing your mother skipping down the stairs, I quickly crawled behind it.

My back caught on the edge of the door. Curiosity and my competitive spirit took over. I inched it open and slipped inside. The room was pitch dark and I sat against the wall, listening out for your mother. I heard her footsteps come closer, but she didn't venture near this end of the kitchens. I felt the thrill of thwarting her efforts to find me. But then in the silence that followed, I heard something altogether different.'

Oskar kneaded the furrow in his brow. 'It sounded like a whine. At first, I thought it was a kitten, and I remember straining my eyes to see in the dark. The sound continued and so I shuffled towards the noise. As I got closer, I realised it didn't sound much like a kitten at all – it was more like a child's whimper. I wondered whether someone else was hiding there too, whether someone had joined the game that I didn't know about.' Oskar removed his glasses and shook his head. 'So I whispered in the dark, *Who's there? This is my hiding place!* There was no answer, but the whimpering stopped. *Who's there?* I asked again. Obstinately, I shuffled forward, wanting to know who it was.' Oskar pointed his torch to the wall where the pile of wood and rags lay. 'I think I had crawled over to that side. Before I could say anything else, a freezing cold hand grabbed my arm. I shouted out, and another hand, just as cold, clamped over my mouth.' Oskar looked straight at me. 'When she whispered, I recognised her voice at once. It was a girl I knew very well. Her name was Eva. Eva Schwartz.'

I started. 'Eva?'

'That's right,' he replied. 'She worked in this house. She used to play with us from time to time. We were quite fond of her.'

I shook my head. 'But in my mother's notebook, she writes of Eva going away – to Salzburg. I assumed she'd got away.' I leaned against the wall, closing my eyes. 'What happened to her?' Part of me was reluctant to know.

'I could hear the sound of clinking chains each time she moved. I remember how tightly she gripped me. Of course, I realise now that I was her means of escape, but back then, as a little boy, her desperation frightened me. I couldn't understand why she was hiding in that room and why she was restrained. *Find Frau Albrecht. Please, Oskar*, she said over and over again, until she thought I understood.'

'And did you?'

'I was just a child, Max. How was I ...'

'*Did* you?'

'I think ... I think I understood that something was wrong. I understood that I needed to get out of that room. I shrank away from her and edged my way back to the door. But then ...' He nodded towards the tunnel. 'Then that door opened up. Bright torchlight filled the room. When my eyes had got used to the light, I saw three men. They looked at me, then at Eva. I remember turning to her to see her properly, and when I did' – he shut his eyes – 'I don't know how I've managed to shut out that image all these years. She was just skin and bones, with bruises and cuts all over her body.' He bowed his head.

'Who were the men?' I knew the answer but I needed to hear it from Oskar.

'One I didn't recognise. I just remember his black uniform and the *Totenkopf* badge on his hat. One was the butler who worked for your grandparents.' Oskar looked at me, his face wrought with anguish. 'The third one was your grandfather.'

I pictured that man, my grandfather, seated next to Eva Schwartz. 'Did you run?'

'I couldn't move. The butler made a grab for me, but your grandfather held him back and told them to go back up the tunnel. Then Herr Albrecht smiled at me. I was petrified. I hunkered down close to the wall. He crouched down in front of me, lifted up my chin and whispered, *You never saw her, did you, Oskar? You never saw us.* I remember his warm breath on my face, and the smell of tobacco and cologne about his clothes. I was frozen to the spot, Max. He pulled me to my feet and shoved me towards the door. *You're going to England soon, aren't you?* he asked. All I could do was nod. And then he said, *If you say a word about this, you and your parents will be taken away before you even get out of your driveway, and no one will ever see you again.* I pushed past him and ran out of the room as fast as I could, bumping the side of my head on the cupboard as I made my getaway.'

'That's why you didn't say anything. But to keep quiet, all this time?'

'I just wanted to forget, and somehow I did – and then you came along.' A tear escaped from the corner of his eye.

'I'm sorry, Oskar.' Those were the only words I could summon up.

I thought back to our first conversation on the telephone: *I hope she wasn't seeking to atone for the sins of her forebears.* The oddness of the statement, the language he used, had stayed with me. Still, I had been completely blind to the truth in that remark.

'But my mother – I think she knew,' I said. 'All she would've needed was to hear it from you.'

Oskar rested his hand on my shoulder. I brought my hand up to his, feeling the bumps of his knuckles, the wrinkles of his skin, loose and cold.

'It's not for you to apologise,' Oskar said. He took his hand away. 'You said you experienced a presence here in this house – that it took the form of a girl – and when you told me about the anagram, I knew she – Eva – was calling me.'

'No Oskar. Please.' Ever since I had seen her in that photograph with my grandfather, I had wrestled with the suspicion that the presence was Eva Schwartz. But I didn't want to accept it, clinging to the belief that Eva was the one who got away, just like my mother had thought. Maybe she had discovered the truth too. Fear flowed through me, colder than the air in the room.

He put his hand on my arm. 'It's me she wants. I need ... I need to tell her that I'm sorry.'

'Let's just leave it. Coming here, what you've just told me – that's enough.' I clasped his hand and tried to draw him away from the room, but he wouldn't move.

'Let me be, Max,' he said.

And then I smelt it. The stench infiltrated the room, clinging to its walls. I pressed my hand against my mouth and nose, trying to stem a wave of nausea. Oskar did the same. But it wasn't just the smell. The atmosphere in the room changed too, shifting from a calm stillness to a restless creeping silence edging around us. I stole a glance at Oskar; he seemed to feel it too. Just then, our torches and every single light in the cellar went out. Both of us stood there, side by side, waiting, my older companion, I was sure, more willing than me to face what was coming. I tried to swallow away the dryness in my throat, to slow the beat of my heart. I tried to move my feet, but they refused to comply. I could hear nothing save for the steady rise and fall of Oskar's breath.

The door leading back to the cellar slammed shut. I jumped.

'It's all right,' Oskar said calmly.

Somehow, I knew he wasn't addressing me. In the darkness, I felt her presence penetrating the silence, filling the room. The torch that I'd set down on the workbench flickered, then emitted a weak shaft of light, casting dark shadows on the opposite wall. One of the shadows moved. Then I realised it wasn't a shadow – it was her, the girl. It was Eva.

She had her back to us. She was a slip of a thing, with dark matted hair straggling over her shoulders. A black ragged dress hung on her, skimming her shins, exposing white legs that appeared lacerated, as if she'd been whipped. But those wounds paled in comparison to the others: red, raw bands around each ankle, matching the welts cuffing her wrists. The torchlight grew fainter. It threw only a sliver of yellow into the room, although it was still enough to show the girl turn around, ever so slowly, to reveal her face.

She was a mere echo of the child captured in sepia in 1937. I couldn't wrest my eyes away. It was the same face that I'd seen in the cellar before, that had been reflected in the French windows on my first visit: a white translucent mask, pulled tight over her skull, throwing into sharp relief the lines of her cheekbones and jaw. She turned her head from Oskar to me, her vacant eyes, like pools of ink, staring at me as she contorted her lips into a sneer.

I felt myself pushed back against the concrete wall, its cold bleeding into my body. I glanced over at Oskar: Eva had turned her attention to him. The sneer had gone and in its place was an altogether different expression, like the quiver of a delicate frown, making her look like the vulnerable child she once was. I watched as she held out her hand to Oskar. He took a couple of steps forward and knelt down, taking her hand in his.

'I'm sorry, Eva. I'm so very sorry.'

She tilted her head to one side, then kneeled beside him. He took her in his arms and held her, rocking back and forth. They remained that way, lost in the past, holding one another as though afraid to let go, and making me feel as though I were intruding on a private reunion. But when I tried to move, I found I was pinned to the wall. Fear, terror, claustrophobia smothered me. I couldn't breathe; I could barely call out. Only my mind whirred on, knowing that somehow I needed to wrench Oskar away from Eva.

'Forgive me,' he said.

Just then, his body seemed to spasm and he let out a gasp. Eva scurried to the corner of the room from where she watched Oskar crumple to the ground as he fought for breath. I tried to go to him, but I still couldn't move. I looked at Eva. She was hunched up against the wall, hugging her knees, staring all the while at Oskar.

I shouted out his name. He tried to turn his head to me. I could see the pain creasing his face. I needed to go to him. But the moment I tried to push myself away from the wall, Eva turned to me, her head tilted in my direction. Her childlike innocence was gone. The twisted smile had reappeared on her face. I tried to move again but couldn't. Surely this was nothing but a bad dream. I felt my eyes close, my head lolled forward ...

When I opened my eyes again it was dark once more. My paralysis had gone. I edged towards Oskar and crouched down beside him. I groped around for his hand. It lay limp in mine. I felt for a pulse, first on his wrist, and then on his neck, detecting a faint beat, but I wasn't sure. The stillness of his body contrasted with the shivers that wracked mine. I bit down on my fist, hoping to jolt myself into action. It seemed to work. As I picked Oskar up, an ice-cold hand upon my wrist stopped me.

The torch's beam came back on, but it was no more than a faint glow. Eva stood on the other side of Oskar. She was still smiling her crooked smile. She raised her arm, her finger pointing at my chest.

'Albrecht,' she said. It was only a whisper, but my grandfather's name rang clear.

It was as if someone yanked me up to standing. I was turned around, then shoved towards the workbench, my feet dragging on the floor as I tried to resist. My hips slammed into the workbench. My right arm reached out for the cigarette lighter. I could only stare, powerless to stop my hand as it picked up the lighter. Then my body spun around and lunged forward. Eva was dictating my moves. Nothing withstood her hold over me. Chilled fear coursed through me, sending the sour taste of bile up my throat. I looked down at the lighter lying in my palm.

I turned to the girl.

She nodded.

I moved as though I were learning how to walk again, to the corner of the room where the wood and petrol cans lay. My left foot took a swing at the cans, sending them toppling to the floor. Clear dark liquid pooled at my feet. I was made to crouch down, to flick the lighter, to lower it to the petrol. A large blue flame leapt up towards my face. I managed to jerk my head away. This sudden ability to control my own movements made me lose my balance and I fell, hitting my head on the concrete floor.

So this is it. This is how it will end.

OBER ST. VEIT, VIENNA, 1968

Annabel comes out of the study and helps Maria with her coat and umbrella. Her former nanny has just returned from her afternoon off – doing what, Annabel has no idea, for Maria has swatted away her enquiries as if they were nothing more than pesky flies.

These days their roles are much reversed. Maria's age and her arthritic knees stop her from doing most things. Really, she's more like a beloved elderly relative than anything else. Even though Christopher has suggested that they let her go, Annabel can't bear to part with her. Shared memories entwine the two of them like the branches of the honeysuckle covering the front of the house.

Even though it's not that cold, Maria shivers, pulling her grey shawl tightly around her. Annabel leads her to the drawing room and Maria sits down on the small sky-blue armchair in the corner, her favourite spot in the house. Age has curved her back and shoulders. It's slowed her down too, and sometimes it's too much to watch her when she walks from room to room. As her duties have diminished, her chatter, her anecdotes of the everyday have grown. Her voice, her sharply accented German, has since filled the house. It's music to Annabel's ears, and anything but to Christopher's, though he'd never admit it. Today, however, Maria is mute.

'What's wrong, Maria?' asks Annabel. She watches her old nanny rubbing her fingers, clearly agitated about something. Her silence draws out, and as it does, Annabel feels the worry tick inside her, keeping time with the staid cadence of the ancient grandfather clock in the drawing room.

'It's time,' Maria says.

Maria's words squeeze Annabel's heart and make her want to cry out in pain. 'But where will you go?'

227

'I have family – I told you that.' Maria looks up at Annabel, her cataracted eyes appearing even more glazed with the tears welling in them.

'So you'll leave for Warsaw?' says Annabel, hardly able to control her shaking voice. She goes to Maria and kneels beside her, resting her head on her lap. Maria strokes her hair: slow, smooth motions over her head. A single tear leaks from Annabel's eye, taking her by surprise; she hasn't wept in so long.

'Too many years have gone by. I made a promise to watch over you. But you're happy now.'

'Am I?'

Maria kisses Annabel's head and sings her favourite song:

> *Sleep now, my hungry little girl,*
> *Close tight your dear little eyes,*
> *Your mother also is hungry,*
> *But she doesn't cry or make noise.*
> *Learn something, child, from your mother dear,*
> *Try to look on the bright side —*
> *When you awake in the morning,*
> *The house will be full of fresh bread.*
> *Ay lyu lyu, ay lyu lyu lyu,*
> *So, sleep now, my precious, my crown.*

CHAPTER SEVENTEEN

I came to. My head throbbed and my eyes stung. Heat flooded the room, the walls danced orange and yellow. The smell of burning filled my nose and I coughed, struggling for air. Then I remembered – the room, Eva, Oskar.

I crawled on my hands and knees to reach him. His body still lay in the middle of the floor. I hoisted him up. For all his frailty, I staggered with the weight of him. I looked at the doorway back to the cellar – flames barricaded our exit. I turned to the door to the tunnel – it was shut. Fighting for breath in the smoke-filled room, I dragged Oskar's body over to the tunnel entrance and pulled at the door. It didn't budge. I glanced over my shoulder. Eva was standing in the far corner, her skeletal body surrounded by the blaze. Her face was expressionless, yet the hollows of her eyes bored their way into me. I tried the handle again and yanked at the door as hard as I could. For the first time, I prayed.

Please God …

The door swung open. The fire surged forward. With Oskar's arm draped over my shoulder, I hauled his body into the tunnel, pulling the door shut on the furnace and its raging flames.

I gulped down the cool smokeless air, feeling it soothe my throat and lungs. A draught streamed down the tunnel, circulating the smell of mould, damp and dead leaves, lending me some hope. I dug in my pocket for my mobile phone and checked for a signal. There was none. Worse, the battery was low and its screen light had faded, making it little use as a torch. I tried not to think about it and shuffled Oskar into a more comfortable position, but as I attempted to stand tall, my head hit rock, forcing me to stoop. I stretched out my arm, grazing my elbow against more rock. My muscles stiffened, refusing to play. For a moment I thought Eva had taken my body captive again. My panic resurfaced.

We had escaped the fire in the room; I just needed to navigate the tunnel, that was all … That was all? I had no idea how long it was, whether it was blocked, how safe it was …

A muffled explosion from behind the door jolted me into action, sending me stumbling forward over small rocks and what felt like clumps of mud and wood. Fear spurred me on, yet the threat of claustrophobia, of the way it could hold siege over my body was never far away. I didn't want to die in here. I didn't want Oskar to die in here. I didn't want him to die full stop. And though the awkwardness of his frame slowed me down, I couldn't just leave him while I explored the length of the tunnel, for time was on the side of the fire that hunted us down. I clung to the hope that Oskar was still alive, fighting for his life, just as I was struggling through this tunnel to get us out, determined we wouldn't succumb to the fire, hissing and rattling behind us. Sweat beaded my face as I tried to quicken the pace, my legs straining against the incline.

We're close, so close.

I repeated it over and over with each step, trying to disregard the faint smell of smoke now snaking through the passage. I wished I had thought to ask Matthias about its length, whether they'd kept the tunnel's exit open or sealed.

If it was closed ... Oh God, if it was closed, it would be the end of us. I wished my mother had never willed the house to me. What kind of gift was this to give your son! The bitterness of the thought came out as laughter, which turned into a shout coming from deep within my lungs. I held on to Oskar's body more tightly, feeling the bow of his ribs under my fingers. Ignoring the exhaustion dragging at my legs, I ploughed on, refusing to stop.

But the dark, the confines of the passage, handicapped any sense of distance covered. Every step forward brought with it a vicious circle of faith, relief and despair that we'd never reach the end of the tunnel. Doubts came at me – the tunnel was too long, we'd never make it, over and over until my shoe stubbed against rock. I'd no idea how far I had walked. Only my ragged breath, the sweat, ice cold and damp, soaking through my shirt, spoke of the effort to get this far. I reached out in front of me, groping around in the dark, searching for the telltale signs of a door, but there were none. Nor was there anything to my left. Panic scraped through me. I reached over to the right: my fingers brushed against a vertical metal rod. I slid my hands up and down it and across, feeling metal rod after metal rod above and below, forming the rungs of a makeshift ladder. I stretched one arm above my head, expecting to touch the tunnel's roof, but there was nothing but air. I could stand to my full height without fear of knocking my head.

I lowered Oskar to the ground, flailing in the darkness to find my scarf to put under his head. A boom echoed from the depths of the tunnel behind us. I leapt on to the ladder and counted each rung as I scaled it, hoping the rods wouldn't give. Without the weight of Oskar, I moved quickly, almost effortlessly, and soon I felt fresh air brush against my face. At the count of twenty, I became aware of the faint smell

of pine, and running just above my head was a thin line of
light. I made out the form of a square metal plate encased
in the ceiling. I traced its perimeter, feeling the rounded
bumps of hinges and the curved dip in the metal's edge
where my fingers caught against a jagged lever. I pulled it
down, then tried to push the trapdoor up, but it didn't give.
I tried again without any luck. I paused. The air below blew
warmer and reeked of smoke. Panic taunted me again. We
were not going to perish in the belly of a hill. I wedged my
knees between the ladder and the wall and pounded on the
trapdoor, willing, forcing it to open, knowing that Oskar's
life, my life, depended on it.

All at once daylight flooded the shaft, and sweet woodland
air filled my lungs. I ducked back inside and raced down the
ladder. The stream of light revealed a swirl of smoke, and no
more than twenty metres away, the fire was inching forward,
feeding on the oxygen and debris that lay scattered in its path. I
slung Oskar over my shoulder and began to climb.

Each rung brought us closer to escape.

I counted them off – *one, two, three.* My back, arms and legs
screamed, but that square of heavenly light kept me going. I
didn't look down.

Eleven, twelve … when would this end? Smoke billowed up
the ladder, reaching the top before me. I could feel the heat
from the fire tonguing my heels.

Eighteen, nineteen, twenty … I summoned up the last bit of
strength left in me to haul us out into the woodland.

Slipping and sliding through the snow, I made my way to
a tree trunk a few metres away and set Oskar down as gently
as I could. I collapsed next to him and cradled his head in
my lap. He lay quite still, his face curiously bare without his
glasses. His eyes were closed, and although his lips were a

faded pink, it looked as though death lay beneath his skin. I put my cheek close to his mouth and nose, wishing for a sign of life, a sigh, anything. I reached into my coat pocket and tugged out my phone to call the emergency services. Snowflakes flitted about us. I looked over at the tunnel exit: black smoke and flames spouted up through the trap door. I smoothed back the tangle of Oskar's hair, unable to stop the tears tracing their way down my face.

'We'll see you for dinner next week, Frederik,' says Annabel, closing the door on her friend.

Right from the beginning she had warmed to him. She tries to describe it to Christopher, but can't find the right words. It's something like déjà vu, she tells him, something she can't explain without it sounding sentimental and unhinged.

'If he didn't bat for the other side I'd be worried,' Christopher says.

She laughs, then shakes her head as they return to the drawing room. How she loves Christopher's dry English humour.

'He's obsessed with that painting of yours too,' he adds.

Annabel glances over her shoulder at Egon Schiele's Mother with Two Children. *Sunlight pouring through the French windows lights up the mother's face and Annabel shivers in spite of the warmth in the room. Until Frederik saw it, she had been the only one who had been drawn to it.*

Christopher had chided her for wasting her money on an artist whose work was akin to junk. 'In a few years' time you'll have me selling it in a jumble sale back home.'

'You can be terribly unreasonable at times,' she says, throwing him a look that tells him not to argue with her. 'I wager that I'll never sell it.'

'And I know better than to bet against you, my darling,' he says, kissing her on the lips.

Even though they've been married eight years, his caresses still make her heart skip. It can't last, she keeps thinking. But it has lasted, for longer than she expected.

Christopher looks at his watch. 'I better collect the boys. I'll be back in twenty minutes.'

Ludmilla has the afternoon off so Annabel takes the tea tray to the kitchen and begins to wash up, all the while admiring the garden through the window. The roses are just beautiful, she thinks to herself, and she makes a note to go out and cut a few before Christopher and her sons return. She's never felt happier – a husband she adores and two beautiful boys. Her hand goes to her stomach. She wonders whether this little one will be a girl, but it's early days yet. Given her last two miscarriages, she's promised Christopher she won't tell anyone about this one – not even Vivienne.

Annabel leaves the things to drain and shakes the water off her hands before drying them on the towel. Ludmilla's prepared something for dinner so Annabel needn't worry about that. She goes into the hallway and readies herself for the garden, but then she stops in her tracks, frowning at the sky through the glass-domed atrium. Despite the sunshine, the entrance hall seems dark. An ice-cold draught brushes against her arms and legs. Annabel turns around to face the statues of the saint and angel. They look strangely alert in the dim light, with their O-shaped mouths, their glimmering eyes staring at a point over her shoulder. Annabel follows their gaze.

A shadow draws away from her own and slips towards the cellar door, which opens, then clicks shut. Annabel's heart freezes. Cold despair roots her to the spot. Suddenly, all she wants is to see the faces of her loved ones.

There's a knock on the front door. Annabel doesn't move, unaware of the rat-a-tat-tat. Then the doorbell chimes, louder and louder, insistent, until it rouses Annabel from that other world.

Thank God! They're back.

She hurries to the door and opens it to two policemen, their caps cradled in their arms.

The pain sears through her, never allowing her to forget her loss. Friends come and go, but it's Vivienne who stays close. She moves in temporarily to watch over Annabel. Frederik visits daily, and one afternoon, when she's lying on the sofa in the drawing room, he whispers in Annabel's ear that he'll look after her, no matter what.

From somewhere in the fog of her mind, a memory dislodges itself. She stares at Frederik in wonder. There's something about him – is it the eyes, the voice? What is it?

But then the sleeping pills take over and the memory vanishes. Annabel slips back into Neverland, dreaming of her family, and the crash, and the surviving son, Max, who lies in a hospital bed, fighting for his life.

CHAPTER EIGHTEEN

Here's what I remember: the rising wail of sirens; the dancing swirl of snow; the static of walkie-talkies; voices hollering through the woodland. What they said, I can't recall, but I do recall my reluctance to let go of Oskar. Some man or a woman, their face a blur, prised him gently from me. I remember the cold surface of a stethoscope numbing my chest while my eyes followed the ambulance that carried Oskar away. I remember smoke curling through the air, and two fire engines – one of them wedged in my mother's driveway – poised to fight the frenzied flames. And then there was a roar that must have come from me. I saw bystanders waved away by Detective Thomas Schmidt's men as I remained dumb to his *whats, whys* and *hows* before breaking down in Vivienne's arms, longing to forget. And I remember Frederik Müller pulling up in a vintage silver Mercedes R107 convertible, demanding to know why Schmidt wanted to take me away.

'Suspected manslaughter,' Schmidt said.

'On what grounds?'

Schmidt nodded to the house. 'And he won't talk.'

Frederik laughed. 'Are you surprised? He's not going anywhere.' He turned to me, putting a hand on my shoulder. 'I'll deal with this.'

I didn't need to go to hospital, but the doctor who visited me later at Vivienne's administered a sedative. I slept for a dreamless twenty-four hours.

The day after, I stayed in bed with the curtains drawn. Although I'd only torn a calf muscle and pulled my shoulder, every part of my body throbbed. I had no appetite and barely touched the tray Vivienne brought me. My mother's notebook, the photograph, the letters and photo album lay undisturbed on the bedside table. I heard intermittent rings from my mobile and from Vivienne's house phone, calls which she quietly fielded. When she came to my room, she just sat by my side. Preoccupied with her own thoughts, she merely touched my forehead, held my hand or adjusted my pillow. Her actions reassured me, but I didn't want the pain to stop. I wanted to suffer. It was all my doing – chasing memories and ghosts – and in the end I was the one who lost. While I registered the destruction of the house and the Schiele, it was the loss of my mother's childhood, the degradation of the family name and my inability to save Oskar that left me feeling hollowed out. I could have uttered a word or two to tell Vivienne how I felt, but no words could convey the depth of the emptiness inside me, so I said nothing. That night I took another sedative.

I was woken late the next morning by the sound of the doorbell. A few moments later, I heard Vivienne's footsteps along the landing, followed by a knock on my door.

'It's Thomas Schmidt,' she said. 'He wants to talk to you again. He said he's prepared to wait. Shall I call Frederik?'

I rubbed my eyes. My temples ached. 'No. It's all right. Tell him I'll be down.' Vivienne nodded before shutting the door behind her.

A hot shower failed to wash away my numbness and my stomach knotted at every memory of Oskar. I did, however, scoop up the things on the bedside table, intending to give them to Schmidt. I didn't want them anywhere near me.

I walked into the living room to find Vivienne pouring tea for us all. Then she went to sit on the armchair by the fireplace, reluctant to leave, eyeing Schmidt from across the room. The detective sat on the sofa, rubbing an oval grey stone between his fingers. 'It's my lucky charm,' he said. 'I've had it for almost twenty years.' He asked me how I was feeling. 'The shock must be huge.' His small talk grated, and I let it show as I sat down opposite him. 'Have you come to arrest me?' I asked abruptly.

'Here's the thing,' he said, pocketing his stone. 'A few weeks back, you ring me up, asking for my help.'

I caught the surprise in Vivienne's eyes.

'You talk to me about cold cases, mentioning a Josef Frank, Elena Markovic and Christine Hintze. You want me to get the facts. I say, okay, I will. You tell me you think you know who did it, and then you mention this so-called witness, Oskar Edelstein.' Schmidt leaned over for his cup of tea and took a couple of sips. 'I'm a little annoyed, to put it mildly, when you say you're going to take matters into your own hands. All I have is a promise of some letters and the date you're meeting him.' He placed his cup back on the coffee table and looked straight at me. 'The next thing I know, there's a fire at your house and Oskar Edelstein is dead. Two things have been bothering me. Firstly, I figured out the anagram was his name.' I couldn't stop a smile from edging across my face. Schmidt noticed, but continued, his expression unchanged. 'So I have to ask myself, was it you who wrote that message to get him to the house?' He glanced at me. 'Your prints were all over that book. You know that, don't you?'

I said nothing.

'Secondly,' he went on, 'it's not entirely clear how the fire started. So understandably, there are questions. With you refusing to answer, it raises suspicions.'

I now wondered whether I should have called Frederik and I checked my back pocket for my mobile phone.

Schmidt jumped in. 'Before you go calling your lawyer, let me finish. My job's to get the facts,' he said. 'Firstly, Frau Fuchs here has very kindly helped with some of them – about your mother, this Oskar Edelstein, the photograph, the letters and your reason for taking him to your house. So I sort of get that. I also checked the years of the cases you mentioned. Frau Fuchs has confirmed that those are the dates given in the articles you found.' He concertinaed his brow. 'But what I don't get is Oskar Edelstein's connection with the murders.'

'He saw my grandfather with a child he'd abducted,' I said quietly. Vivienne paled.

'Which child?' Schmidt asked.

I told him, in a little more detail, what Oskar had seen that day all those years ago, and that my mother must have realised he'd been holding something back.

'So why didn't he come forward before?'

I stared at him, wondering whether his ignorance was just an act.

Vivienne intervened, her brusque tone barely masking her irritation with him. 'Isn't it obvious? Oskar was only a small boy. He must have been terrified. Then he left for England and the war started. Besides, he was probably unaware that there were others.'

'The child Oskar saw with my grandfather – it wasn't Elena or Josef or Christine. It was Eva. Eva Schwartz,' I said. 'My mother probably worked the connection out, but it was too late.' A multitude of regrets swam around me. I should have picked up the phone earlier and tended to her request. If I had done that, then the house would have been saved and Oskar would be alive and well. I wanted to shout it out loud, to scream.

'Strange that this Eva wasn't reported missing,' said Schmidt.

'No doubt the others weren't reported missing either until their bodies were found,' said Vivienne.

Schmidt popped a piece of gum in his mouth. 'So tell me, Max, how did the fire start?' His casual tone didn't fool me.

'We were downstairs, checking out the room and tunnel that the builders discovered. Oskar collapsed. Then the lights went out – a problem with the electrics, I assumed. I went to help him but slipped in the dark and knocked my head on the floor. When I came round, I saw the fire and knew we had to get out.' I looked Schmidt square in the face. 'He was my friend.' I took hold of the bundle of things that I'd brought downstairs with me and threw them to him. 'Here. Perhaps if you took the time to read these you'd understand.'

I got up to leave the room.

'I have to ask, Max,' he said, flicking through the things I gave him. 'You see, we found a blue cigarette lighter in your coat pocket. Obviously your prints were on it.'

I stopped. I had my back to Schmidt, my hand hovering over the doorknob. I turned to look at him over my shoulder.

'So I picked it up. There was also a packet of cigarettes lying next to it. I picked that up too, but it must have fallen out of my pocket. I wasn't happy about the mess, particularly given there were two old cans of fuel down there. You think I started the fire to claim insurance? The next thing you'll be saying is that I colluded with the Serbs about the break-in too.'

I walked out and went to the bathroom.

Splashing cold water on my face did nothing for me. I leaned over the basin. My hands shook. I gripped the edge of the sink to steady them. I didn't want to relive the events of a couple of days ago. I didn't want to recall Eva's control over me. I wanted to forget about her, just as Oskar, and possibly my mother, had tried to do. And I wanted Schmidt out of Vivienne's house.

I dried my face with a towel and returned to the living room to find Schmidt finishing a phone call.

'Look, I know it's difficult for you,' he said, stuffing his phone into his jacket pocket. 'And I'm sure at some stage we'll get to the bottom of the fire, but there's ...'

'I couldn't care less about your theories,' I said. 'Oskar died of a heart attack. Haven't they confirmed that?'

'Yes. The initial post-mortem results seem to indicate that.'

'Fine,' I said. 'And have you talked to his housekeeper, to his friends and doctors to confirm his ill health?'

'Yes, we have,' said Schmidt. 'And that corroborates your story. But let me ask you this – if you knew of his ill health, why put him under more stress by insisting on this visit?'

'I didn't insist on it. *He* wanted it. You should confirm that too.'

I went to the window, pushing my trembling hands into my jeans pockets. The outdoors didn't bring much solace. Mild weather had ushered in sleet and rain, turning the ground into a muddy slush.

'You know,' I said, 'it should be those closest to him who ask me that, not you.'

'Max.' Vivienne's voice brought me back to the room. She wanted me to take a seat, but I couldn't sit and listen to Schmidt's constant questioning.

'The main reason for my visit,' he said, 'is that we found some human remains.'

I wheeled round.

'We found a skeleton behind one of the walls of the bunker.'

'What?'

Suddenly everything slowed down; sounds were muted. Schmidt mouthed the words, repeating what he had just said.

I turned to Vivienne and saw the shock painted on her face, her fingers pressed against her lips. I hadn't misheard, then. My feet felt unsteady and I reached for the windowsill, my fingers desperate for the touch of its solid edge. Everything went black.

'Are you all right?'

Schmidt's voice seemed to echo from some faraway room. I came to on the sofa. Vivienne was sitting next to me, holding a glass of water. I took it, but I struggled to hold the glass steady.

Schmidt chewed his gum, furrowing his brow into a vee. 'Looks like they're the remains of a girl, possibly twelve to fourteen years old. Hard to tell.'

I curbed the rush of nausea with a sip of water. 'Eva,' I whispered.

'It's impossible to know without any records. But if that's your assumption ...' He tapped his finger on the bundle of memorabilia I'd given him. 'These will help, no doubt.'

'So what happens now?' Vivienne asked.

Schmidt shrugged. 'We record everything, including the things you've given me.' He waggled the bundle in the air. 'Then we close the old cases. The suspect's dead – we can't question him or press charges.'

'But I could have all honours, titles and so on retrospectively removed, correct?'

'I've no idea,' said Schmidt.

'And if I wanted to disinter a body?'

Vivienne stared at me, her eyes wide with alarm. 'You're not thinking of removing your grandfather's remains?'

I gave Vivienne's hand a squeeze.

'Not my department,' said Schmidt. He lifted his shirt cuff to look at his watch. 'I'll be in touch again. You'll be here?'

I nodded. Despite his and Vivienne's protests to stay put, I got up to see him out.

At the door, Schmidt hesitated. 'Can I say something?' I nodded.

'The photograph. I had a good look at it, front and back, and then at that anagram in the novel. The handwriting's the same.' He leaned against the doorframe. 'Like I said, there was no way those Serbs could've done that. It wasn't your mother's handwriting was it?'

My hand began to shake again but I kept my face blank. 'Impossible to know, but if that's your assumption …'

He gave me a wry smile, then took his leave, pausing at the gate as if he wanted to say something else. But then he shook his head and departed with a mock salute.

That night I joined Vivienne for dinner in the kitchen. She had made a simple *spätzle* supper, which I ate for her sake rather than my own. Following Schmidt's visit, I expected her to ask questions about what had happened at the house with Oskar, and I wrestled with whether or not to tell her the truth. With the death of my mother and recent events at the house, she had been through enough. Thankfully for both of us, she didn't ask.

'I still can't believe it,' was all she said, pushing her plate to one side. Then she added, 'You were lucky, Max. I could have lost you too.' She placed my hand in hers.

I stared at my plate, my knife and fork slipping out of focus. I squeezed my eyes shut, plugging the sting of tears.

After a while, Vivienne cleared our plates away. She hummed to herself while she washed the dishes, her voice conjuring up pictures of my mother. There were two contrasting images

I had of her, flipping through my mind like a zoetrope: the Annabel Vivienne knew, and the Annabel I knew as my mother, all angles and frowns. For me, there was nothing in between.

'Vivienne?'

She turned from the sink and dried her hands on a towel.

'What made you take me under your wing?'

She sat back down at the table. 'Your mother was in a bad place.'

'I know that, but *when* did you step in? When did I start spending more time with you? Was it straight after the accident, or sometime after?'

'Does it matter?'

'Yes it does.'

'Very well. It happened a few months after your brother and father passed away. Your mother was quite depressed. You were playing in the garden. Something made her run out to you, she ... Well, you remember.'

I had been talking to my friend, Chanoo, who, by virtue of his death in the same car crash as my father and brother, had become my imaginary friend.

'And that's when you stepped in?'

'Annabel asked me to. She told me that you'd had a run of bad dreams and she couldn't cope with your screams in the night. She suggested that it might be better if you stayed with me from time to time.' Vivienne wiped away some stray crumbs on the tablecloth. 'But she was always your mother – I made sure of that.' As an apparent afterthought she added, 'She chose to keep you at a distance. She was afraid she couldn't be a good enough mother ... But that's all in the past now.' She pushed back her chair, went to one of the cupboards and took out the Stollen she had intended to keep for Christmas Eve. 'Now, what about some of this cake? A slice might cheer us both up.'

On our way through to the living room I thought about what she had said, mulling over my own conclusion: that perhaps I would have done the same. Maybe my mother and I weren't so different after all.

I went through Vivienne's music collection to find something light-hearted. I really didn't know what to choose, and in the end I decided on *The Mikado* on account of its cartoonish CD cover. When I put it on, Vivienne let out a laugh.

'An admirer of your mother's gave that CD to her. She was going to throw it away, but I thought it a waste, so she gave it to me – even though I hate Gilbert and Sullivan. Your mother did too.'

Vivienne bent down to light the fire.

'Here, let me,' I said, taking the box of matches from her hand. I struck a match against the side of the box and instantly became transfixed by the flame, its voluminous shape feeding on the matchstick. The smell of singeing skin brought me back to myself. I threw the spent match into the fireplace and blew on my burnt fingertips. I tried again, but the same thing happened. Vivienne, her back to me while she cut the cake, was oblivious to it all.

'Vivienne, actually …'

She came straight over, starting the fire without a fuss while I stood at the hearth, watching the flames, replaying Eva's last act in my mind.

'It'll take a while,' Vivienne said, drawing me away to the sofa and handing me a plate and a small pastry fork. 'I know it's the last thing on your mind,' she went on, 'but thank goodness the art was saved.'

I looked at her. 'What do you mean? The Schiele and two others went up in smoke.'

She returned the quizzical look on my face with an expression of mild surprise on hers. 'But Max,' she said, 'they were copies.'

I sat forward, almost sending the plate and cake resting on my lap tumbling to the floor. 'They were what?'

Vivienne stifled a laugh. 'I was sure you knew. But then I couldn't understand why you wanted them in storage.'

'My mother knowingly bought forgeries?'

The trill of 'Three Little Maids' in the background made the moment all the more surreal.

Vivienne put her plate on the coffee table and turned to me. 'Of course not! I told you Annabel bought the Schiele and some others from galleries back in the Sixties. Several years ago, when she saw how their value rose – notably the Schiele – she decided she needed to do something to safeguard them. She still wanted to see them each day, but she didn't want to bother with an alarm system – she was worried about setting it off by accident and all that. So she put the real paintings into secure storage and had copies done. It was Frederik's idea. When you saw him that day for the will, I assumed he'd told you.'

I didn't recall any mention of it. There was just the pack of documentation he'd handed over.

'I'm sorry, Max.' Vivienne laughed – a proper tinkle of laughter – and shook her head. 'You must have thought me quite careless.'

I tried to think of it as a very thin silver lining. It was something to hold on to – the Schiele was safe.

'There's a chance the Schiele originally belonged to Oskar's family,' I said, spoiling Vivienne's fun. 'It makes sense. If Mama bought it from a gallery then I'm sure I could find out where they got it from. Did she ever say why she bought it?'

Vivienne frowned, her mirth quite gone. 'Not that I remember. I never really liked it, so we rarely spoke about it. But then, her entire collection was quite personal. She bought for herself, not for show. So what will you do?'

'What's right,' I said.

OBER ST. VEIT, VIENNA, 1974

Annabel drifts into the drawing room, still wearing her nightdress and dressing gown, even though it's early in the afternoon. Vivienne's in the kitchen with Ludmilla preparing their lunch, but like most days, Annabel will just pick at her food. Her mouth is permanently dry. Her body has rejected most things since it rejected the little one inside her.

I should be dead, she thinks, but somehow she clings on. It's because of Max, people tell her, her little boy, who came back from the edge of death. You wouldn't know he had escaped the serious car crash, what with the way he runs about in the garden, two sticks clutched in his hands, shouting, yelling, screaming. How can he forget so quickly? Though Annabel tries hard to quell her anger, she can't help but feel it simmer within her. She swallows – the ulcers on her tongue pinch at the saliva in her mouth. Settling herself on the sofa like an elderly woman, Annabel's a far cry from the person who had a spring in her step just a few months before.

Bubbles of laughter draw her gaze to the French windows. Bundled in a navy-blue jacket and the bright red scarf that Ludmilla knitted him, Max is still all legs and arms, although the kugel belly Annabel was fond of kissing after his bath has returned. And the love she has for him stirs deep in her womb, like one of his kicks when he was still inside her. Annabel's heart swells and beats again. And again. And again. Yes, my dearest boy, meine Maus, I'll get better. For you.

More of his boyish chatter trickles through. Much of it is pure nonsense and Annabel smiles, her eyes following him as he leaps back, then stops, a frown on his face, his head shaking, saying no. What's he

*saying no to? She has no idea, but she delights in his imagination, which
has proven to be as inventive as her own. Pushing his long dark fringe
out of his eyes he takes two steps towards whichever imaginary foe he's
confronting, and as he parries with one of his sticks she briefly remembers
the little boy she had once played with, whose name she can't for the life
of her remember.*

*Max is talking again, his aqua eyes narrowing, his face scowling.
Regarding this little theatrical show of his, she has the urge to join him,
to take him in her arms, to shower him in kisses she knows he'll squirm
from. Annabel doesn't care that it's cold outside, that she's just recovered
from a prolonged chest infection. Annabel pulls on her slippers and goes to
the French windows. Unlocking them, she hesitates, her breath catching
in her throat. The curtain cuts off part of the scene, but she sees – she's
sure of it – the twist of a black ragged dress. She draws back the curtain.
Her hand is shaking as it goes to her chest, then her mouth. She sees a
girl, raven-haired, rakish, with skin as grey as the winter sky, wandering
towards the back of the garden. And Max is skipping after her.*

No. Annabel shakes her head. No. No, no, no, no!

*She wrenches the door open and races outside, across the terrace and
on to the grass, the damp seeping through her slippers, her dressing gown
coming undone and flying wildly out behind her.*

'Max!'

*Oblivious to his mother's shouts, Max trots down the garden
towards the back wall, which the girl scales and glides over, disappearing
out of view. Annabel watches in horror as Max drops his sticks, reaches
for the wall and begins to scramble up without any fear for his own
safety.*

*Annabel's heart lurches as though someone is trying to yank it from
her body. She screams but no sound comes from her mouth. She can't
run any faster. She slips and falls, mud splattering her face and her eyes.
Grappling to get up, she screams again, 'Max. Stop!' But by this time,
Max has pulled himself up to the top of the wall. Crouching down, he*

peers over the edge. Then he stands up with an ease and poise that he's never had before, unperturbed by the sheer drop on the other side.

You're not taking him away from me!

Annabel sees her precious son, his back towards her, teeter on the wall just as she draws near, panting, fighting for breath. She grabs him firmly by the waist and hauls him down.

Down they both tumble. She is holding him so tight she's afraid she'll suffocate him.

'Who were you talking to?' she asks him. She can't keep the panic out of her voice and she catches the fear in his wide eyes, brimming with tears and hurt. 'Who were you talking to?' Oh, she wishes she could speak more softly, that she could whisper, as she sees the tremble of his bottom lip.

Through his tears, he blurts out the name of his dead friend: 'Chanoo.'

Guilt mixed with melancholy douse her and she rocks Max gently in her arms. 'I'm sorry, meine Maus. So sorry.'

As she strokes his hair and kisses his head, her mind rushes through the ways she can protect him. From the top of the garden she hears Vivienne calling. Her friend would understand if Annabel asked her to take care of him. She'll come up with something plausible. And in that instant, she knows it's her only choice. The realisation drives a knife into Annabel's heart, the blade twisting until the pain is unbearable.

Crumpling against her son, she cries out because now she understands the wrenching hurt her Mama felt when they took her away all those years ago.

CHAPTER NINETEEN

Felix Llewellyn, a friend of Oskar's, came to Vienna to collect his body. The British Embassy had stepped in and arranged the handover to an English coroner. Based on the full autopsy report, it was likely that Oskar's death would be ruled the result of a heart attack. Felix wanted to meet me, but I told him I was unavailable. I couldn't bring myself to face him and admit what I still believed to be my culpability in Oskar's death. The day before Felix flew back, he telephoned me. Being as considerate as he could, he asked me what had happened. Angela had given him some details, painting too glowing a picture of my character for my liking, and telling him about Oskar's search for the truth. I repeated the same story I had told Thomas Schmidt and Vivienne.

'No one's blaming you,' said Felix. 'If anyone's to blame it's Oskar. He never should have got on that flight in the first place.' Then he told me that Oskar wished to be cremated. 'Like his wife. He wanted his ashes scattered off Prussia Cove. It'll be a small ceremony, quiet – just as he planned. Please join us.'

'I'm not sure …'

'Oskar would've wanted you to be there.'

Quelling the choke in my voice I promised I'd think about it. 'Before you go,' I went on, 'there's a painting my family had. There's a chance it belonged to Oskar.' I described the Schiele and asked for details of Oskar's lawyer in London.

'But are you *quite sure*?' he asked.

The press soon got wind of the news that a child's skeleton had been found in my mother's house, and that my grandfather was allegedly involved in the deaths of three other children. Headlines ranged from the mundane to the extreme: *The Dis-Trust of Albrecht! Albrecht: Lies Lies Lies!* They raided archives for images of both my grandparents, but their favourite – it appeared most days – was one of my grandfather dressed in hunting regalia and brandishing a shotgun. The news spread beyond Austria's borders. Tanned anchormen and women endlessly analysed and discussed the case, as well as The Albrecht Trust, my grandparents, my mother and me.

I tried not to pay much attention to it – until journalists discovered I was staying close by, after which they set up camp outside Vivienne's house, impatient for a glimpse and a sound bite. They were hard to ignore. Frederik got involved when the public and politicians called for an investigation into allegations of child sexual abuse at The Albrecht Trust. As a trustee, he did his best to limit the damage, organising a publicity campaign to highlight its history of good work and exemplary standards. Tempers flared. Frederik and Schmidt had a heated exchange over the leak about the skeleton. I stepped in and we agreed to issue a joint statement. With the discovery of Eva's remains and the news centring on my grandfather, Oskar's passing went almost unnoticed, enabling us to keep his death relatively concealed from the public. But no matter how we spun the rest of the story, it always came across as sensationalist. And in the end we had no choice but to hold court to the press.

The three of us stood in fresh snowfall outside Vivienne's gate. Schmidt spoke first, and before I knew it, it was my turn.

I read out some lines that Frederik had drafted. Although I had learnt the words off by heart, I still held the piece of paper in front of me as a distraction from the sea of faces.

'We want to be clear,' I said, 'that during the period in which The Albrecht Trust had the children under its care, they did not come to harm. Sebastian Albrecht was never involved on a day-to-day basis – he merely gave his name to the organisation. Since the war, and since my mother Annabel Albrecht took over, the Trust has grown from strength to strength, becoming a beacon of charitable care for women and children.' There was more, but the flash of cameras, the clamour of questions interrupted my flow.

'When did you come to know about all this?'

'Just a few days ago,' I said.

'How did you find out?'

'We can't comment on that at this point in time.'

'Did your mother suffer at the hands of your grandfather?'

Faltering, I shot a cold stare at the anonymous reporter, certain that my face had the truth written all over it.

When my ex-boss saw the impromptu news conference on CNN he called me, wanting to know whether *everything was okay*. I was half truthful, telling him, between his mutterings of *Jesus H. Christ*, that I was shaken but all right. Before he hung up, he mentioned he was leaving my old firm too and that he planned to set up a corporate finance advisory business.

'I'd like you to join me,' he said. 'As a partner.'

'I'm not sure.'

'Just think about it.'

I told him I would, in my own time.

Lana also phoned me. 'I'll be here, when you need me,' she said. 'Whenever you're ready.' And that was all I wanted to know, that perhaps there was an opening, another chance for us.

The reality was that Oskar's passing dominated my mind. I couldn't bring myself to venture near Himmelhofgasse either. It was genuine fear that held me back – fear of confronting the cadaver of my ancestral home, fear of reliving what had happened to Oskar, fear of seeing Eva again. On the one occasion I did leave Vivienne's, I went directly to Hietzinger Hauptstrasse, rather than veer towards Adolfstorgasse or beyond. And I was painfully aware of my loss of privacy. Well-meaning people passing in the street gave me brief smiles or nods; in Biedermayer and other shops, people asked me how I was. All I could do was mumble a few assurances, desperate to get back to Vivienne's.

Immediately after Christmas Day, Vivienne and I decided to go away for a while. At the last minute, we went to the alpine town of Kitzbühel. A friend of a friend arranged for us to stay at the Tennerhof. Of course Vivienne didn't ski any more, but she didn't mind – she just needed a change of scenery. My injuries had improved and I went out skiing most mornings, joining Vivienne in the afternoons for walks along the river.

We made a pledge to not talk about what had happened. On the first day, the effort not to mention it left our conversation stilted as we tiptoed around the subject, afraid to stir up memories we'd rather forget. But thereafter, we managed to find other things to chat over, and returned to near normal topics of politics, business, the Albertina and books. I even got round to buying her a belated Christmas gift – a sky-blue cashmere shawl that I hoped would replace the green one she wore most days.

Some friends of mine were also in Kitzbühel. They invited me to their house for a New Year's Eve party. Given recent events I was tempted to shy away, but just a few days earlier a massive earthquake had struck in the Indian Ocean. It was the only thing people were talking about, and eclipsed everything that had happened to me. So, cajoled by Vivienne, I changed my mind and went to the party after all. My friends put a makeshift donations box in the hallway. By midnight, close to five thousand euros had been collected. The loss of life, irrespective of where it was, put things into perspective, not just for me, but for everyone at the party. When we later went out to see the fireworks, we watched them jewel the night sky with muted cheer. Standing on my friends' terrace I made one wish: to somehow find the means to move on, to get on with my life. My mother had; Oskar had. So could I.

A week later, we returned to Vienna feeling the better for our time away. I received a phone call from Schmidt with a brief update, but he had nothing new to tell me, other than who had been the source of the leak to the press about the skeleton.

'It came from a member of my team – he was pissed that he missed out on promotion.'

I thought Schmidt might have wanted to discuss the messages on the reverse of the photograph and in the novel, but he didn't mention them. 'One day, though, I'll get to the bottom of the whole thing,' he said, before ending the call. That was the last time I heard from him.

Frederik also called to see how things were. His manner towards me had softened again. I half expected him to revert to his usual distant self, but his continued goodwill seemed to suggest otherwise. I told him I wanted his help to retrieve the Schiele from storage and to discuss a couple of other things, so the day before my flight back to London, I went to his office.

Although it was a Monday, he was dressed casually in corduroys and a dove-grey cashmere sweater worn over a pristine white shirt. The Stepford wife assistant was absent.

'I've made some changes,' he said. 'I've decided to take a back seat – let a couple of others take the helm. Let's call it a New Year's resolution.'

He signalled for me to follow him to his office. I sat down on an armchair beside the bookshelf.

'The Albrecht Trust – it's taken up a lot of my time,' he said, lowering himself into a chair next to mine.

'I wanted to talk to you about that,' I said, helping myself to some water. 'I think we should change the name of the Trust.'

'I see.' He crossed his legs. 'On what basis?'

'It's obvious – the association with my grandfather's name.'

'Do you think it's necessary?'

'Tell me you're kidding? What with the media, the remains found in the house, my grandmother's letter …'

He said nothing as he stared back at me.

His reaction unnerved me but I refused to let it weaken my resolve. 'You're one of the trustees, you can propose it.'

He leaned back in his chair. 'What would you suggest?'

'Anything that's as far removed from that name as possible. I don't know – The Children's Trust or something.'

'But it's for women too,' Frederik said with a slow blink.

'It's the spirit of it, that's all. Look, it's just a suggestion. I'm sure there are better names out there. But not Albrecht.'

'Very well, but I don't think now's a good time to do this.'

I stood up, digging my hands into my pockets. 'I disagree, Frederik. I don't want some sensational news story killing off the Trust on account of a name. And I want to do something in memory of those children.' That seemed to have got his attention. 'I thought …' I swallowed. 'I thought about turning the site where the house stood into a garden, open to the public – a family space with a playground and so on. But I wouldn't know where to start.' I looked down at my shoes, then at Frederik. 'Will you help me?'

He rubbed his chin. 'So you won't rebuild?'

I shook my head.

He closed his eyes and took a deep breath. 'If that's what you want, then yes, I can assist,' he said eventually. 'It's a pity,' he added.

'You went back there?'

'Yes,' he said. 'You know the art was stored away – the Schiele and the others – don't you?'

'Mama never mentioned that the originals were in storage – and neither did you.'

'You were slightly distracted at the time. I assumed you'd look through everything at your leisure.'

I shook my head again.

'The Dorotheum arranged it all,' he said. 'You should have a letter with all the contact details.'

When I explained the Schiele may have belonged to Oskar's family before the war, Frederik didn't comment, but he seemed to close in on himself, folding his arms, giving a slow nod of his head. I wasn't sure why he was reacting that way but I gave it no more thought. I was more concerned with how I was going to present my next question. My gaze skimmed along the rows of books, lingering on the photograph of him and my mother on the middle shelf.

'Why are you really here, Max?' he suddenly asked.

His question made me smart for some reason, and I sat down again. Frederik took off his glasses, put them on the coffee table and rubbed his eyes. In that moment, he seemed to have aged ten years.

'In the last letter my grandmother sent to Claudia Edelstein, she made reference to sending her son Thaddäus away.' I brushed imaginary fluff off my trouser leg. 'What if he never died as a baby?' I looked up.

Something close to panic skittered across Frederik's eyes. 'Do you realise the absurdity of what you've just said?'

I carried on with my theory. 'What if he was sent away to safety and my grandmother was never able to fetch him because *she* was sent away? I want to disinter his body – I need to know what happened to him.'

Frederik swiped his glasses from the coffee table. He didn't put them back on, just held them in his hand. 'Your grandmother had a mental breakdown. She killed her son. What are you hoping to find? An empty coffin?'

About to utter a defensive retort, I stopped and looked at him. I was certain Vivienne said that no one else knew about the real reason behind Thaddäus's death. 'How did you know she killed him?' I asked.

He glanced away from me, his hand opening and closing over his glasses like a clam.

'What else do you know?' I was determined to get to the truth. My patience was wearing thin and he took too long to answer me. 'Frederik?'

'It's a long story.'

'I don't care,' I said. 'Give me the condensed version, if that helps.'

He leaned forward, his fingers rubbing the bridge of his nose. 'Very well.' The phone rang. He hazarded a glance at me, then looked over at it but didn't get up. When the ringing stopped, he began.

'I was born during the war and left at the doors of The Albrecht Trust before I turned one. I didn't spend long there. After about two or three months, a family who lived in Lienz adopted me. They gave me a happy childhood. I excelled in school, went to university, got my law degree and began practising in Vienna. I'd been working as a lawyer for a couple of years when I received a visitor at my office. She was an elderly lady, dressed all in black. Her name was Maria Lemanski. I thought she was a prospective client, but when she sat down in my office, she broke down in tears. Once she had calmed down she started from the beginning.' Frederik trained his eyes on me. 'She had come to tell me that my real parents were Sebastian and Isabella Albrecht.'

I shot forward in my seat. 'What?'

'That's right,' said Frederik. 'When Isabella, my mother – your grandmother – discovered her husband was a threat, she planned to flee with me and your mother, but she needed to do it in a way that wouldn't draw attention. She confided in Maria, our nanny – the lady who had come to see me – swearing her to secrecy. Your grandfather was away for several days, and the women decided to take the opportunity to make their escape. So in the middle of the night, Maria took me away, slipping through a tunnel under the house. She said she left me at the steps of The Albrecht Trust. A letter from your grandmother had been tucked into my clothes, requesting Frau Werner at the Trust to contact her in the strictest confidence. But as luck would have it, the letter disappeared.'

Frederik reached for his glass of water, balancing its base in the palm of his hand. 'Your grandfather, however, returned from his trip two days earlier than expected, the day Isabella, Annabel and Maria were due to leave. He noticed that the baby boy was missing. So Isabella claimed that she had killed his son, that she had, in her words, *thrown the body away*. Maria claimed that Isabella had had some sort of breakdown. The household was turned upside down. Shortly afterwards, your grandmother was taken away. Your grandfather wanted to avoid any undue attention so allegedly the staff and police were paid to keep quiet. A few days later, Maria managed to visit The Albrecht Trust to seek the baby out. She said she saw me. She even took me in her arms. The staff told her they had named me Frederik. They thought it suited me. The name change prompted her to do what she believed was the right thing – she said nothing about my identity and left me there – and prayed for my safety every day after that.'

He returned his glass to the coffee table.

I had a fleeting moment of satisfaction at the neat ending, but then the real impact of his story sank in, negating any sense of happy fulfilment. Over a matter of weeks, I had dredged up disturbing things – murder, abuse – that tarnished my family's history. Secrets had kept the Albrecht name intact, until now. Frederik's tale, even when related in his frank, unemotional manner, told of acts that were both horrific and desperate.

How could he be a living relative? I regarded him, wondering whether he had ever really absorbed the story, whether he ever felt the gravitas of it. He appeared quite numb to it all. He was an innocent in this, just as my mother had been. Just as I had been. Yet he had covered it up, just like my mother had covered up so much.

'I presume my mother knew?'

'No.'

'Oh come on, Frederik!'

'There was no birth certificate – no record of my birth whatsoever, in fact. And after that meeting with Maria, I never saw her again.' He smoothed down his trousers and put on his glasses. 'I did seek out your mother. I was sure she'd know about me. We met through a mutual acquaintance. She invited me to her house where I also met your father. I saw the Schiele hanging in her drawing room – I believe she'd just acquired it. Unprompted, she told me it reminded her of her family, saying only that her mother had died, as had her younger brother Thaddäus.' He smiled. 'I came away from that meeting with two things: a new client, and knowledge of the name I'd been given at birth.'

'So she had no suspicion of who you really were?'

He shook his head. 'Not as far as I ever knew.'

'But didn't you try to tell her after you got to know her?'

'I thought about it, but we'd become good friends. Her reputation – the reputation of The Albrecht Trust – meant everything to her, and to me. I didn't have the heart to shatter that illusion, and besides, I had no real proof other than the words of a woman I never saw again. Your mother looked out for me, I suppose, like an older sister would. That was sufficient. And when she died …' He ran his thumb around the palm of his hand. 'I saw you that day I visited her grave. You were jogging towards the cemetery entrance. I didn't want you to find out either. You'd been through enough already.' He looked over my shoulder where I knew the picture of him and my mother was standing. 'Until recently, I had no idea what type of threat my father was supposed to have been. Maria refused to go into details when I asked her. Like you, I try to avoid thinking about it. But it's hard.'

I studied his face. 'You look nothing like my mother.'

'Long ago I noticed we both had a mole, shaped like a comma in the same spot just above our left wrists. Perhaps she saw that too.' He shrugged his shoulders. 'I used to notice we had similar mannerisms. They were enough for me.'

There were too many questions jostling for attention, though one shouted louder than the rest. 'Do you think my grandmother did have a breakdown?' I asked.

Frederik thought about it, then with a wry smile said, 'She didn't murder me, did she?'

But there were other things that still didn't fit. 'That day you saw me at the cemetery – was it you who left the coat of arms at her grave?'

Frederik nodded.

'How come you had that?'

'I went through a sticky patch with my law firm. I didn't agree with the practices of a couple of my fellow partners. I could've walked away, but your mother told me to stand firm and gave the small shield to me. The motto – *teach me whatever's true* – seemed appropriate at the time.'

'But why leave it at her grave?'

'I felt she had only loaned it to me. I had tried to return it to her on several occasions, but she had always refused – *over my dead body*, she would say. So that's what I did.'

It was bittersweet, this reunion of sorts between Frederik and me. When I left, there was no film-ending hug; we did embrace, but it was with a stiff-limbed awkwardness that only time could loosen. Our embrace turned into a handshake, a gesture of intent that our common cause – The Albrecht Trust and the memorial garden I wanted to create – would draw us together.

Later that day, I left Vienna. Frederik's story began to sink in, but it did little to fill the hollow in my heart. I knew it would take a long time to recover from what had happened, but I decided to face it head on rather than scurry away from it, as I had tried to do after my mother's death. Besides, there was too much to hide from.

In London, I filed through security, passport control, the airport, lost in my own world. When I arrived at my building on Wimpole Street, I nodded at the familiar Coade-stone head with something like relief. Yet on entering my apartment, it came as a surprise to see my own belongings. For a moment, I wondered why I felt like that. Then I realised how much I had changed in the time I'd been away.

OBER ST. VEIT, VIENNA, 26TH AUGUST 2004

Footsteps outside on the driveway draw Annabel to the hallway. The jar of painkillers jangles in her dressing-gown pocket, reminding her of the tiny bell Mama used to ring to signal the departure of the Christkind on Christmas Eve. The cancer's so far gone now, the tablets do little to deflect the pain; they just send her into a dream-like state that she can't bear. At first she wondered if the pills had conjured up the sounds outside, but the light from the chandelier in the atrium triggers voices, foreign and quite unfathomable. As she listens to the footsteps running out of her driveway, she smiles. If someone did break in, she wouldn't mind if they killed her while they were at it. Rather that than this sloth-like death she's having to endure. Then again, she'd like to see the look on their faces when they discover that almost everything in the house is a fake or hails from foreign flea markets she's visited over the years. Perhaps she should invite them in for a cup of tea.

Annabel grimaces as her stomach cramps, and for a moment she doubles over, her arms wrapped around her torso. Really, she should sit down; really, she should be lying down, as Vivienne keeps urging her. Her friend is forever telling her to rest, to stop rummaging through old memories in the attic. But she can't help it: the discoveries she's made keep her going back for more. She's pieced together scraps of information that suggest her father was more of a monster than she had ever imagined. It's a cruel realisation, and an obvious one, in light of everything.

Guilt presses down on her. Hiding her own trauma seemed to be the best thing to do. And then Christopher had come along, a conduit for her to get it all out, and she'd felt better for it. But maybe she should have pressed further to find out more about her father. Jumbled memories, snatches of conversations, scenes she walked into as a child that she shouldn't have – one could read anything into them. And then Christopher died and she had swallowed her secret again, when really she would have been better confronting the truth and facing it head on. Perhaps I would never have had to push Max away, *Annabel thinks.*

If only Max would call her. She wants some word of him, some sign from him, but his silence is to be expected, she supposes. It was never easy for her to distance herself from him. There were times she thought she'd capitulate, but that scene in the garden – seeing her precious boy being led away to his probable death; the prelude to the car accident and the arrival of the police – these things always returned to her without fail, stoking her fear for him.

But now? If Max could help her find her forgotten childhood friend Oskar Edelstein – if he's still alive – he could help fill the gaps, because he had seen something too. The You *knew on the back of the photograph pointed at Oskar as well as at Annabel. And if that was the case, then maybe this could all be put to rest and Max could finally come home to her. Then Annabel could tell her son how sorry she is and hold him in her arms again without any lingering trepidation. She blinks away the tears.*

Shaking her head, Annabel goes to the study intending to call her son. Time won't wait. She picks up the phone and frowns. There's no dialling tone. She presses the on–off button several times, but the telephone's about as useful as a child's toy. She could go to the drawing room phone but she hasn't the energy, and without anything to distract herself, the pain's become all encompassing.

She slumps down on the chair behind her desk, taking slow deep breaths through her nose and exhaling through her mouth. It's like labour all over again, *she thinks. With an unsteady hand, she pulls out the jar of painkillers from her pocket.* What would it take – five? ten? twenty? *There are at least fifty in the bottle. She eyes up a glass of stale water sitting on her desk, another thing Ludmilla's forgotten about. The woman's become worse as Annabel's health has deteriorated.*

But it doesn't matter any more.

Annabel unscrews the top of the bottle and takes out the recommended two tablets. Poised to swallow them without liquid, she hesitates. Goosebumps ripple along her skin and the hairs at the nape of her neck stand up. She sees the cloud of her breath hang in the air. Strange, her pain's vanished too. In the hall, the chandelier lights flicker and a calm stillness descends on the house.

Turning to the doorway, Annabel says, 'Well, you've been away a long, long time.'

CHAPTER TWENTY

As soon as I set my things down, I went straight to the drawer in the spare bedroom to fetch the folder of paperwork Frederik had given me and found the envelope marked with the insignia of the Dorotheum. Its contents provided information on the location of the *genuine* Schiele, together with the necessaries to retrieve it and the other two paintings, which I noticed were two early works by Franz von Zülow.

Felix Llewellyn had passed on details of the lawyer in charge of the Edelstein estate, telling me that Oskar had left everything to his housekeeper, Angela. I set the ball rolling to verify the provenance of the Schiele and then handed everything over to Oskar's lawyer. On hearing the story, all he could say was, *She's incredibly lucky*. It made me think of luck's erratic pendulum, swinging away from me; any hope I had of the painting remaining in my hands disintegrated with each passing day. I struggled to shrug off the sadness at losing so much. Wherever I went, it hung like dust particles in the air around me.

I didn't jump into finding a job and I took my time to get back in touch with my ex-boss. I also dropped the case against my old firm, wanting to distance myself from it and its ivory-tower world. Besides, even if I did win, it wouldn't fill the hollowness I felt.

The memorial garden was my only focus. I worked with a Hietzing-based landscape architect who designed a beautiful space, with quiet enclaves for reflection and a large wooden play area for children. A white stone wall was to mark the far end of the garden, with steps leading up to a small platform from where visitors could look out over Vienna. Frederik laughed at my suggested name for it – *The Brosel-Anakan Gardens* – but then agreed the anagram was a fitting gesture.

He also personally stepped in to establish a case for the garden with the city authorities on my behalf. We pulled the memorial garden under the umbrella of the newly named *Noble Stone Trust*. His connections assisted with obtaining the necessary permissions and it looked likely that we would get the green light. A complicating factor was what to do about Eva Schwartz's remains: I thought it right to have them buried there; Frederik argued against it. Eventually, he accepted my decision.

On the first Saturday in February I drove down to Prussia Cove. A southerly breeze seasoned with brine brushed my face as I joined the gathering at the cliff's edge. There were only a few of us: Angela, Felix and his wife, and a couple of others – and Ripley, of course. He sat on his haunches by Angela's side, his eyes downcast and his tail still, but when he saw me, he padded over, his tail gently wagging. And I, in turn, crouched down to greet him, burying my face in his coat, ruffling the hair between his ears, hearing only sorrow in his low whine.

We took it in turns to scatter Oskar's ashes over the grey corrugated sea below. It swept in and out, in and out, accepting our offering while a lone gull swooped beneath the clouds, its wings outstretched.

We didn't stay long. As I turned to leave I noticed Angela hanging back. I went over to join her, noticing a postcard in her hand. The wind had pushed strands of hair across her face,

269

which she made no attempt to push away, and I could see the faint tracks of tears on her cheeks.

'Mr Edelstein wrote just two words on this one,' she said, bending down to clasp Ripley's leash back on his collar. 'Another adventure.' I took the leash from her as she pressed a tissue to her eyes. 'I hope he's with Mrs Edelstein.'

'Do you believe that? That we get to see our loved ones again?' I asked, stroking Ripley once more.

'I like to think so. Gives us something to look forward to after we go.' She flipped the postcard over to the picture of the Donnerbrunnen. 'He was very fond of you, you know – talked a lot about you, he did. I can't believe he's gone – just like that.' She swallowed and took a moment to compose herself. 'And I can't believe he left everything to me.'

'Do you know what you're going to do?'

Angela shook her head. 'I've no idea. I can't bring myself to go into his house. Not yet.' With a fresh tissue she wiped away more tears. 'But there's one thing I have decided. That painting – I know it's been confirmed that it belonged to Mr Edelstein's family, but I don't want it. I saw a photo of it and …' She pressed her lips together and shook her head. 'I want to sell it. Give the proceeds to the tsunami effort.'

I stared at her. 'Are you sure?'

'I know its value, but money won't bring him back, will it?' she said with quiet determination. She looked up at me. 'I want your help – to sell it, I mean.'

There was no persuading her to do otherwise.

As we expected, the city authority and local Gemeinde gave their permission for our memorial garden, complete with burial plot.

There was one caveat: that Eva's resting place should lie, fenced off, in the furthest corner of the garden.

Work began in late March. Frederik oversaw everything on my behalf, and from time to time Vivienne would wander up Himmelhofgasse and report on its progress. While I still couldn't go near the place, I promised myself that I would visit when it was finished. In the meantime, I patched things up with Lana. This time, there was an intimation that the relationship had the potential to be more lasting. Although I eventually told her about my mother, Oskar and my grandfather, I couldn't tell her about the presence, nor how the fire really started. I knew there would be a time when I'd have to tell her everything, but just not yet.

In mid-July, on my mother's birthday, Frederik and I joined Vivienne in the short walk from her home to The Brosel-Anakan Gardens on Himmelhofgasse. There was no one else there, just the three of us, Vivienne in the middle, her arms looped through each of ours. As we rounded on to that street, panic butterflied in my stomach and the tremor in my hands kicked in. Vivienne gave my hand a squeeze and the dread ebbed away.

We entered through an arched gateway covered in honeysuckle – the only nod to the house – and into the park, for that's what it was in reality. It was larger than I'd imagined and the huge transformation soon displaced any initial misgivings I had. Sunshine dappled the expanse of lush greenery. Roses, begonias and other flowers I couldn't name splashed colour everywhere. There were no ravens or crows to sour the place, just the odd blackbird and a couple of chaffinches perched on the edge of the stone birdbath in the centre. Pleased with the way it had turned out, I could picture families coming here for picnics, or people sitting on the benches under the shade of the trees seeking peace.

I thought I'd feel sad to see the house gone, but I didn't. Now I knew for sure that the garden was the perfect way to seal in the past. I left Vivienne and Frederik and walked over to the far corner of the garden where a small wrought-iron fence framed Eva's resting place. Just beneath the wall stood a small granite statue of an angel resting on a plinth. Engraved on the front were the words:

> *Our children,*
> *Once silenced,*
> *Forever in our memories.*

Crouching down, I laid the white rose I had brought with me and paused for a moment, thinking back to the house and what had come to pass. Mostly I thought about childhood, how it came and went. Oskar's hadn't ended when he left Austria – he had been stripped of it the day he found Eva; my grandfather stole my mother's away; and as for my own – it probably ended the day my mother ran out to me demanding to know who it was I was talking to.

I now had a better understanding of her, the way she had been. There were things that would forever remain an enigma, but now I knew she had her reasons. I still wished for a better outcome – for the ability to go back in time, to make amends with her – but that, of course, was impossible.

Fate. I didn't really believe in it; Vivienne did. For her, things always happened for a reason. Perhaps one day I'd become more accepting of her perspective – that a map of our life exists and we always arrive at the same end point no matter what path we choose.

I suspect Oskar played a role in guiding me through the twists and turns of that period in my life. I wished I'd paid more attention to him as a person rather than as a clue to solving the riddle my mother set. I wondered, then, what he would make of our memorial. I closed my eyes, picturing him again in the snow-filled garden when we had first arrived on that fatal visit, his face quite jubilant as he relived memories of happier times.

THE NATIONAL PSYCHOSIS UNIT, BETHLEM ROYAL HOSPITAL, LONDON. TEN YEARS LATER.

The nurse locks Max's door with a resolute click. Max feels the two pills he's just swallowed buffet their way down his throat. The doctor's reduced his dosage, but even so, it still feels like his mind's encased in polystyrene. They'd talked about switching medication – a breakthrough, according to the doctor. But right now, after this last session with her, he doesn't want to change his prescription. The tremors have returned. So too has the darkness.

Over the last few weeks Max has lifted the shroud of his mother's death and its aftermath. He's omitted nothing, telling the doctor his story without embellishment. But when she'd asked him, during that afternoon's session, to talk about his wife Lana, he'd faltered. His mouth had turned to sand. He'd felt the torment seep into his body. But still the doctor had waited, tap-tapping her pencil on her notepad.

It wasn't that he couldn't remember. He could play out the events, minute by minute. But this part of the story lay on an altogether different plane from the experiences he'd recounted to the doctor so far. How he wished that he and Lana had visited The Brosel-Anakan Gardens in the summer or spring as they usually did. He hadn't seen Eva since the fire at his mother's house and he really believed that her spirit had been put to rest. But when they went there, on the eighteenth of December, a little over a year ago, there was something different. It wasn't the frost dusting the grass, or the wintry bare bones of the Gardens. It

274

was the creeping silence, a stillness he had never forgotten, that enclosed him.

'I should have known,' Max had told the doctor and that had been all he could manage.

'Why not write her a letter,' the doctor had suggested gently. 'Put it down on paper. Explaining how you feel may help.'

And that's what he sits down to do now. He grips the blunt pencil and stares at the blank sheet of paper.

Dear Lana … *he begins. Even that seems inadequate. He scores it out and begins again.*

Dearest Lana,

Your name is engraved on my heart. I can't believe you're gone – the fact that you're no longer here with me is my fault alone. You should never have married me – and I should never have taken you to that place.

He stops writing. This guilt, it's been a constant for so long now. The pencil slips from his fingers. Images of his wife flicker in his mind – strands of her hair caught in the sunlight, the spray of freckles on a flushed cheek.

As she'd climbed up to the viewing platform to take in the city, one hand on her swollen belly, she'd seemed oblivious to the strangled quiet in the Gardens. But Max had recognised it. And then he'd glimpsed Eva lingering by the statue of the angel. Fear had clamped down on him; he'd tried to call out to Lana, to tell her to leave – that was all he wanted – but it was too late.

Lana's scream had splintered the silence. It was a sound that would never leave him. Nor would the sight of the platform suddenly collapsing, his wife and unborn child plunging down with it. He can't put into words how he'd felt as he and others scrambled to recover her lifeless body, as he'd held her in his arms.

His Lana. Her heart was his heart. That day in the Gardens, his had stopped beating. The guilt, carried by his mother for most of her life, shouldered by Oskar Edelstein, had reared up once more and become his own burden to bear.

Max picks up the pencil and writes two more words.

Forgive me.

ACKNOWLEDGEMENTS

This story has been almost three years in the making and I wouldn't have been able to get to the finish line without a host of people. First and foremost, my editor, Averill Buchanan: your adept touch and critique helped me hone a novel that was 70% there to 100% complete. You were effectively my creative writing tutor. Thanks also to Victoria Woodside for cutting your teeth on my final draft. My fellow Faber Academy classmates: your feedback was brutal but honest. The Literary Consultancy and their reader, Ashely Stokes, whose manuscript assessment gave me the encouragement to keep going. My *Better Half*: thank you for introducing me to Vienna. Little did you know I'd end up dragging you around the city multiple times. You enabled me to fulfil my ambition to write a novel, even though it meant losing me to a set of troublesome characters who kept me up at night. Lastly – Dad, you inspired me to put pen to paper. One day – I promise – I will read *War and Peace*.

FURTHER ACKNOWLEDGEMENTS & INFORMATION

The lullaby which Annabel Albrecht's former nanny sings is a Yiddish folk song – *Your Kitten is Hungry* – by Mordecai Gebirtig. Gebirtig was born in 1877 in Krakow, Poland. He had three daughters, for whom he wrote and performed his poems. The words were set to improvised melodies, and most of his songs resemble entries in a diary. Many of Gebirtig's poems contain themes of eastern European Jewish life in the 1920s and 1930s. *Your Kitten is Hungry* dates from the early 1920s. The lyrics, addressed to a hungry child, evoke the themes of hunger and deprivation.

Mother with Two Children III by Egon Schiele currently hangs in the Belvedere in Vienna.

In some of his work, Schiele explored the theme of motherhood and the relationship between mother and child. He had a difficult relationship with his mother and he wove this conflict into his images, playing with ideas of motherhood in ways which were counter opposite to the classical paintings depicting this theme. For Schiele, motherhood was perhaps more about sacrifice and subordination than joy and happiness. Despair, melancholy and bitterness shrouded his paintings, and in a series of earlier pictures he juxtaposed motherhood and death.

Mother with Two Children III is slightly different from those and other versions of this painting: perhaps he was slowly coming to terms with his own conflict with his mother. Yet even though the matriarch in this picture is more 'alive', she appears withdrawn and glassy-eyed. There are innumerable ways to interpret it, but for me, this painting (and Schiele more generally) inspired my novel. Given one of the themes running through my story, I wanted to give this picture a 'cameo role'. Of course, I've exercised my creative licence and placed it in a fictional setting — in this case, in somebody's own home, and I've removed the roman numeral, III from its title.

I'd like to thank Bernhard Brandstaetter at Sotheby's, London, for being a helpful source of additional information on the works of Egon Schiele.

BIOGRAPHY

Amna K. Boheim worked in investment banking before turning her hand to writing. She has embarked on two Faber Academy writing courses, including the six-month Faber Academy Writing a Novel (online) course. She authors a blog under the title, *Djinn Mamu … & Other Strange Stories*.

The Silent Children is her debut novel.

For more information please visit her website www. akboheim.com or via Facebook/akboheim. Feel free to follow Amna on Twitter @AmnaKBoheim and she will follow back.

To receive updates and her latest blog posts, please contact Amna via amna@akboheim.com

Translating Research into Healthy New Life

I will be donating 50% of the royalties from The Silent Children to the charity, Borne (registered charity number 1067412-7) to support their research into preventing death and disability in childbirth.

Borne aims to prevent disability and death in childbirth and create lifelong health for mothers and babies. It was created in response to a real need:

- In the UK alone, more than 1 in 10 babies are born too soon – that's nearly 80,000 every year.
- Premature birth is responsible for 70% of disability and death in newborn babies

Borne was set up by the maternity team at London's Chelsea and Westminster Hospital, the hospital's charity, CW+, and a group of parents – our Founding Donors. So far they have already raised over £3 million, which has enabled them to:

1. Identify possible treatments which should reduce the risk of preterm labour in high-risk pregnancies from 35% to 10% or less.
2. Train medical teams to deal with obstetric emergencies in resource poor countries.
3. Conduct a study highlighting the link between maternal diet and a baby's brain development.

Going forward, if they succeed in raising a further £3 million, they will:

1. Identify ways to reduce the risk and complications of preterm birth

2. Develop ways to prevent pre-eclampsia, a life threatening pregnancy condition.

3. Investigate how to prevent necrotising enterocolitis (NEC), a bowel condition which is the second most common cause of death in neonatal intensive care units in the developed world.

CPSIA information can be obtained
at www.ICGtesting.com
Printed in the USA
LVOW04s1210311016

511007LV00004B/332/P

9 781784 625160